DEADLY COMPULSION

by

Shirley B. Garrett

Positive Directions LLC
Huntsville, Alabama

This is a work of fiction. All of the characters, organizations, and events portrayed in this novel are either products of the author's imagination or are used fictitiously.

DEADLY COMPULSION

Paperback ISBN-978-1-943065-02-8

Published by Positive Directions LLC, Huntsville, AL.

Cover design by Dan Thompson

ACKNOWLEDGEMENTS

Creative works come to fruition with the help and guidance of many people. I'd like to thank the Huntsville Literary Association Critique Group, The Coffee and Critique Group, and the North Alabama Mystery Writers for their valuable insights and wise guidance. My beta readers, Tom Mailey, Lisa Malice, Edi Peterson, and Ron and B.J. Moore offered many good suggestions that improved my book.

Many thanks to the following editors worked on this project before its acceptance for publication. My colleague, Barbara Higgins, MA was of great help regarding the psychological aspects. Jeremy Bronaugh helped me to eliminate an unnecessary character. Christine Brown and Lisa Prince performed their editorial magic by smoothing many rough edges.

Special thanks to Sgt. Luna of the Ardmore Police Department. He offered his expertise on the sections of the story that occurred in Ardmore.

None of this would be possible without the love and support of my husband. Behind every great woman is a guy like Bob Garrett.

Table of Contents

Table of Contents, Continued

Table of Contents, Continued

CHAPTER 1 - THE HUNT BEGINS

"If left unchecked, any desire can become a deadly compulsion. It can drive behavior and consume the human mind." Shirley B. Garrett, Psy.D

The Huntress spotted the Huntsville police cruiser when it pulled into the parking lot of the Night Owl. *That's all I need. A nosy cop.*

She ducked low on the seat of her green Mustang convertible, waiting for him to leave. A short while later, she peeked over the dash. The cruiser had moved on. She sat up and smoothed down her skirt with moist palms.

Her watch showed midnight. It was time to begin the hunt.

She exited the car and walked toward the entrance. A nippy March breeze ruffled her long hair and caused her nipples to become erect under her silk blouse.

The club's neon beer signs reflected off the bald ebony head of the bouncer, a tree trunk of a man.

"Hey, pretty lady." He cast a wink in her direction.

Eager to blend into the crowd, she gave a quick nod as she glided past. A haze of theatrical fog tinted by colored lights drifted across the packed dance floor. The bass guitar reverberated inside her chest.

Closing her eyes, she filled her lungs with the scent of her prey: smoke, perspiration, and cologne.

She scanned the room in search of the best spot to lure her quarry. Groups of women, ten years her senior, sat scattered at the scarred wooden tables that filled the expanse between the dance floor and the bar. Dozens of men eyed the women as they walked among the tables. Like her, they were on the prowl.

She suppressed a smile of satisfaction. *This club looks to be an ideal hunting ground.*

"Can I buy you a drink?"

The Huntress pivoted, her heart pounding in her temples. She raked her gaze over a man with blond hair combed to hide a receding hairline. He wore a navy blazer and a tie sporting red chili peppers that screamed "traveling salesman."

He's not the one.

Folding her arms across her chest, she stepped away to create distance and ignored him while she continued to peruse the room.

He took several steps toward her. "I'm in town on business for a few days. Do you live here, honey?"

The bastard won't take a hint. She skewered him with a look guaranteed to crush the hardiest of male egos.

He took a hasty step back and held up his hands. Mumbling something unintelligible, he walked away.

The Huntress wove her way between the tables toward the bar. As she passed, she saw several men smile.

The women glared daggers.

A group of men already occupied the expanse of the U-shaped mahogany bar, conversing and nursing their drinks. She slithered onto an available stool and crossed her tanned legs, allowing the short skirt to inch up her thighs. Several of the men nudged each other and raked their fingers through thinning hair.

The liquor bottles that decorated the bar stood at attention like soldiers, guarding a large mirror. The bartender was busy restocking gleaming glasses onto a hanging rack.

She caught his attention by raising a finger. He nodded and worked his way to her side of the bar.

"What can I get you?" He wiped the area in front of her. Boredom flattened his expression. Pierced and tattooed to the point of self-mutilation, he looked out of place in this country music nightclub.

"Corona, with a lime."

As the bartender stepped away to fetch her beer, the Huntress spied a dark-haired man on the downward slide of prime, seated across from her.

He rubbed his chin as he let his gaze glide over her.

She squinted, searching for a wedding band. When she found none, a smile wound its way over her glossed lips.

He may be the one.

He gulped the last of his whiskey with one smooth motion and set down his glass. Wiping his sleeve across his mouth, he signaled for another. Nodding to acknowledge the request, the bartender turned and plopped down her Corona.

She tossed bills on the bar. "Keep the change."

He scooped the bills into his tattooed hands. In blue ink, the left said, *love*; the right, *hate*. Prison ink.

The Huntress squeezed the lime into the beer, aware that her mark was watching. Holding his gaze, she placed her index finger in her mouth and sucked the lime from it. She intensified her provocative smile as she brushed dark locks over her shoulder.

He dismounted from his stool, stumbled, and righted himself. Squaring his shoulders, he swaggered toward her with a confident stride.

"May I join you?" he asked, with a deep, melodious voice.

She nodded and moistened her lips.

He hoisted himself onto the stool next to her. "I'm John Harper." He held open his arms, palms up as if to say *tadaaa*.

Silence raced by and his hundred-watt smile began to dim. "Do you ever listen to my radio show? *John in the Morning* on W-N-K-S? You know, Winks?" He winked at her to demonstrate.

"Can't say that I do. I'm not an early riser." She shifted on the stool to face him.

His smile dimmed even more, and his shoulders slumped.

Gazing at him from under her lashes, she said, "You see, I work late, so I sleep in. I've never met a radio personality."

The bartender plopped a new whiskey on the bar beside John. He reached for it. "What do you do?" His gaze never left her face.

She looked deep into his dark eyes as her foot caressed his shin.

He paused. His hand dropped to the polished surface of the bar, leaving the whiskey untouched.

"I help people feel better." She offered him a sultry smile.

3

"You're certainly helping me feel better." His gaze dropped lower.

She threaded fingers through her hair and allowed it to cascade over her shoulders. "I'm glad to hear that." She winked.

A reptilian smile oozed onto Harper's face. He reached behind her and traced her spine with his fingers.

Arching her back, she purred. "Oooooh, that feels good."

"Wanna dance?" He shifted as if to leave the stool.

The Huntress glanced at her watch and shook her head. "I have a better idea. Why don't we get out of here? Maybe go to your house, have some fun, and get away from this crowd?"

"Um…sure. We can do that." His dark brows arched as he leaned back.

"You do live alone, don't you? I hate it when roommates barge in while I'm having…fun." She ran her hand up and down his thigh.

"No chance of that, Baby Girl. We'll be all alone." He placed his hand over hers and squeezed.

The Huntress stiffened and narrowed her eyes. "My daddy always called me Baby Girl." She reached past him and downed his shot. "Mmmm, good whiskey."

He paid his tab, and they left the club, arm in arm. She insisted on driving him home since he was unsteady on his feet. Twenty minutes later, she pulled into an upscale neighborhood in southeast Huntsville.

John pointed at a two-story brick home partway down the block. "That's the house, the third one on the right."

Nice, she thought, as she pulled into the driveway.

"Pull around back and park in the garage," said John. "Pull into the bay on my left. My neighbors don't need to know all my business, the nosy bastards."

He opened the car door and hung onto it to steady himself. "Damn room's spinning," he mumbled, as he pulled his keys from his pocket.

He opened the door to the house and let her enter first. The moment they were inside, he pinned her to the wall. Sliding his hands under her shirt, he cupped her breasts.

A light switch was digging into her back. She moved it up with her shoulder blade. The crystal chandelier in the split foyer to her right lit to reveal a stairway. She pushed him away, ducked under his arm and ran upstairs.

He pursued her, huffing from the exertion. "I'm coming to get you, Baby Girl."

When she reached the top, she flipped a switch to her left. It lit a long hallway.

"Come and get me!" Laughing, she pulled her blouse over her head.

He paused on the landing, his gaze glued to her bare breasts.

She ran one hand through her hair and slid the other one over her heated skin caressing her breasts, as she gyrated to a tune playing in her head.

He climbed the remaining steps and reached for her.

"Not yet," she teased.

She whirled and raced down the hallway into a bedroom. Once she turned on the lights, her gaze took in the unmade bed, the girlie poster and the porn DVDs scattered across the top of the dresser.

You've been a bad boy. You must be punished.

CHAPTER 2 - CHARLIE'S FIRST CASE

The phone rang, jerking Charlie awake.

"Nooo," she moaned. She wondered which insomniac patient on her caseload had slid into despair while watching perky late-night infomercials. *I hope nobody relapsed.*

She reached a hand out from under her warm comforter and groped for the handset.

It fell to the floor.

She dived over the side of the bed to retrieve it.

"Hello," she rasped, hanging half off the bed.

The clock showed 4:15 in red glowing numerals.

"May I speak to Dr. Charlene Stone?" The male voice was deep and resonant.

"You've got her." She pulled herself back into bed and tugged the covers up to her chin.

"This is Detective Ryan Roberts with the Huntsville Police Department. I understand you're our new consultant?"

She yawned and sat up in the bed. "Yes."

"We have a case at 1312 Lewis Drive, and we need you here right away."

"What happened?" Charlie flung off the covers. She scooted her beagle puppy, Spanky, off her bed and scrambled to her feet.

"There's been a murder." His voice sounded tired.

Charlie yanked open the drawer of the bedside table, nabbed a pen and paper, and jotted down the address. "On my way."

She looked at her yawning pup. "Spanky, it's my first profiling assignment with the HPD."

She pulled her, "I Love my Beagle" sleep shirt over her head and raced for her closet, where she'd laid out her clothes the night before.

****

The house was easy to spot in the early dawn. Yellow and black crime scene tape greeted her a block before she saw the red brick two-story set back from the street.

Four blue-and-whites, two Crown Vics, and a crime scene van didn't leave much available parking. Three television news vans hugged curbs as close to the scene as possible. Crowds of neighbors congregated in the next yard, gossiping as they answered questions from the reporters.

Charlie parked behind a black news van that dwarfed her Honda and got out, careful to lock her doors.

Her pulse was racing along at twice its normal rate. She took a deep breath, straightened her shoulders, and marched toward a pair of uniformed officers who were guarding the entrance to the driveway.

The older of the officers resembled her steadfast Uncle George, with a bulldog face and barrel chest. He oozed authority as he stepped forward to block her passage.

"Hi, I'm Dr. Stone," she told him. "Detective Roberts called me to assess the crime scene."

With a voice as gritty as sand, he said, "Oh yeah, he told me to watch for you. Sign here. I need your I.D."

She signed the log sheet he gave her. "Det. R. Roberts" was scribbled toward the top of the page. After she had extracted her license, the officer took it, did a visual check, and nodded as he stepped to the side.

He pointed over his shoulder with his thumb. "Go on in."

Charlie read his nametag. "Thank you, Officer Dennison. You remind me of my uncle, George Moore. He just took a disability retirement from the sheriff's department."

"George and I went through the academy together," he said, with a tentative smile that spread to a full grin. "I may retire myself in a year or two. What happened to George?"

She sighed. "Arthritis. It's so hard for Uncle George to move nowadays."

He shook his head as he shifted his weight. "Hate to hear that. Tell him Frank Dennison said hello." He stood taller and pulled up his utility belt.

Stationed several yards to Dennison's right, the younger officer monitored the media extravaganza that was edging ever closer to the crime scene tape. He looked over his shoulder, eyed Charlie with a quick up and down, then sauntered closer, flexing the massive muscles that strained the seams of his uniform shirt. His gaze sleazed over her, stopping at her breasts before heading south.

Feeling X-rayed, she took a step back and balled her fists.

Officer No-Neck reached Dennison's side and gave him a nudge. "Hey Dennison," he whispered, "I could protect and serve a woman who looks like that."

Charlie saw Dennison's expression harden. He turned to face the younger officer, stepping between him and Charlie. No-Neck leered at her over his shoulder.

Face flaming, Charlie was taking a step forward to confront the disrespectful cop, when a hand touched her left arm. She whirled to glare at a dark-haired man wearing a blue suit.

He wasn't looking at her. His icy stare was directed at the younger officer. "That's enough, Jackson."

Jackson's eyes darkened with malice.

Dennison pointed toward the crowd. "You've got company."

Jackson turned and pounded over to shoo away a reporter who was trying to slip under the crime scene tape.

Dennison looked over his shoulder, nodded to Charlie, and gave her a conspiratorial wink. "Don't forget to tell George I said hi, you hear?"

"I will. I know he'd love to hear from you. Thanks."

The man in the blue suit directed her toward the house with an open palm. "This way, please."

They strode down the cracked sidewalk toward the two-story brick house. She noticed the shrubbery was in dire need of a trim. Several bushes intruded on the concrete front porch.

He stopped before they reached the porch and turned to her. "I'm Detective Roberts." He gave her a warm handshake, flashing a brief smile of welcome. "I'm the homicide detective who spoke with you on the phone. Sorry about Officer Jackson."

Still flushed with anger, Charlie managed a nod. She could feel her hand tingle where he'd just touched it.

"I've heard of you, Dr. Stone. Don't you treat work-release prisoners who have addiction problems?" A wind gust blew his thick dark hair across his brow.

The respect she saw in his eyes soothed the Mexican jumping beans in her stomach. The whole incident with Officer-No-Neck had unsettled her adrenaline-overloaded system. She found she could smile. "Please call me Charlie."

"Ryan."

Charlie nodded toward the house. "What have y'all got here?" She dodged behind Ryan to avoid a cop coming down the steps.

"A forty-year-old, white male named John Harper. He's divorced and a local D.J. on WNKS, a country music station. Have you heard of his show?"

"I'm more of a rhythm and blues fan, but my friend Marti will be upset to hear he's dead. She calls him 'Mr. Sexy Voice'."

"He's pretty well known." He tipped his head toward the news vans. "Hence all the media coverage. The next-door neighbor leaked it to the press."

"Who found him?" Charlie shifted her purse to her other shoulder.

"The daughter. Station called this morning when he didn't show for work. He'd been late before on a Monday, but they usually could reach him. She found him dead in his bedroom." Ryan grimaced. "He's been beaten, and it looks like a sex crime."

Charlie followed Ryan up the stairs to the porch. He stopped and scanned the area before returning his attention to her.

"Have there been any other cases with the same M.O.?" she asked.

"None that I know about." Ryan loosened the knot of his tie. "We called you because the murder was so brutal — not the usual. I thought you might provide some insight on the crime scene because of your training with the FBI Behavioral Science Unit."

Once he was on the porch, he donned latex gloves, zipped himself into a Tyvek suit, and pulled on a mask and paper booties. When Charlie followed his example, one of the booties caught on the heel of her right shoe. She wobbled dangerously on her left foot as she struggled to get it in place. Regaining her balance, she entered the door he held open for her and trailed behind him up the staircase of a split entry foyer.

"The bedroom is at the end of the hall." Ryan indicated the direction with a nod of his head. "Don't touch anything."

As they approached, Charlie held her breath, unsure what to expect.

"Have you ever been on an active crime scene?" asked Ryan.

"No, the FBI's Community Profiler Program consisted of a mixture of classroom, crime photos or processed scenes. Locally, I was called in after-the-fact on the Fiancé murder case."

"That was a bad one. Joe and I caught that case. Did you consult with the Army?"

Charlie nodded. "A former classmate was a captain working with C.I.D. He asked me to look at the photos. Those pictures were disturbing."

He shook his head as if to clear the troublesome images from his mind. "It's worse in person."

When they reached the master bedroom at the end of the hall, Charlie stood in the doorway to absorb the crime scene. Deciding to break the scene down into sections, she methodically scanned the room from left to right, one wall at a time.

To the left, a flat-screened TV sat on a narrow chest. Beyond it, taped to the blue wall, Charlie saw a poster of a blonde in a yellow bikini. A mirrored dresser stood against the long wall opposite the door. The angle prevented her from seeing the deeper side of the room that held the bed.

She turned to Ryan. "May I go in?"

He nodded. "Just watch where you walk and —"

"Don't touch anything."

"You've got it."

Charlie picked her way across the room to the dresser. A neatly stacked pile of DVDs sat on it. By its title, the one on top looked to be porn. She resisted the urge to pick it up and check the rest. His keys and wallet were nearby, lined up with precision along the dresser's edge. The whole layout of the items smacked of Obsessive Compulsive Disorder.

There was no dust on the dresser. Charlie closed her eyes for a moment and sniffed. A faint smell of lemon furniture polish lingered.

A bright flash of light bounced off the mirror into Charlie's eyes, leaving spots dancing across her vision. Another blinding flash, followed by another.

Blinking, she raised her hand to shield her eyes and turned toward the source. The broad back of the police photographer blocked her view of the victim, but not of the blood splattered on the wall and headboard.

When the photographer moved to shoot another angle, she gasped and took a reflexive step back.

CHAPTER 3 - DON'T BARF

"Oh shit!" Charlie's hand covered her mouth. *Don't barf, don't barf, don't barf,* she chanted in her mind, as she swallowed down the bile burning her throat.

"That pretty well covers it," said Ryan.

She tore her gaze from the mutilated body and looked around. Ryan looked concerned, but the other three members of the forensic crew were eyeing her. If their crinkling eyes above the masks were any indication, they were grinning. Charlie could tell from what she could see of their faces that they expected her to hurl breakfast at any moment.

Great, now that was a good first impression. Very professional, she scolded herself. *Thank goodness I skipped breakfast.*

"This is Dr. Stone," Ryan announced. "She's our new psychological profiler."

Charlie cleared her throat, swallowed, and raised her chin. "I noticed his wallet on the dresser. Has anyone checked it yet?"

"Nope. We're waiting for Jason to finish and for the rest of the forensic team to arrive. We had a shooting in the projects. Not our only murder this fine day." Ryan nudged the photographer. "You done yet?"

"Yeah, you're good to go in here. I'll shoot the rest of the house."

Within minutes, the rest of the forensic team arrived. Their paper slippers swished across the dark hardwood floor as they worked with quiet efficiency on their assigned tasks.

A technician opened the wallet with forceps. "The credit cards are here. There are two of them, with a driver's license issued to John Harper. He's got sixty dollars in cash. There's a photo of two little kids. That's about it." He inserted the wallet into a clear plastic evidence bag, sealed it, and passed it to another team member, who tagged it as evidence.

That rules out robbery as a motive. Charlie took a deep breath and walked toward the victim. The body lay face up, spread-eagled on the bed. Blood soaked the rumpled light blue sheets and congealed beneath the body. The splattered headboard and wall reminded Charlie of morbid modern art.

"If you notice, there's an area on this wall where there's no blood splatter." Ryan pointed to a spot behind him, to the right of the bed. "This is probably where the killer stood."

Charlie walked around the bed, watching where she stepped. "There's no blood on the floor. I'm not a blood splatter expert, but wouldn't there be blood somewhere on the floor?"

"The killer probably stepped in it and cleaned it up," said Ryan.

The victim's entire body had sustained damage. The primary focus of the attack was the head and genitals. The face was a gory mess, beaten beyond recognition. Torn flesh peeled away in places from the crushed bones. Even the victim's teeth were cracked.

Charlie scrunched her nose. "What's that in his mouth?"

"It's his, umm…testicles," said Ryan. "The M.E. will be able to confirm that later."

Charlie swayed and reached to steady herself on the bedpost, but jerked her hand back. Instead, she rubbed the area between her brows.

"Are you sure?" She chanced another quick glance. Her stomach felt like a fist had just squeezed it.

Ryan nodded and jammed his hands into his pockets. Grimacing, he rocked back on his heels. Silence fell over the room.

The glare of the overhead ceiling light gave the dried blood a garish quality. *So much blood.* Charlie remembered one of the instructors at Quantico stating that an adult male would have 1.5 gallons of blood in his body.

"At least he was practicing safe sex." Ryan nodded toward the condom, still in place on what was left of the man's flaccid penis. "Man, she beat his dick, umm...penis to a pulp!"

"Apparently, his safer sex wasn't safe enough." Charlie shook her head, trying to take her focus off the blood. "Why did you say 'she'? Isn't it too early in the investigation to eliminate the possibility that a male could have committed this crime?"

"That's true," said Ryan, crossing his arms.

Charlie couldn't peel her gaze from the brown gelatinous goo of congealed blood between the victim's legs. The FBI trainer's voice reverberated in her mind. *"Dead people don't bleed."*

"He was alive when the killer sliced off his testicles and tortured him." Charlie blinked back tears and attempted to breathe through her nose to avoid gagging.

"Did you notice the restraint marks on his wrists?" asked Ryan, gesturing toward the wrists.

Charlie bent over the body for a better view, careful to touch nothing. "Doesn't look like rope burns. What do you think caused those marks?"

"My guess would be handcuffs. See the cuts on the heels of the hands?" Ryan leaned over her, pointing toward the victim's wrists. "When you struggle wearing cuffs, they slice you to pieces."

"His wrists are mangled." Charlie grimaced. "Is that duct tape goo on his face?"

"Probably so," said Ryan. "The lab will analyze it."

Always sensitive to smells, Charlie wrinkled her nose at the acrid metallic smell of blood and the heady fumes of alcohol combined with the stench of feces. She straightened to back away, bumped into Ryan, and almost toppled onto the bloody corpse.

"Ooooo!" She pin-wheeled her arms in a frantic attempt to regain her balance.

Ryan placed both hands on her waist and pulled her upright. "I've got you."

She sighed with relief. "Thanks, I didn't realize you were so close. I'm a chronic klutz, trip over my own feet all the time."

"No problem. My bad."

His hands remained on her waist. She could feel his warmth. An electrical tingle spread through her.

The forensic team exchanged glances as they dusted for prints.

An older, heavyset man she hadn't noticed before shot a lethal glare at her. Her instinct knew if that narrowed-eyed glower was a bullet, the coroner would haul away two bodies, instead of one.

Charlie eased away from Ryan and glanced around the room. "Ryan, I don't think they'll find any prints."

"Why?"

"Everything's too clean. I can still smell the lemon furniture polish. This is ultra-neat and sterile for a bachelor's bedroom."

"I can't smell much today — allergies. Bradford Pear trees torture me." Ryan shrugged his shoulders, hands in his pockets.

"Lucky you," said Charlie.

She peeked into the master bathroom. Spotless, it still carried the faint scent of bleach. No towels hung on the racks, not even a hand towel.

Ryan tapped Charlie on the shoulder. "Let's move out. These guys need more room to work."

He headed down the hall. Charlie followed him, admiring his smooth athletic stride. En route, she paused to peer into the guest bath to the right. *Pristine, with no towels on the racks.*

Ryan led her to the living room.

"There are vacuum marks on the carpet." Charlie pointed at the floor.

"Yeah, someone vacuumed, maybe the perp." Ryan frowned down at the carpet's neat alignment of marks.

Resting her elbow in her palm, Charlie tapped her index finger against her chin and eyed the surroundings. The room was tidy. A Swedish modern couch and love seat covered in matching royal blue fabric sat at right angles to each other. Two orderly stacks of porn and fishing magazines were centered to perfection on the kidney-shaped glass coffee table.

From her peripheral vision, she saw Ryan walk to her left, toward the kitchen. She followed.

"The kitchen is immaculate," she said.

The "clean" light on the dishwasher panel glowed. Walking to it, she held her hand close to the vent.

Ryan cocked his head like a bird. "What'd you find?"

"This dishwasher is still warm. I bet if we knew how long the cycle runs, we could estimate when the killer left."

"Interesting, that may require an Internet search," said Ryan. He pulled his mask from his face for a second and gulped some air.

"The techs could take the front off. The spec sheet is usually behind the dishwasher's front panel. They probably already know that."

"Maybe we'll get lucky and find the murder weapon in there," said Ryan. "What's this?"

"A broom closet or maybe a pantry." Charlie moved closer for a look. The scent of Ryan's Polo cologne caught her attention. "Mmmm."

Ryan turned and looked at her, brows arched. "What?"

She felt her cheeks prickle from embarrassment and edged away. "Nothing."

"There's the vacuum! Damn, it looks like the perp took the bag." Ryan pointed at the upright.

"Too bad."

"The vacuum will still have trace evidence in the brushes and pipes," said Ryan.

Charlie raised her brows. "Hadn't thought of that."

Ryan strode out of the kitchen and down the hallway. She peeked around the corner and watched him as he poked his head into the bedroom. "Hey guys, when you make it to the kitchen, Charlie noticed the dishwasher is still warm. No, she didn't touch it, Joe. The vacuum's in the broom closet. The bag is missing."

Charlie heard the babble of several people talking, but couldn't make out the words.

"Sure thing, Joe, I'll question Mrs. Brown." Ryan strolled back toward Charlie.

"I wonder if John Harper's daughter could tell us if he was a neatnik," said Charlie.

"Let's ask her," said Ryan.

"She's still here?"

CHAPTER 4 - DADDY DEAREST

Charlie followed Ryan downstairs to a den filled with expensive stereo equipment, including a pair of six-foot speakers. A part of the room was sectioned off with crime scene tape. Ryan lifted the plastic divider and held it for Charlie to scoot underneath.

"We can take the gear off here," said Ryan as he pulled off his protective gear and gloves.

On a massive sectional sofa, a diminutive, puffy-eyed brunette with smudged mascara had turned to stare at them.

"Bless her heart, she looks traumatized," whispered Charlie to Ryan.

"Mrs. Brown, I'm Detective Roberts, and this is Dr. Stone. Would you be willing to answer a few questions about your father?" Ryan stopped a few feet from her.

Mrs. Brown looked up at Ryan and gave a slight nod. Her reddened eyes and sorrowful expression brought a sheen of tears to Charlie's eyes. *I can't imagine how I'd feel if my dad were upstairs, dead and mutilated.*

"Mrs. Brown, I know this is a terrible shock. I'm sorry about your father." Charlie took a seat next to the woman. Sensing the mushiness of the cushions, she slid forward and planted her feet on the carpet.

Mrs. Brown cradled her head with her hands and sobbed, her hunched shoulders shifting up and down with the force of her emotion.

Looking ill at ease, Ryan fastened his top button and straightened his tie. He sat on the other side of the woman and offered her his handkerchief.

She dabbed it under her lashes, leaving streaks of black mascara on the snowy white fabric. "I'm sorry to lose it like this. It's just so, so … awful." She honked into the handkerchief and handed it back to Ryan.

Charlie saw his eyes narrow to focus on the white square of cloth.

"Mrs. Brown —"

"Debbie."

"Debbie, do you know anything about your father's whereabouts yesterday?" Ryan's gaze was riveted to the glob of snot in the middle of his handkerchief. His brows drew together as he tried to fold it so as to isolate her generous deposit.

"He was probably out clubbing and drinking like every weekend." Debbie sat back and crossed her arms, wrinkling her reddened nose. The sofa was so deep it forced her to slouch. She reached in her purse, removed a wrapper, and popped something into her mouth.

Charlie sniffed. *Peppermint?*

Ryan leaned forward, resting his elbows on his knees. "Do you know what clubs your father frequented?"

"Oh, my dad went to several, but his favorite was the Night Owl. He called it 'Menopause Heaven.'"

Ryan adjusted the crease in his pants. "What other clubs did he like?"

"Murphy's and the Roustabout." Debbie crossed her right leg over her left and bopped her foot. She was gripping her upper arms so tight her French manicured nails indented the flesh. Crying had mottled her complexion to a combination of pink and puce.

"Did your father date anyone in particular?" Ryan was jotting notes on a small pad he'd taken from his pocket.

"My parents divorced two years ago, and he's done nothing but whore around ever since. You see, my father is…was…an alcoholic. All he cared about was booze, himself, and screwing sluts." Her tone reeked of rancor. She swiped her eyes with the palms of both hands and crossed her arms, sniffing. Then she burst into tears again.

Charlie spotted a box of tissues. Rocking to her feet, she walked to the table and passed one to Debbie, acknowledging with a nod the grateful smile she received from Ryan.

"Debbie, despite all your anger, I can see you still loved your Dad." Charlie patted her arm.

Debbie looked up. "Yeah, isn't that crazy?" Dark rivulets of mascara coursed down each cheek.

"No, it's not crazy, he was your father."

Debbie dabbed at her eyes. "He used to be a different person before the drinking. When I was younger, he was a great dad. Every so often I'd see glimpses of that man, and I'd have hope. Then the booze would take over again." She shook her head and looked down, a tear dropping to stain her canvas shoe.

"Was your father a neat person?" Charlie made a sweeping gesture around the room.

"Are you *kidding*? I don't mean to speak ill of the dead, but he was a real slob."

"Did he hire a maid?" asked Ryan.

She shook her head. "He liked things messy. My mom always complained about it. She's a bit of a neat freak."

Charlie straightened and exchanged a quick glance with Ryan.

"Debbie, do you know why anyone would want to kill your father?" Ryan rubbed the stubble on his chin, creating a faint scraping sound.

"No. I've tried to think of anyone who'd do this, but I can't think of a soul. Maybe one of those sluts he brought home killed him? Was he robbed?"

"We considered that possibility. The motive doesn't appear to be robbery. Your father was still wearing his watch, and his wallet was on the dresser."

Debbie rubbed her temples, still sniffling. "Can I leave now? I have a pounding migraine, and I need to tell my children their grandfather's dead." She took a deep, shuddering breath. "Oh God, how do I explain it to them? Dr. Stone, what do I say?"

"I would keep it simple," Charlie told her. "Someone killed him. Don't mention any of the gruesome details. If they ask why someone one would hurt him, say sometimes people do bad things. They may worry that someone will try to harm y'all. Assure them that you and the rest of the family are safe." Charlie shifted on the soft cushion. "You'll know what to say when the time comes."

She added, "Children have sonar ears. Be careful that they don't overhear you discussing what you saw with anyone else. Protect them from the media. Reporters may try to interview you or take photos of your family. Don't watch the news with them in the room until this blows over."

Debbie nodded her head. "I hadn't thought about the media." She used the soggy tissue to wipe a tear that was tracking down her face.

Ryan cleared his throat and jerked his head toward the wall to Debbie's left. "All the major stations are in the next-door neighbor's yard, so I'll get an officer to escort you to your car when we finish. Just a few more questions, how long has it been since your mom saw your dad?"

Debbie glared at him. "My mother had *nothing* to do with this. She loved that man her whole life."

Ryan stared at her while he waited for his answer.

"She's on a cruise to the Bahamas that left this morning."
Icicles hung from every word.

"We'll verify that." Ryan wrote a note on his pad. "Where were *you* yesterday?"

"At home with my husband and children. We had a family day. I dropped my Mom off at the airport at six this morning." She rubbed her temples again. "Can I leave now?"

"Right after we get your prints," said Ryan, pointing upstairs.

"You think I did this to my father!" Her mouth dropped open, revealing a half-dissolved peppermint.

"It's for elimination purposes," Ryan told her. "We need to be able to separate your prints from the perpetrator's. We have your number, so we'll contact you if we have further questions. Here's my card, in case you remember something that may help us identify your father's killer."

Debbie took the card without a glance and stuffed it in her purse.

"I'll need to speak to your mother when she returns from her cruise. When will that be?" Ryan looked up from his notes.

"Saturday, but I'm telling you my mother had *nothing* to do with this. She — is — a — good — woman." She slashed him with a fierce look that should have left claw marks.

Feeling the escalation of tension, Charlie said, "I'm sure she is, Debbie. Your mom may know information about your father and possible suspects that you don't."

"Oh." Debbie sat back, relaxing her rigid posture a bit.

"I guess that's all for now. Do you have any more questions, Dr. Stone?"

"No questions." Charlie scooted closer to the edge of her seat. "Debbie, finding your father this way this is a hard thing to handle. If you or your children start to have any problems, I'll be glad to make a referral to a professional who may be able to help you." She offered her card.

"Thank you." Debbie accepted it. Her hand trembled as her gaze scanned the card. "Could you jot down a name, just in case my kids need to talk to someone?"

Charlie scribbled three names and numbers on the back and returned it to Debbie. "The first two therapists work with children."

Debbie placed it with care in her wallet and returned it to her large purse. She struggled to free herself from the person-eating sofa.

Charlie stood and pulled Debbie to her feet. Debbie reached out and hugged her. Charlie stiffened in surprise, but then relaxed and patted Debbie's back. "Take care of yourself. That will help you to take care of your little ones."

After giving Charlie a watery smile, Debbie took a final look around the room. Giving Ryan a curt nod, she walked up the steps.

After Debbie had left, Ryan sat to write some notes. Charlie sank to the edge of the sofa, feeling tired.

Someone pounded down the stairs sounding like a herd of water buffalo. Ryan and Charlie looked at each other.

"Who's that?" Charlie asked.

CHAPTER 5 - CHARLIE MEETS JOE

Ryan's partner rounded the corner into the room. Huffing, he pulled off the protective gear, his face florid by the time he finished.

"Joe, this is Dr. Stone, our new consultant," Ryan stood and said, "This is my partner, Lieutenant Joe Sparks."

At five-eleven, with gray hair styled in a buzz cut, Joe was built like a concrete block. A navy blazer pulled tight across his shoulders and no longer buttoned across his gut. A crisp, white shirt set a perfect backdrop for his mustard-stained tie.

Joe's brooding gaze met Charlie's. His mouth turned down, he crossed his arms and widened his stance, settling back on his heels. He looked immovable.

"So you're the new consultant? A shrink no less. You need to be more careful. You nearly contaminated a crime scene back there." He pointed in the general direction of the bedroom. "If you screw things up, we can't defend the evidence in court. Then another scumbag gets away."

Charlie looked down and shuffled her feet. "I'm —"

Ryan interrupted. "Joe, I was the one who bumped into her and knocked her off balance." Joe threw a sour glance in Ryan's direction and then refocused on Charlie. "What we do here is serious business."

"I'll be more careful in the future," Charlie rolled her shoulders back and lifted her chin.

Joe nodded, turned to Ryan and said, "You wanted her on this case — she's yours to shrink-sit." He turned back to Charlie, "Ryan is your liaison with the department on any of our cases. You have any input or questions, talk to him. If you can't find him, call me."

Ryan could feel his ears burn from embarrassment.

"Yes sir, I'll follow that protocol," said Charlie, almost standing at attention.

Joe unbuttoned his collar and ran his finger inside his shirt. A red rash formed a ring around his neck. He craned his neck and mumbled, "Damn starch. I keep telling Sarah to leave off the damn starch."

"Uh, Joe…you have some mustard on your tie." Ryan nodded toward the stain.

Joe flipped up his tie and looked at it. He wiped the spot with his finger, smearing it, and licked the mustard from his finger. "I grabbed a hot dog from the convenience store on the way in and ate in the car." He grimaced. "Sarah gave me this tie for my birthday. She's gonna be madder than a preacher with no donations after a Sunday church service."

"Wait a minute, Joe." Charlie held up her hand. "I can get out that stain." She rested her purse on the back of the sofa and dug through it, shifting items from one side to the other.

Joe looked at Ryan, who shrugged his shoulders.

Charlie held a tiny orange packet aloft. Tearing it open, she pulled out a small wet cloth. She advanced on Joe and grabbed his tie before he could say or do anything. His eyes shot wide as she invaded his personal space, and he backed up several paces.

Charlie followed him, scrubbing his tie with the cloth. "Be still! I've almost got it out. There, it's good as new. Sarah will never know."

Charlie retreated, and Joe reached down to examine his tie. After a moment, he grinned and nodded. "I've got to get back upstairs to supervise. Ryan, why don't you take Doc here for some coffee to hear what she has to say? Bring me back a cup. Doc, I want the paperwork on my desk by Wednesday."

Charlie nodded.

Joe looked at his tie again and shook his head. He completed the ritual to reenter the crime scene by putting on fresh gloves and a Tyvek suit.

He grumbled, "They probably make the damned wear these things in Hell," as he trudged back up the stairs.

"Sorry he acted that way, that's just Joe." Ryan ran both hands through his hair. "He's committed to what he does. He didn't see me bump you, so he probably thought you were careless. Joe sees every crime scene he works as *his* crime scene. Under all that tough-guy crap is a hell of a nice guy and a good cop."

"I'll take your word for it," said Charlie.

CHAPTER 6 - COFFEE HONEY?

Tucked away in a corner booth at Mullins, a long-time institution in Huntsville, Charlie scrutinized the décor while they waited for their coffee.

"I hope you don't mind if I take a minute to check my office email before we get started." Ryan thumb-printed his phone to access its contents. "I'm waiting on a ballistics report about another case."

"No, go ahead." Charlie waved her hand and glanced around. *This place looks interesting. Dad would have called it a "meat and three."* Despite living in Huntsville for the past thirteen years, she'd never eaten at Mullins. *Nathan's tastes always did run to the expensive.*

The owner appeared to be quite a collector. Colorful caricatures of famous movie stars covered the wall behind the lunch counter. Many of the paintings and photos in the open dining area were of historic Huntsville. The majority of the patrons were older; the rest were blue-collar workers, grabbing breakfast before going to work.

Charlie propped her elbow on the table and rested her chin in her hand. Laughter drifted from the round Liars' Table in the front room, where the mayor was holding court with several prominent business owners. Her orientation in the booth allowed her a clear view of its occupants.

She shifted her gaze back to Ryan. The stubble on his face reminded her that both of them had had an abrupt start to their day. The corners of her mouth twitched to form a smile as she assessed him. His thick hair, blue eyes, and lean muscled body reminded her of his touch and its effect on her.

Interrupting her thoughts, the waitress placed two sturdy white mugs of steaming coffee on the table. Directing a bright smile at Ryan, she winked and drawled, "Honey, are you sure you don't want to order some eggs, maybe some pancakes?"

Ryan glanced up and focused back on his phone. "No thanks. Just coffee."

The waitress pursed her lips and planted a hand on her ample hip. Almost as an afterthought, she dropped several white plastic containers of cream next to Charlie's mug, without ever looking away from Ryan. One bounced into Charlie's lap, but the waitress never noticed.

Arching a brow, Charlie plucked the cream container from her lap.

"You sure I can't get y'all anything else, hon?" the waitress said, eyeing Ryan from top to bottom. "We have good biscuits."

After what Charlie had seen at the murder scene, the thought of biscuits made her stomach churn.

In unison, she and Ryan said, "No, this is fine."

They looked at each other and laughed.

The waitress frowned and flounced off toward the swinging metal doors that guarded the kitchen.

Charlie, a cream-and-sugar kind of person, stirred her coffee and placed the spoon on a napkin before bringing the mug to her lips. She closed her eyes and sighed with contentment as the fragrance of Ryan's Polo cologne commingled with the coffee's aroma. She inhaled the scents, savoring the flavors on her tongue.

She opened them to see Ryan's eyes twinkling with speculation. She thought, *Jeez, I need a sex life.*

"Well Doc, what do you think? Were you able to tell anything from the crime scene?"

Charlie folded a paper napkin and placed her cup on it. "The killer's organized. From what we saw, it appears that handcuffs, and possibly the murder weapons, were brought to the crime."

"I agree. I'm hoping the knife will be in the dishwasher." Ryan reached for his cup.

"I'll be surprised if that's the case. This killer's thorough. The house cleaning, the removal of the bag from the vacuum, all point to careful planning. In my opinion, this rules out a severe mental illness like schizophrenia."

A group of older adults walked past on their way to the register. Their loud talking led Charlie to suspect that some of them had left their hearing aids at home.

After they had passed, Charlie continued. "I believe a mental disorder is involved. The neatness, the placement of objects on the dresser and coffee table would be consistent with Obsessive Compulsive Disorder."

"Like the detective on that television series, what's his name? Oh, yeah, Monk."

"Yes, I love that show. It's possible the killer is under psychiatric care since many OCD patients are placed on antidepressants."

"We haven't had much luck with the local shrinks regarding access to records." Ryan sipped his black coffee, winced, and blew on it.

"As a psychologist, I can understand why that's the case. In our field, we have our hands tied by state and federal laws, the ethics of licensing boards, standards of care, and now HIPAA. Not many doctors or therapists are willing to risk a ten-thousand-dollar HIPAA fine, a year in jail, a lawsuit, and the loss of our license to practice, by releasing records in an inappropriate manner."

Ryan held up his hands as if in defense. "All they ever say to us is 'the records are confidential.' How would you suggest we approach the issue with the local docs?"

"I can put together a letter that the department can distribute to the mental health and substance abuse agencies, as well as the private practitioners in town. If the profile matches one of their patients, and any threatening remarks are made in the session, a therapist or doctor is required by *Tarasoff* to report the incident to the proper authorities."

Ryan nodded. "Sounds like a plan."

Charlie's gaze tracked a tall, well-dressed man as he strode toward the Liars' Table. Something about his walk seemed familiar. The mayor stood, shook hands, and directed him to an empty chair. When he turned to face her direction, she recognized him.

Nathan Stone. Her lack of visceral reaction to seeing her philandering ex for the first time in almost a year surprised her. *I thought I'd want to rip out his eyes, or at least feel anxious.* Instead, she felt nothing. No, that wasn't quite true. She felt stupid. *I can't believe I married that man and allowed him to betray me.*

"What else did you notice?" asked Ryan.

Charlie fingered her spoon and herded her thoughts back to the case. "Can we talk about the blood splatter, or rather, lack of it?"

Ryan shifted in the booth to lean his back against the wall and propped one leg on the seat. "The guys fluoresced the bedroom floor while we were talking to Debbie. There was a definite cleanup effort. They also found blood in the shower and sinks in both bathrooms and the kitchen."

"So the killer did step in the blood and cleaned it up, just as you said. That's why the bathrooms and the kitchen were so clean."

Sipping her coffee, Charlie watched the mayor rise from the Liars' Table to shake hands with everyone within reach before he left. She wrenched her attention back to the situation at hand and gathered her thoughts.

"To clean up that much blood, the killer had to use something. I didn't see any bloody towels or paper towels. I looked for them. In fact, there were no towels in sight, none beside the sink or on the towel racks in either bathroom," she said, smoothing the napkin in her lap.

"I didn't notice any missing towels," said Ryan. "I did notice the trashcan liner was missing. Too bad the garbage truck ran early." He shook his head and stared into his cup.

"This killer is too careful to risk letting bloody towels be found by the curb in a garbage bag. I think the trash was taken and dumped elsewhere, perhaps in a dumpster."

"That makes sense. We can check all the dumpsters located nearby. Let me call Joe." He picked up his phone. "He can get somebody started on that."

While Ryan phoned his partner, Charlie took the opportunity to pull a small notepad out of her purse to jot some notes.

The call complete, Ryan downed some coffee before he asked, "Any other observations?"

"We shouldn't rule out a stalker. Radio and television personalities sometimes attract them. I think the killer knew John Harper lived alone. This assured privacy and plenty of time to torture and to kill him."

27

Ryan nodded. "That makes sense. It could be a crazy fan. We'll check the station to see if Harper had any threatening fan mail. One thing is clear, the sex occurred before the torture because they found ejaculate in the condom."

Charlie sipped her coffee and mulled over Ryan's comment. "I'm surprised he was able to perform with that much alcohol in his system."

Ryan cocked his head. "How do you know he was intoxicated?"

"I could smell the lingering aroma of alcohol in the bedroom. It was on his clothes and body. I work for an outpatient substance abuse program, so I'm quite familiar with the smell."

Ryan's eyes crinkled as he smiled. "Dr. Bloodhound, if you're so good, what cologne am I wearing?" He shifted in the booth to face her, leaned back, and laced the fingers of his hands behind his head, blazing a wide "double-dog-dare-you" grin.

"Polo." Charlie sat back to watch his reaction.

His mouth dropped open, and his arms fell to his sides.

With a "got you" tilt of her head, Charlie flashed her teeth in a grin. "It's my favorite cologne."

Eyes gleaming, Ryan leaned forward and propped his forearms on the table. "Your *favorite* cologne. I'll keep that in mind." His gaze intensified.

Heat crept up her neck. She resisted the urge to fan herself with the laminated menu smashed between the napkin dispenser and the ketchup bottle.

"Hi, Charlie, how's it going?" Her ex-husband stood beside their booth, smirking as he straightened the knot on his silk tie.

Charlie rolled her eyes and sighed. "Nathan, I hate to be rude, but —"

Shifting his attention to Ryan, he said, "I'm Nathan Stone." He reached out and shook Ryan's hand.

"Stone?" Ryan looked at Charlie. "Is this your husband?"

"Ex." Charlie looked up at Nathan. "Nice to see you, Nathan. I hope you're doing well. Give your boyfriend Eric my best." The dismissive tone said it all.

Nathan shifted his feet and stuffed his hands into his pockets, his usual suave façade fraying at her mention of Eric's name. Nathan was *not* out of the closet yet. "Sure, I'll do that. Gotta go." He turned and walked toward the register, jingling his change.

Charlie watched his retreat for an instant before refocusing her attention on Ryan's face. He had a quizzical expression, but asked no questions.

Determined to get the meeting back on the rails, she said, "I heard Joe talking to the coroner. Do we know for sure that John Harper died Saturday night? Could he have been killed on Friday?"

Ryan leaned back in the booth. "We have two witnesses who saw him in his backyard Saturday afternoon around three o'clock. He sawed a limb off his Bradford pear tree that broke during Friday night's storm."

"That was a bad storm." Charlie shivered, remembering. Spanky had taken cover under the bed. It had taken her thirty minutes to coax her out.

"Saturday night and early yesterday are both possibilities. The M.E. at the state lab will be able to give us a more accurate time of death." Ryan tapped the side of his cup with his index finger. "Do you still think the perp may be a man?"

"If the killer is the person who had sex with John Harper, it's likely to be a woman. His daughter said he was a womanizer. I'm sure you noticed the poster on the wall in the bedroom. His choice of porn indicated no same-sex interest. However —"

Ryan interrupted. "The killer may not be the person who had sex with him. My guess would be a jealous spouse or boyfriend of one of his lovers."

"That's a possibility." Charlie nodded and drained her cup. Their waitress was nowhere in sight.

Ryan shifted to place his back against the wall again on his side of the booth. "We'll also check out anyone who's obvious, like a jilted lover, girlfriend, family member, or his ex-wife."

"I feel certain it wasn't his daughter," said Charlie. "Her shock seemed genuine."

"I agree, but we need to check her alibi to clear her and her husband. If Harper was killed on Saturday night or the wee hours of Sunday, the ex-wife could have murdered him."

"The timing is interesting. She leaves the country on a cruise the morning her ex-husband is found murdered in his bed. If she doesn't come back, will the State Department try to extradite her?" Charlie dabbed her lips with a napkin, keeping an eye out for the waitress. She needed more caffeine.

"Not unless we can find some solid evidence. Right now, she's only a person of interest," said Ryan. "Did you notice how defensive Debbie Brown became when I mentioned her mother as a suspect? A little over the top." He ran his hand over his head.

"Maybe," said Charlie. "In dysfunctional families, it's not unusual for the kids to divide the household into good parent and bad parent —"

"Like good cop, bad cop?" Ryan swallowed more coffee and chased it with water.

"Right. Debbie placed her mother high on a pedestal in her mind. Since she's the good parent, she's capable of no wrong." Charlie wondered how Debbie was doing and hoped her children would be all right.

"It's clear she has a high opinion of her mom." Ryan rubbed the stubble on his cheek.

They both sat for a moment, contemplating, as Ryan finished his coffee.

Ryan broke the silence. "This crime was as vicious as the Fiancé Murder."

"There are similarities." Charlie shuddered at the memory. "Both crimes have elements of anger, control, and punishment. Only in the current murder, the attack was on the victim's masculinity, through the castration and the beating of the penis. It was a way of assuring that John Harper *never* had sex again."

Ryan cringed. He emptied his glass of water, condensation dripping on the table and his lap. Wiping his pants with a napkin, he glanced around for their M.I.A. server.

30

Charlie frowned, remembering the nightmares that had plagued her for weeks. "In the Fiancé Murder, the killer removed the victim's femininity and reclaimed his territory. He wanted to make sure she would never be attractive to another man, even in death."

"I get that he shaved her head and reclaimed her by raping her," said Ryan. "Why do you think he cut up her clothes?"

"Cutting up clothes is a psychological indicator of extreme rage," Charlie told him. "Harper's killer was enraged too, and tried to make a point."

"Oh yeah, the perp made a point all right," Ryan shook his head. "Oh, I forgot to mention that the garage was empty. So we're going to search the local clubs for Harper's car."

"Good. Let's summarize what we know so far. The killer is organized, maybe has OCD, and based on statistics I learned at Quantico, is Caucasian, between the ages of twenty-five to forty. A female is involved, but may not be the killer."

"That's a start," said Ryan as he suppressed a yawn.

Glancing at her watch, Charlie reached for her purse and searched for her keys. "I have a new patient in twenty minutes. I'll write up a report before Wednesday for the case file."

Ryan nodded. "I'll call you when the autopsy report and the data from the State Lab return so that we can go over it. I've found your observations to be helpful."

Reaching across the table, they shook hands. Both stopped for a brief second and looked at each other. His eyes widened a tad as if surprised.

Did he feel it too?

CHAPTER 7 - D.M.R.

Charlie barreled through the staff entrance and rushed down the grey-carpeted hallway to her office. Dumping her purse into a drawer of the credenza, she double-timed it into the front office to retrieve her messages.

Kathy Hinkley looked up from her computer at the reception desk. "You're cutting it close today. Your new patient is here. There's the paperwork." She pointed at a vanilla colored chart to her left.

Charlie stuffed several messages into the pocket of her blazer and grabbed the chart. "Thanks, Kathy. I got a call to assess a murder scene and lost track of the time."

Kathy turned in her chair to face Charlie. Her pink lips formed an O.

Charlie scooted out the door before the curious receptionist could ask questions. Kathy had the gift of slipping secrets out of people with a wink and a smile.

As a part-time psychologist for Hope Returns Treatment Center, Charlie had adjusted to the no-frills facility. The Intensive Outpatient Program offered reduced rates for the patients. This meant meager paychecks for the staff.

"Miss Major?" Charlie's gaze tracked across the faces of the three females seated in the narrow rectangular lobby.

An attractive dark-haired woman of slender proportion looked up from her magazine. "Yes?"

"Will you come with me, please?"

Melissa Major sighed and stood, rolling her eyes. She tossed the magazine she was reading down on the end table.

"I'm Dr. Stone. I'll be your therapist if you choose to enter our program." Charlie offered a welcoming smile.

Melissa gave a sharp nod.

Charlie gestured Melissa into her office, "Have a seat. Please make yourself comfortable."

Because attorneys, the court system, or probation officers referred many of her patients, Charlie had set up her rectangular office for safety first, beauty second. Her large wooden desk divided the room into thirds, with the largest portion on Charlie's side of the desk. On her right side, a matching wooden credenza sat against the wall. Behind her, a twenty-gallon aquarium rested on an enclosed wooden stand, and a filing cabinet was wedged in the corner.

The door was to Charlie's left, offering a quick exit from behind the desk if needed. In front of her desk sat two standard-issue chairs with wooden arms and covered in scratchy charcoal-gray fabric. Several large potted plants lined the wall behind them, including a Schefflera that had once belonged to her mother. Her friend Marti referred to her office as the "tropical forest."

Melissa fidgeted in her seat and glared at Charlie. She was wearing a loose tee shirt smeared with paint and faded blue jeans.

"Have you been painting today?" Charlie inquired.

Melissa glanced down at her shirt as if surprised to see paint splatters. "I paint apartments for a living."

"I see. Today I'll be doing an alcohol and drug intake to assess your needs. If I.O.P. is appropriate, I'll explain the program and requirements to you. Then you can make a decision about your treatment options. If not, I'll make an appropriate referral." Happy to have that spiel out of the way, Charlie studied her new client to see if she understood.

"What's IOP?"

"Intensive Outpatient Program."

Melissa offered a slight nod and squirmed in her seat. Charlie spread the chart across her desk.

"You were referred by the Huntsville Municipal Court." Charlie scanned through her paperwork to confirm.

"Yeah, I was arrested for DUI. I forgot to turn on my lights when I left a club, so the cop pulled me over. He was camped there just waiting for an excuse to pull someone over. Pure entrapment." Melissa reported this with an indignant look and tone as if she were the one wronged and the cop had committed the crime.

Charlie knew she had to confront Melissa's rationalizations about the reasons for her behavior and her denial about any wrongdoing. It was a necessary part of the therapeutic process to reduce addictive thinking, but it wasn't always a pleasant task. "It's my understanding you were arrested for drinking and driving, not driving without lights."

"Whatever." Melissa sat back and crossed her arms.

"You're court-ordered to complete this treatment program. I hope *if* you make a choice to start the program, you'll *stay* in the program because you feel better and want to get your life in order. Not just because you're court-ordered." Charlie gave Melissa a kind smile. Her many years of work with addicts proved it was near impossible to stay entrenched in a nasty frame of mind when someone was nice. *There are exceptions to every rule. I hope she won't be one.*

Melissa looked at Charlie as if she were daft. "I have no choice."

Charlie thought, *If her brows inch any higher, they'll become part of her hairline.* "Yes, you do. You always have choices."

"Here or jail, that's a choice?" Melissa's voice rose an octave. She leaned forward and rolled her eyes as if Charlie was stupid.

"Not one you'd prefer, but it is a choice. Your decisions and actions often set up the choices you're offered in life." Charlie met and held her new patient's caustic gaze. This important point would make a repeat performance if Melissa entered treatment.

"Yeah, sure, whatever you say," Melissa slumped further down the seat. She watched the goldfish flitter about in the aquarium.

Charlie steeled herself for the next part, which to her was the most difficult area of a substance abuse assessment. Pinning a patient down to truthful answers about the amount and types of substances used wasn't easy. Her patients often played a lethal game of, "if you don't ask, I won't tell." Misjudging the volume and length of use of some chemicals could place a patient in physical danger from withdrawals, or possibly death.

"Melissa, when was your last drink?"

"Two days ago." She reached down and rooted around in her purse before extracting a piece of gum.

"How much did you drink?"

"Maybe a six-pack of beer and a few shots." Melissa unwrapped the gum with slow deliberation and placed it in her mouth.

Charlie noted Melissa's response and asked, "At what age did you start drinking?"

"Twelve." With rapt attention, Melissa folded the silver liner in half, long ways.

Charlie paused and assumed her best poker face. *Twelve is a young age to start drinking. I wonder what happened in Melissa's life at that age.* "How many days a week do you typically drink?"

"Most weekends. I only started drinking again about a year ago." Melissa laid the shiny foil on the edge of the desk and smoothed it with the tip of her index finger.

"Really. How long were you clean and sober?" *This bodes well. If Melissa was able to maintain sobriety for any length of time, it will be easier for her to do so again.*

"I stopped drinking when I moved to Denver when I was seventeen." Melissa focused her attention on folding the foil into a triangle.

"What days during the weekend do you drink, Melissa?"

Charlie found this question was helpful in clarifying what a "weekend" actually meant to the patient.

Melissa raised her chin. "I drink Friday, Saturday, and sometimes Sunday." She began twirling her hair around her index finger.

"How much do you drink a day on weekends?" Charlie scribbled information on the form.

"It's just a couple of beers with friends. It's no big deal." Melissa slid even further down the seat, twirling her hair faster.

Charlie raised a brow. *If she slides any further down that chair, I'll have to pick her up off the floor.* "What does 'a couple' mean?"

"Maybe a half-case of beer, I guess. It's not that much." Melissa straightened in her chair and held the triangle football with one finger on the edge of Charlie's desk.

Charlie looked up from her notes in time to see Melissa flick the triangle of paper with the index finger of her right hand. It sailed over her head and bounced off the side of the aquarium behind her.

Shit! Charlie arched her brows in disbelief.

Melissa laid the outer paper wrapper on the edge of the desk and started to fold it.

Snaking her hand across the desk, Charlie retrieved the paper, crumpled it in her fist, and threw it away.

Melissa sat back, folded her arms, and pooched out her lower lip.

Charlie studied Melissa for a moment, estimating her weight. For a slender female, she consumed large amounts of alcohol. *This means she has a high tolerance, consistent with the diagnosis of alcohol addiction.* "Melissa, women lack an enzyme that men have to metabolize alcohol. That volume of beer would knock most women on their butts. How many DUI's is this for you?"

Melissa looked frightened for a fleeting instant. "My third."

"Have you retained an attorney yet?"

"Yeah, Leo Splunker. He said I should come to this program."

Charlie nodded without surprise. Splunker focused his practice on DUI cases. He often referred people to treatment to strengthen his plea for a reduced sentence.

"Your third DUI. That's pretty serious. Did you know that the next DUI will be a felony?" asked Charlie, tapping her pen on the assessment form.

"Yeah, Mr. Splunker told me." Melissa began twirling her hair again.

"Have you been arrested for any other reasons?"

"I had a Disturbing the Peace charge last year, right after I relapsed. This bitch got in my face in a parking lot. She started it, and I finished it." Melissa smirked her dark eyes hard pebbles.

"Were you drinking when you received the Disturbing the Peace charge?" Charlie asked, wondering how honest Melissa would be. Charlie already knew the answer, having spoken to Melissa's probation officer the day before.

Melissa smacked her gum. "That was the night I got my first DUI."

"Melissa, sometimes when people drink a lot they have blackouts, where they don't remember events or things they did while drinking. Have you had anything like that happen to you?"

"Yes," Melissa shifted in her chair, "but just a couple of times."

"How do you feel after your weekend drinking binges?" Charlie swallowed a yawn. *Geez, I wish the waitress had poured a second cup of coffee this morning.*

"Tired. Grumpy. I feel bad for a couple of days, nothing serious. Everybody feels bad after they drink a little." Melissa jutted her chin forward, jaws flexing as she gnawed on the gum.

There was no doubt in Charlie's mind. Melissa had DMR — denial, minimization, and rationalization.

"Melissa, we have a very simple definition at Hope Returns. If alcohol and drugs are causing you problems, then you have a problem with them."

She sat back to look past the defiant posture to see the real Melissa. *That is one angry little girl, wearing rebellion like a shield and stuffed into a woman's body.*

Charlie and Melissa parried their way through the complete assessment. Melissa admitted to heavy past marijuana use, but her recent use was one joint a month. This decline, she reported, was due to availability and the rising cost of the drug.

Charlie jotted down the following note in the chart: *Melissa's drug of choice is alcohol, and she's a weekend drinker. I need to address the marijuana use too. Exhibits defiant behavior. Possibly a complicated case.*

Charlie acquainted Melissa with the rules and requirements: three therapy groups a week, three AA or NA meetings a week, acquiring a sponsor, and a weekly individual therapy appointment. Glowering her displeasure, Melissa gripped the pen and scrawled her name across the paperwork.

"I'm sending you home with a goal sheet, so you can help me understand what you want to accomplish while in the treatment program. In our next session, we'll talk about your family history and go over your goals. Remember, you start tonight at six." Charlie stood, reached across the desk, and offered Melissa her hand.

"Uh huh." Melissa ignored Charlie's hand, turned, and stopped by the door. After spitting the gum into the waste paper basket to the right of the door, she looked over her shoulder at Charlie. Melissa nodded. With the paperwork clutched to her chest, she opened the door and clomped down the hall.

I need a whiff of fresh air to perk me up Charlie decided. She eased out the rear door of the facility. Standing beside a large bush, she yawned and watched a squirrel scamper up a tree.

Melissa stomped through the parking lot toward a dark green Cherokee SUV that wasn't far away. Charlie stepped back out of view and peered through the sparse foliage.

Melissa fumed, "Why me? Why do I get stuck with all this bullshit?" She slung the paperwork onto the passenger seat. "If she thinks I'm making all those stupid AA meetings every week, she's crazy. There's got to be a way around this shit." She got in, slammed the door, and powered down the driver's window. "This is total crap!" She pounded her hand on the steering wheel. She backed up the Cherokee and roared through the lot, tires squealing.

Charlie stepped around the bush to watch as Melissa turned right onto St. Clair Avenue and only just missed the front bumper of a Volkswagen Beetle. It beeped its squeaky horn. Charlie gasped at the sight of the near collision.

CHAPTER 8 - TOXIC DREAMS

Charlie shot upright, her chest heaving as she fought to breathe. The dream image of Harper's mutilated corpse, demanding she find his killer, scorched her mind. Tears welled in her eyes, and she wiped them with the back of her hand.

Sensing her distress, Spanky jumped on the bed and licked her salty cheeks. Charlie pulled her close, finding comfort in the steady beat of the pup's heart. The fragrance of warm puppy helped her muscles to relax.

Easing off the bed, she jammed her feet into her fur-lined moccasins. She padded toward the kitchen, turning on lights as she entered each room to banish the shadows.

Her favorite cup, with a photo of a beagle on the side, sat on the drying rack. She filled it with water and popped it in the microwave. Rummaging in a cabinet, she found a chamomile tea bag that she placed in the cup of steaming water. She perched at the breakfast nook table with her journal and favorite pen. Dunking the tea bag helped to soothe her ragged nerves. With a sigh, she lifted her pen and wrote, "I could hear his screaming...."

CHAPTER 9 - RELIVING THE EXCITEMENT

The Huntress stretched and yawned. She usually didn't wake this early. Turning on the radio, she listened to the new DJ that had replaced John. "This is Suzy in the morning, bringing you the latest hits, traffic, and news."

A malicious grin settled on her face as she remembered John's words, *"Do you ever listen to my show on the radio? John in the Morning?"*

"You'll never be on the radio again, you alcoholic prick."

Looking at the mirror secured to the ceiling above her bed, she whipped back the covers, exposing her nakedness. She remembered John inside her, stroking. Reaching down, she ran a finger inside her moist vagina. She watched herself in the mirror as the scene flashed in her mind. *The sex. The release. His muffled screams inhibited by the tape. The blood streaming down his arms as he struggled against the handcuffs. The metallic smell of the blood as it sprayed with each blow.* Her body quivered as she climaxed.

Focusing back on the scene in her mind, she remembered the gleam of the knife as his balls dropped to the sheet between his legs. *The way his back arched as he screamed. The blood as it gushed from his body and pooled on the bed.* Her right hand slid down, bringing her to another shuddering climax. With a satisfied smile, she pulled the covers to her chin and rolled on her side. After fluffing her pillow, she switched off the radio and closed her eyes, a peaceful expression on her face.

CHAPTER 10 - DRUGS AND SEX

Charlie gulped her latte, hoping the caffeine would infuse her system and jolt her awake. Stretching, she dropped the empty cup into the wastepaper basket. She yawned as she plodded to the lobby to greet her first intake of the day.

Janice Knight seemed to vibrate in her seat. If her pop-eyed expression was any indication, she was terrified, therefore cooperative. In fact, she vomited information on Charlie that normally took several sessions to acquire.

"I'm referred by the Alabama Board of Nursing. If I don't complete this program, I'm at risk of losing my license to practice."

Janice also had an upcoming court case, which meant her attorney had advised her to complete the program.

"So Janice, you forged a prescription. How did you manage it?" Charlie tapped her pen against her chin.

"I stole a pad of prescriptions from a doc who works at the hospital. I thought I got away with it, but the pharmacist got suspicious about the prescription. He phoned the doctor's office, so I got busted." She rubbed her palms over the smooth wooden arms of the chair.

"Is that the first time you forged a prescription?" Charlie jotted a few notes and looked up.

"Yeah. I won't do *that* again." Janice fluttered her hand in the air as if dismissing the notion.

"So how do you get your drugs when you're not forging prescriptions?" Charlie sat back in her chair and crossed her legs.

"This is confidential, right?" Janice looked left and right as if someone was hiding in Charlie's office plants.

"Did you read the paper you signed about confidentiality? Was there something you didn't understand about the limitations? Is there anything I need to explain?" Charlie gave her a level gaze. As a nurse, Charlie knew, Janice was familiar with issues of confidentiality, as well as the HIPAA regulations.

"No, I understood it all." Janice shifted in her seat and placed her purse on the floor beside her.

"In the past, I just stole a few pills from work or bought them on the street. I know it's wrong. I *should* stop." Janice raised her hand in the universal signal for stop.

Charlie leaned forward, placed her elbow on the desk, and rested her chin in her hand. She nodded for Janice to continue.

"I certainly won't be doing *that* anymore. I need to straighten out my life. If I lose my nursing license, the hospital will fire me. My career will be kaput. I'm already on probation with the hospital, so I can't screw up again." Reaching into her bag, she extracted a bottle of water and guzzled half of it.

"It sounds as though you have a great deal to lose," said Charlie.

"Hell, yeah! My attorney told me if I complete this program and stay straight, I might get probation since this is my first offense. Is that true?"

"That's a strong possibility, Janice. It'll also help your case with the Nursing Board. When did you start using pain pills?"

Janice looked at the ceiling as she considered her response. Charlie had begun to write her observations when the pen stopped writing. Frowning, she reached into the drawer to pull out a new pen and tossed the old one in the trash with a clink.

"Umm, about three years ago. You see, I was in a car accident." Janice started rubbing the arms of the chair again. "I was driving on Memorial Parkway's access road. This guy in a big-ass pickup truck ran a red light. Bam!" She rammed one palm into another, making a smacking sound. "He T-boned me. I broke a rib and my wrist."

Charlie shook her head. "Life is strange. One day everything is fine; the next, your whole world has changed because of an idiot in a pickup truck."

Janice nodded. "You've got that right. It did change my whole world. At first, I took the pain pills because I was in agony. Every breath hurt." Janice moved a hand to rest on her ribs.

"I've heard broken ribs are agonizing." Charlie rested her forearms on her desk, leaning closer to hear the tale.

"It hurt much worse than my wrist. The Hydrocodone made me feel great like I had more energy — more focused."

This wasn't the first time Charlie had heard patients addicted to opioids describe this high.

"So you have a paradoxical reaction to the drug. Most people feel groggy or unable to function. How much were you taking and how often?" Charlie documented the facts with her neat, efficient script.

"That depended on what I could score. Anywhere from six to ten pills a day." Janice gulped more water. The bottle crackled when she tightened her grip.

Charlie looked up from her note. "You're not using to get high anymore. You're using to feel normal."

Janice nodded. Tears filled her eyes.

"You're a nurse. You know how drug use affects your body. Promise me you'll have a physical and some blood work done."

"Okay, I will. You're right. I need to get checked out."

"Pills on the street are expensive. How were you supporting this habit?" Charlie cocked a brow; combining it with the expression Marti called her "fess up" look.

Janice looked down at her hands, tears leaking over her lower lashes. Charlie scooted a box of tissues toward Janice, who dabbed under her lashes and inhaled a deep shuddering breath.

"If I don't have the cash, I sleep with my dealer or whoever has the pills. My last boyfriend…um, he thought I had a problem with sex."

"How long has this been a problem for you, Janice?"

"Since my teens. It sounds so bad to say it out loud. When a guy gives me a little attention, I have sex with him. This is embarrassing — I'm glad you're a woman." Janice sat back in her chair and placed a hand over her mouth like she wanted to hold in the confession.

Charlie pasted on her best "Oh no, you didn't just knock me out of the chair" face as she waited for Janice to continue. She leaned back and interlaced her fingers over her stomach.

Janice gulped more water and fidgeted. "I like sex. I'm, like, really into it at the time. It makes me feel in control and beautiful when a guy goes crazy over me."

Charlie asked, "Is it always a positive experience for you?"

"Sometimes…afterward, I feel…you know, crappy." Janice screwed up her face as if she could smell the crap. "I don't feel good about the sex when I sleep with some scumbag that I find disgusting just to score pills."

Charlie twirled her pen between her index finger and thumb. "Sex can be just as dangerous an addiction as drugs."

"Tell me about it. I'm a nurse. I know it's dangerous, but I keep doing it. Sometimes after I do it, I hate myself. Especially when some guy or his ex-wife treats me like I'm a slut." With drooping shoulders, Janice dropped her gaze back to her hands.

I can see why Janice would have no shortage of willing sex partners. At a slender five foot seven, Janice had all the mandatory

43

curves. Everything about her exuded pheromones that sent a chemical message of "Yoo-hoo, come get me."

I wonder if Janice was sexually abused as a child. Charlie decided to broach that charged subject on a subsequent session. "One of the dangers of sexual addiction is STD's. Have you contracted any diseases because of this behavior?"

"Yeah." Janice screwed the top of her water bottle on and off. "I got Syphilis once." She looked down and back up to lock gazes with Charlie. "Now I have Genital Herpes. I'm so ashamed." Color crept up Janice's neck, pinking her cheeks. "It's incurable, you know."

"I'm sure it's embarrassing for you since you're a nurse."

"Damned right. I drive to Nashville to see a gynecologist. If I saw someone here, it would be all over the hospital."

"So much for privacy and H.I.P.A.A.," said Charlie.

"You see why I asked about confidentiality?" She held her hands out, palms up.

"Have you been tested for HIV?"

"I get tested every six months." The plastic of the water bottle crackled again. Janice looked at it and loosened her grip.

"Are you using protection now?"

"Sometimes…I know, I should every time, but if I'm drinking…." Janice tilted her head to the side and shrugged her shoulders.

"How much are you drinking?" asked Charlie.

"Not much, really, it's kinda sporadic. One or two drinks every couple of weeks." She shrugged her shoulders again as if it wasn't a big deal.

"Janice, are you drinking while taking the Hydrocodone?" Charlie leaned forward to better hear her answer.

"I know. I shouldn't do that either."

Charlie thought of the Twelve Step saying, "Insanity is doing the same thing over and over again and expecting different results." She passed the Sex Addicts Questions test across the desk to Janice, along with a pen. "Answer those questions, please. Be honest."

Janice looked wary as she reached for the test. Chewing on her bottom lip, she read the form and marked her answers. She slid the test back across the desk toward Charlie and dropped the pen in her purse.

Charlie winced when she saw how high Janice scored for sexual addiction. *Thank goodness my certification to treat sexual addictions is current.*

Finding the underlying triggers to her addictive behaviors would be the key to setting up a successful relapse prevention plan. "I'm curious, Janice, are you craving sex or is it more about the attention?"

Janice screwed up her face as if she were thinking. "I like the attention. It makes me feel special."

"When a man wants you, does it make you feel loved?"

"Sometimes, yes. Most of the time, it makes me feel beautiful. When I feel that way, I like myself. I feel powerful. To be honest, sometimes sex is just a tool to get what I want."

"Like drugs?" said Charlie.

"Yeah, among other things," Janice said, with a shrug of her shoulders. She flashed Charlie a wicked little grin.

Cocking her head to one side, Charlie thought, *Sex for some women is a multipurpose tool. I wonder what monster stole her innocence and at what age?* "Janice, let's talk about group therapy. We have a basic dress code for our program. You need to tone down what you wear to group. I want to lessen temptation so all the group members, including you, can keep their minds on recovery. No low-cut shirts, short skirts, or skin-tight clothes."

Janice whined, "That rules out most of my wardrobe."

Charlie eyed the low cut blouse that threatened to spill Janice's ample breasts across her desk every time she leaned forward. Charlie shook her head and thought, *Janice qualifies as an addictive substance. If she doesn't dress down, none of the men in the groups will hear anything said for the next ten weeks.* "Do you have scrubs?"

"Oh yeah, I have plenty of those."

"Then wear scrubs to group until you can purchase less provocative clothing."

Charlie followed Janice out of her office and stood in the hall, waiting for the restroom to be available. She watched Janice sashay toward the lobby, hips swaying.

On the way, Janice passed a tall man with dark hair. She stopped and turned. "Hi there, are you in this program?"

The guy, who was checking her out, said, "I'll find out in a few minutes. Have you seen a therapist yet?"

"Just finished, I'm starting tonight. Hope to see you around." She touched his muscled bicep. "I'm Janice Knight."

"Kevin Humster." His gaze roamed over Janice's body, and a lazy grin spread across his face. "Are the requirements stiff?"

"Pain in the ass." She plopped a hand on her hip.

"Damn." He frowned and ran his hand through his shaggy hair.

"I'm sure we'll become friends," said Janice.

Charlie watched the interaction and shook her head. *Life is about to become more interesting at Hope Returns.*

CHAPTER 11 - REACHING OUT

Charlie stood rubbing her lower back, staring morosely at the charts piled high on her desk, when the phone rang. "Dr. Stone."

"Hi, Charlie, just a courtesy call. We got the preliminary autopsy report back. Harper had severe blood loss, broken ribs, fractured hips, a shattered shinbone, fractured knees, and internal injuries. The cause of death was cerebral hemorrhage due to head trauma. The injuries were premortem," said Ryan.

"So the autopsy confirms that the killer kept Harper alive during most of the torture. That tells us something more about the unsub."

"Specifically?"

"The killer didn't just go into a blind rage, beating Harper until exhausted. This killer delivered the blows in a strategic manner, to maximize his suffering. I'm curious, what was his blood alcohol level?" With the phone cradled between her ear and shoulder, Charlie tried to organize the paperwork from her last patient.

"You were right. 1.82. He was legally intoxicated."

"A sensitive nose can be a blessing or a curse. This means Harper was an easier target," said Charlie.

"Well, Dr. Bloodhound, we'll just call you in the next time the department sets up a DUI checkpoint."

They both laughed. His was nice, deep and throaty.

I like a man with a sense of humor. Humor was how she coped with tough situations. The work release cops she worked with on some of her cases used morbid humor to get over the tough spots. Sometimes psychologists did, too.

"The approximate time of death was between 1 and 4 a.m.," said Ryan.

"Since he was drunk, he was probably out clubbing. Was his car found?"

"We found it at the Night Owl. The theory is the perp drove him home and parked in the garage. There are old oil stains on the right side of the garage, but fresh ones on the left side. Samples are at the lab. We also checked with the neighbors. No one saw or heard anything."

"I once lived in that neighborhood. I would guess Harper left well before the two o'clock closing time. If he was at the Night Owl, the drive time from that club to his house is about twenty minutes. Then he had sex with someone. Whoever annihilated him needed plenty of time to kill him and then do all that cleaning. If I were the killer, I'd want to disappear before sunrise."

Charlie turned her phone on speaker as she stood, and closed her door for privacy. She stretched her lower back, twisting from side to side with her arms extended over her head. Audible pops brought a smile to her face.

"One of the waitresses saw Harper sitting at the bar, talking to a woman she described as 'some hot chick.' Joe did the interview and believes she may be our unsub."

Charlie heard papers crackling.

"Ah, here's the report. The waitress told Joe that the woman was 'pretty, slender, with long brown hair and big tits.' Unfortunately, she didn't get a good look at her face."

"What about the bartender?" asked Charlie.

"He only worked there a week and was fired at the end of the shift for skimming money off the cash sales. So far, we haven't located him." Ryan sounded resigned. "We're searching through the credit card receipts, but the club owner says they get a lot of cash business."

"Ryan, I work with a counselor here, Marti Hathoway, who went through the same profiler training I did. In fact, she was one of the candidates considered for my position in your department. We act as a clinical team. Am I allowed to discuss this case with her, to bounce ideas off her?"

"I don't know." There was a long pause and more rattling of papers. "Can she be trusted to keep the facts and details of the case confidential?"

"Marti's like Fort Knox. She's a mental health professional."

"I shouldn't do this, but I trust your judgment since she's had the training and you work with her. If there's a leak, it's on your head."

"I'll make sure she understands the confidentiality issues."

"We'll have officers waiting for the ex-wife when she gets home on Saturday. I'd like for you to be there during the interrogation. We need to get a crack at her before she lawyers up."

"There's nothing like a sneak attack. If there isn't anything else, I have a stack of paperwork." Charlie walked over and looked at her fish. One of the males was chasing a female with unusual ardor. After checking the aquarium's thermometer, she understood the passionate pursuit. *Oh great, the tank's too hot. The male thinks it's mating season. I need to cool things off, fast.*

"A few of the guys are going out for a beer after work. You're welcome to join us."

Charlie stood straight, stunned by the invitation. *None of the work release officers ever asked me to join them for drinks.* "Excuse me?"

"I asked if you wanted to hang out with the guys tonight."

"Do you mean to discuss the case?"

"Mainly just hanging out, but yeah, we can discuss the case. One of the guys is having a birthday."

"Ryan, I wish I could, but I'm not a drinker. It sets a bad example for my patients if I'm seen hanging out in bars, and rumors are so easy to start. Thanks for asking." Charlie knew her decision was rational, so why was her heart doing a tap dance in her chest?

"Okay, let me know if you change your mind." Ryan disconnected the call.

Charlie smiled as she pictured Ryan at the diner. *He's the only man who's ever made me tingle.* She was thinking about the color of Ryan's eyes when the image of Nathan standing in their bedroom invaded her mind, shattering Ryan's smiling face the way a collision shatters safety glass.

****

Nathan stood moaning, his head back and his eyes closed. The designer silk tie she'd bought him for their anniversary was knotted to perfection, but his pants pooled around his ankles. His newest stock analyst knelt in front of him, cupping his buttocks while blowing him. Eric stopped, turned his blond head, and stared at her wide-eyed as he wiped Nathan's cum from his mouth. Nathan opened his eyes. She saw shock, shame, and then regret tickertape across his face.

****

Someone knocked on her office door.

Charlie's hand flew to her chest and she swayed.

Marti peeped in. "I hope I'm not interrupting anything. Kathy said you didn't have a patient."

Charlie turned to face her best friend.

"Hi Marti, I just got off the phone with the homicide detective about my consulting case. He gave me permission to collaborate with you. Are you interested in being my Watson?" Charlie waggled her eyebrows.

"Sure, I'm willing to help. What would I do?"

"Be a sounding board, make sure I'm not missing anything, and offer ideas. You'd have to treat this with the utmost confidentiality."

Marti laughed. "I'm a therapist, I know about confidentiality. How's the case going?"

"They just found the victim's car at the Night Owl."

"Menopause Heaven! That's where some of our patients hung out before they entered the program." Marti slid into a chair.

"This guy was a mid-lifer and an alcoholic. A waitress saw him talking to an attractive woman, but she didn't see them leave together."

"Wait, is this case about John Harper, the D.J.? I used to listen to his show on the drive in to work. He had a drop-your-panties sexy voice. I saw on the evening news that he was murdered in his home."

"One and the same, only he no longer has a sexy anything." Charlie scrunched her face at the memory of the blood and gore. "Ryan thinks the killer gave John Harper a ride home."

"A friend could have given him a ride home, or maybe he took a taxi," suggested Marti. Today she wore navy slacks and a freshly ironed turquoise blouse. Silver and turquoise earrings dangled from her earlobes. They looked to be pieces of the Navajo jewelry she'd collected during the years she lived in Albuquerque.

"If that's the case, anyone could be the murderer." Charlie sat down at her desk and tapped her index finger on her chin. "If the killer is a woman, she could drive him home, have sex, and then kill him."

"Maybe you need to start at the beginning and tell me about the case and your profile."

Charlie sat bopping her foot while she brought Marti up to speed on the case. Marti's eyes widened when Charlie described Harper's body.

"I'm leaning toward a female, only women don't tend to bludgeon people to death," said Charlie.

"I agree, but stop worrying about the statistics and trends. They're guidelines, not the holy grail of forensic psychology. There are always exceptions. Let the facts of this case be your guide."

"That's good advice," Charlie agreed. "Ryan thinks it could be a jealous spouse or boyfriend."

"Ryan, huh, so now you're on a first-name basis with this detective. Is he cute?" Marti leaned forward, eyes twinkling with interest.

"Oh yeah, he's hot." Charlie fanned herself and grinned. "He's also off limits."

"Married?"

"No, word is that he's single. In fact, he just asked me to go have a drink with the guys." Charlie sat back in her chair.

Marti had scooted to the edge of her chair. "Did you say yes, tell me you said yes?" she demanded, her earrings bouncing with her emphatic nods. She didn't approve of Charlie's foolproof plan to avoid heartache by not dating and had been on a rampage for several months for Charlie to improve her social life.

"No, we're working together. Besides, it's best if I'm not seen in bars since I work in a treatment facility."

Unlike Marti, Charlie wasn't a recovering addict. She still felt it best to avoid addictive substances. Her parents had never exhibited addicted behavior, but her family tree was laden with alcoholics and addicts.

"Uh huh, we'll see." Marti rolled her eyes, her signature response when Charlie avoided her matchmaking attempts.

"Marti, I'm just not ready to take on a guy right now." Charlie shuddered as she saw Harper's beaten body in her mind, like a gruesome photo. "One thing was clear to me; this murderer was not just angry, but in a rage. Marti, it was a controlled brutal attack to inflict suffering."

Marti winced. "Sounds gruesome. I'm glad I didn't get the profiling job."

"Maybe we'll get some answers tomorrow when the ex-wife arrives home from her cruise. I've been asked to sit in on the interrogation."

"Tomorrow's Saturday. You're working on your day off?"

"Yeah, one of the downsides of the job." Charlie stood and stretched. "I need a cup of coffee so I can focus on this mountain of paperwork."

"I'll go with you. I need a cup of tea."

Walking side by side, they strolled toward the break room.

"So Ryan invited you to join the guys. Maybe he'll ask you to dinner or something?"

"Drop it, Marti, it's not going to happen."

Marti nudged her with her elbow. "We'll see."

CHAPTER 12 - THE EX-WIFE

Charlie leaned forward in her seat behind the one-way mirror, watching for every nuance that might provide a clue to John Harper's murder.

An atmosphere of despair loomed within the gray walls of the Huntsville Police Department interrogation room. Charlie wondered if that was contrived to break down a suspect's resistance. A long rectangular table dominated the space.

Ryan held the door open for Sherry Harper and directed her to a seat on the long side of the metal table so that she faced the one-way mirror. Following behind, Joe closed the door. Ryan sat in a scarred wooden chair diagonally across from her. Joe was to her left, closest to the door. Sherry clutched an oversized purse to her chest as her gaze roved between the two men.

"Ms. Harper, we're going to record this interview." Joe reached over and pushed a button. Small microphones sat in the middle of the table, one facing each of them.

"Do I need a lawyer?"

Joe's wooden posture gave nothing away. "You haven't been arrested or charged with a crime. You're here to answer questions regarding your husband's death."

"Ex-husband. We divorced two years ago." She scowled at Joe and clutched her purse tighter.

"Sorry, ex-husband. If you wanna hire an attorney and spend your hard-earned money, that's your choice. Do you want an attorney?" Joe picked up his pen and tapped it on the yellow legal pad in front of him. Charlie noticed his tie was askew and the top button of his shirt open.

Sherry's face contorted with what appeared to be indecision. "I guess it's okay for now."

Joe leaned over and recited into the mike the preamble required before every interrogation that confirmed the time, date, and those present. "Would you state your full name please?"

"Sherry Ann Harper."

"Would you please state your current address?" Joe tugged at his collar. Charlie noticed a rash and assumed his wife was still having his shirts starched.

"2533 Melodi Lane, Huntsville."

Joe leaned back in his chair, fingers laced over his gut. "Ms. Harper, when did you learn of your ex-husband's death?"

"Today, when my daughter picked me up at the airport. The police were waiting at my house. I didn't even get to unpack." Her expression was grim as she fingered the handle of her purse.

"When was the last time you saw your ex-husband?" Joe ran his hand across his thinning hair.

"A month ago at my daughter's house during my grandson's birthday party." She was hiding behind her purse, only her French manicured nails visible.

Charlie leaned closer. *She's using that purse as a shield.*

"How would you describe your relationship with John Harper?" Ryan looped an elbow over the back of his chair. He looked the picture of ease from the waist up, but Charlie could see under the table, and his right leg was bumping up and down.

She shrugged her shoulders. "After twenty-eight years of marriage, you can't help but have feelings for someone." She looked first at Ryan, then Joe. "We had our differences, but we were courteous to each other for the sake of our daughter and grandkids."

"Did you ask for the divorce or did he?" asked Joe. He began tapping the pen again.

"He did. He said he wanted his freedom." Color crept up her neck, staining her cheeks. Her nails dug into the leather of the purse as her gaze slid over to the tapping pen.

That still upsets her, thought Charlie.

"What did you think about that?" Ryan moved his arm and leaned forward.

"I was upset, of course. He was my husband. I put up with his crap for years, and he left *me*?" Sweat beaded her upper lip and dampened her hairline.

Joe shifted in his chair, scraping it on the floor. "Do you know anyone who might want to kill your ex-husband? Any enemies?"

Sherry heaved a sigh, and her face turned a blotchy scarlet as she pushed her moist hair away from her forehead. "I don't know many of John's *associates*. We went separate ways and lived different lives. John didn't have any enemies when we were married. Have you checked out any of those sluts he's been screwing?" She clamped her jaw shut and gripped the edge of the table.

Charlie sat straighter. *I've seen that body language before. She's jealous.* Charlie bit her lip. *She's still in love with him. He's haunting her heart.*

"We're checking out all of his known associates. If you could provide us a list before you leave, it would be helpful." Joe slid the pad and pen in front of her.

Sherry reached out and pushed the legal pad a few inches away. "I suggest you start with that slut he dated last month. She had the gall to show up dressed like a hooker at my grandson's birthday party! Can you believe it? Debbie asked her to leave, but she refused. John and that whore argued in my daughter's front yard, right there in front of all the neighbors. She was pissed because he didn't invite her. John wasn't stupid; he knew she wouldn't be welcome."

Joe took his notebook from his shirt pocket, along with a pen. "What's the lady's name? We'll talk to her."

Sherry banged her fist on the table. "She's no lady! All I know is her name was Janice. She claimed to be a nurse." A drop of sweat dripped to her blouse, staining it a darker version of the original aqua.

Charlie leaned closer. *Did I hear that right? Did she say, Janice?*

Joe asked, "Ms. Harper, where were you the night before you left for the cruise?"

"Why I was home, packing. I went to bed early. My daughter picked me up at five and took me to the airport. My flight was at six." Sherry's hands were trembling. More sweat dripped from her face to her blouse.

Charlie squinted her eyes to examine Sherry's face. *Is she nervous or having a hot flash?*

Joe folded his hands on the table. "Do you have an alibi, Ms. Harper?"

Sherry stiffened. "I want a lawyer."

CHAPTER 13 - MEMORIES

Exactly at midnight, the Huntress strode past the men loitering around the entrance of the Roustabout. It was Saturday, and the club bustled with activity. The men shifted to create a path for her.

"Oh baby, you're looking hot tonight."

"What's your name, sweetheart?"

"Lemme buy you a drink, honey?"

Ignoring them, she walked the gauntlet. They were easy prey, but they didn't meet her criteria.

Her sexual juices were flowing. She was ready to hunt.

Once inside the club, she slid into the shadows. The Roustabout was a new arena for her. Checking the place for possible escape routes, she scrutinized the layout and planned her approach.

Her need for vengeance was high. Feeling confident, she unzipped her black leather jacket to reveal her white silk blouse and model-walked to the bar with perfect posture. The intensity of each man's interest excited her, giving her moist pleasure.

This was the playful part — the seduction — the game. Eyeing a potential victim, she approached and glided onto the stool next to him. The man shifted in his seat and smiled. She caught sight of his wedding ring and eliminated him. *The last thing I need is a nosy wife coming home while I'm having fun.*

"What can I get you?" the harried-looking bartender asked.

"Corona, with a lime."

"Comin' right up."

In a jiff, he returned and set the bottle on the bar. "You wanna run a tab?"

The Huntress shook her head and handed him some bills. "Keep the change."

The bartender nodded his appreciation and left to fill the next order.

She turned her back to the bar, rested her elbows on the edge, and crossed her legs, letting her black leather skirt ride up her thighs. Her body language was as clear as a flashing neon sign.

She surveyed the club for another potential victim. *Now, that one's promising.* He was about forty-five, graying at the temples, with the mottled nose of an alcoholic.

She narrowed her eyes. *It's time to dangle the bait and reel him in, but first, I want the "worm to squirm."* She stiffened. *Why did I think that? He said that at the river where he took me fishing.*

****

"Come on, Baby Girl, it's just a worm, it won't hurt you."

"It's icky, Daddy, don't make me touch it, please don't make me touch it."

"If I say to touch it, you will touch it."

She knew that growl in his voice. The last time she heard it and disobeyed, he broke her arm. He forced her to tell everybody she fell down the stairs.

Her eyes roamed the wooded area seeking help. There was nowhere to run. They were deep in the woods. Alone. Again.

"That's right, Baby Girl. It's time to make the worm squirm. Wrap both hands around it and stroke it up and down. Not too hard now, oh yes, yes, keep it up."

Tears cascaded down her face as her daddy erupted, squirting white goo across her face and hair.

****

"Can I get you anything else, little lady?" the bartender asked.

The Huntress jumped in her seat and turned. "Umm…no, I'm fine."

Lifting her chin, she snatched her beer and slithered from her seat. She chose an angle that would allow her to pass her mark's table as she sashayed toward the ladies' room.

The crowded conditions forced people to travel along narrow transient pathways. Her quarry sat in a corner in a dimly lit area. She moved closer to check his hand for a wedding ring and saw

57

none. Skimming past him, she pretended to trip and grazed his arm with her breast. Gazing with intent into his eyes, she said, "Oh, sorry to bump you. I didn't cause you to spill your beer, did I?"

"Not a problem, ma'am, no harm done." His eyes crinkled when he smiled.

The Huntress returned his smile and moved on to the ladies' room, where she entered a stall. She was pissed-off now and primed for action. If the place were cleaner, she would masturbate to relieve some of her sexual tension.

After adjusting her clothes back in place, she exited the stall and washed her hands.

Three women were talking near the door. Scrunching her nose, she thought, *Yuck, that heavy makeup makes them look like hell under these harsh fluorescent lights.*

The women's conversation was the same in every ladies' room across the country.

"I thought this guy was different," the blonde whined to her two friends. "He said he loved me."

Rolling her eyes, the Huntress applied lipstick.

"I thought he really cared and that we'd be together." A tear rolled from the blonde's left eye, leaving a smear of mascara in its wake.

The Huntress slid a disgusted glance toward the distraught woman. "Did he tell you he loved you *before* or *after* he screwed you?"

"Before, why?"

Capping her lipstick, the Huntress dropped it in her purse. "Then he won't call. He told you what you wanted to hear to get in your pants. It's time to move on." Shouldering her purse, she brushed past the three women and left the ladies' room.

The Huntress checked the surrounding area before moving toward the man's table.

"Hi." She placed her hand on an empty chair beside him. "Is this seat taken?"

He sat erect, straightened the collar on his western shirt, and removed his Stetson from the seat, placing it on the table.

"No ma'am, you just sit right on down."

"It's so loud and crowded," she said, moving her chair closer to him.

"You're looking mighty fine tonight." He smiled, revealing straight white teeth.

"Thanks. What's your name, cowboy?"

"David, and what's yours, little lady?"

Ignoring the question, she asked, "Do you come here often, David?" She waved her hand to indicate the club.

"I haven't been here in a while. Not since I quit drinking. That was a while back." His shoulders drooped as he rubbed his chin. "I relapsed, and my lady broke up with me, didn't even tell me why. So here I am, back to business as usual." He raised his beer in a silent toast and then downed the remainder. "I've been down lately. Thought I'd come out tonight, hoping it would cheer me up." He picked up the pitcher on the table and filled his mug with care.

"Raising a man's spirit is my specialty." She leaned forward and covered his hand with hers. "She was a fool to let a man like you get away." Her manicured hand ran up his arm to his shoulder and then traced down his back. Moving closer, she pressed her breast against his arm. Her breath caught in her throat as his hand settled on her thigh.

"I guess I was lucky it had happened before I tried to sell my house." His voice sounded disconsolate.

"Do you live alone?"

He nodded, then picked up his mug and took a swallow.

"It must get so lonely." She laid her head on his shoulder.

He nodded again. Unshed tears sparkled in his eyes. Settling back onto his seat, he took a long swig of beer. His hand slid from her thigh.

"I know it hurts, but I'm here to cheer you up, remember? Where were we?" The Huntress placed his hand back on her thigh.

He looked into her eyes. "We were about to discuss how beautiful you are."

The hand on her thigh inched upward and his gaze dropped from her eyes to the swell of her breasts. The Huntress unfastened another button to offer a clearer view.

David sat straighter. "Better watch it, pretty lady, you're tempting me to do things."

"I want you to; it makes me feel beautiful." Reaching for his other hand, she placed it over her erect nipple.

He glanced around and shifted in his seat, using his broad back as a shield. He fondled her breast and squeezed her nipple.

"Ahh, yes," she moaned. She uncrossed her legs and spread them.

Sliding his hand up, he glided his fingers inside her moist depths.

"Don't stop, yes, don't stop," she hissed, as she matched the rhythm of his finger thrusts. Her body tensed and she shuddered with her release. She sighed, leaned against him, and smiled her satisfaction.

A startled expression washed over his face. "I've never done nothin' like that before in public." He looked around to see if anyone had noticed.

Pulling her clothes back in place, the Huntress thought, *and you never will again.*

CHAPTER 14 - HOW DID I GET HERE?

It was almost midnight. Charlie was wide-awake, strung out from her week. She shuffled into her living room with a large bowl of popcorn and a fizzing glass of soda and placed them on the coffee table in front of the sofa. *I need a little cinema therapy.*

She tore the crackling plastic off a DVD. Marti had given her "Runaway Bride," starring Julia Roberts, but she had never watched it. After popping it into the player, she made it back to the sofa and flopped down on it with a grunt. Spanky hopped up next to her.

"Spanky, it's just us girls on a Saturday night. I live *such* an exciting life."

The smells of butter and salt wafted to Charlie's nose, making her salivate. Popcorn was her favorite comfort food, just a smidgen ahead of chocolate and ice cream. She leaned back, melted into the sofa, and propped her feet on the coffee table.

Spanky stretched her twitching nose toward the bowl, sniffing.

"You just keep your nose to yourself, Spanky. This is *my* popcorn!" Charlie moved the red ceramic bowl out of reach. "I've had a trying week. Don't mess with me."

Spanky gave her a reproachful look, then turned around three times and snuggled against Charlie's thigh. Feeling both tenderness and envy, Charlie listened to the gentle snores that matched the rise and fall of the beagle's side. "Gee, Spanky, I wish I could fall asleep that easy. Heck, I wish I could fall asleep, period."

Charlie's sleep schedule had gone awry since the murder. Normally comatose by ten, she was now awake past midnight, her mind whirling. If she passed out from exhaustion, she would wake with a nightmare. She had an appointment on Monday to see if her doctor could suggest something new for insomnia.

I hope this romantic comedy will lift my spirits. She needed something to nudge her mind away from dark thoughts and speculations.

Charlie convulsed with laughter throughout "Runaway Bride." The bride was running from her wedding, with loads of chiffon flying behind her like wings, when Charlie paused the movie. "Drat, I need more Dr. Pepper."

She placed the popcorn on the table and walked to the kitchen for a refill.

When she returned, Spanky was on the coffee table with her head buried in the bowl of popcorn.

"No!" Charlie yelled.

Spanky's head popped out of the bowl and swiveled toward Charlie. The gawky pup lost her balance, all four paws skating in different directions on the table's polished surface. Clawing to gain traction, Spanky skidded into the bowl, showering the whole area with popcorn. She slid off the edge of the table with a thump and scampered away, her tail between her legs.

"Good grief, what's next?" Charlie clapped her hand over her mouth as she eyed the popcorn scattered across the rug. Erupting into giggles, she knelt and scraped the popcorn into the bowl.

Spanky wiggled forward, her body low to the ground in a groveling apology.

Charlie patted her on the head and crooned, "I forgive you, Spanky."

The pup raced circles around the coffee table, scattering the remaining popcorn.

"Calm down!"

After cleaning up the mess, she threw the remainder of the popcorn in the trash, and turned off the TV.

Never a morning person, Charlie pulled out her clothes for the next day and laid them out in her walk-in closet. It was a habit she'd developed while on-call during her psychology internship. Satisfied, she brushed her teeth and crawled into bed around two. Spanky leaped on the bed, circled, and then snuggled close. Sleep blanketed Charlie in its warm embrace.

She woke on the couch. She looked over at the clock on the DVD player. *Four in the morning? How did I get here?* She stood and fell over her purse. She heard her keys jangle to the floor. Feeling confused, she staggered back to bed.

CHAPTER 15 - DANGER

Charlie dragged herself into work on Monday clutching a large mocha latte. While feeding her goldfish, she noticed a lime green sticky note stuck to the middle of her desk blotter. Yawning, she picked it up and read, *Crawfish found in the hall. Almost sucked into the vacuum. Back in the tank.*

Charlie, mouth open, bent down and peered into the aquarium. She spotted Harvey somewhat hidden by a rock. "So you had a little adventure last night, Harvey?"

"Are you talking to Harvey again?"

Charlie jumped and blushed as she turned to find Marti grinning at her.

"Well at present, he's the only male in my life, and last night he stepped out on me." Charlie handed Marti the sticky note.

Marti read it and giggled. "I would have loved to be a fly on the wall when they found Harvey. You look tired. What's up, girl?"

"It's this case."

"You want to talk about it over lunch?"

"Sure, that would be great. Meanwhile, I have an intake waiting."

Charlie sank into her chair and thought, *dear Lord, please let me make it to lunch. Not sleeping is getting to me.*

She shook her head to clear it and swallowed the last of her latte. *Perhaps I should just start a caffeine IV.* She tossed the cup in the trash, popped a breath mint in her mouth, and walked to the front office.

Kathy offered a perky smile and handed her the patient's portion of the new chart. She pointed over her shoulder to the adjoining room. "Nellie has the old one."

"So he's a rerun," said Charlie.

"More like a mini-series," said Nellie. Everything about Nellie screamed, *office mommy.* Her domain was the records room, where she presided behind a large wooden desk.

Charlie shot over to the metal bins along the wall behind Nellie, to retrieve the rest of her charts for the day. En route, she hit her thigh on the corner of the desk.

"Ow!"

"Are you attacking my desk with your thigh again?" Nellie grinned, glasses perched on the end of her nose.

"I'm running low on sleep today," said Charlie, rubbing her thigh.

Kathy chimed in, "You're just a natural born klutz, Charlie. Admit it."

"True, but I'm lovable." Charlie shrugged her shoulders, batted her eyelashes, and hammed it up a bit.

"You are indeed lovable," said Nellie. Her glasses slipped off her nose and dangled by the beaded chain that hung around her neck.

Charlie sat in the chair beside Nellie's desk and flipped through her next patient's chart. His criminal background was extensive. Two DUI's, one drunk and disorderly, two burglaries, one armed robbery, and three domestic violence arrests made it clear he wasn't a choir boy. His name was Mark Walker, IV. Charlie wondered how many generations of Mark Walkers were alcoholics. She noticed in the chart that Max, the clinic's director, had been his last therapist.

Charlie stood, stretched, and walked to the lobby to escort Mr. Walker to her office.

"Mr. Walker, I'm Dr. Stone, come with me, please?"

He sneered as he unfolded from a slouch and stood to face her. Standing well over six feet, he towered over her. Rolling his massive shoulders, he stretched, interlaced his fingers and popped them.

Unfazed, Charlie looked up and met his cold black eyes, "Follow me."

Once in her office, she pointed to the chair across from her desk. "Have a seat, please."

He glanced around the room and took his sweet time pulling out the chair. Slumping into it, he rested one elbow on the back. He crossed his ankle on top of his knee, rested the other hand on it, and smirked.

"I see you've been a guest of ours before," said Charlie. Warning signals clanged in her mind. She sat and opened the top drawer to the left of her desk a bit.

He shrugged, reached into his pocket, and took out a cigarette.

"You can't smoke in here."

He gave her a narrow-eyed glare.

Pasting on an expression of professional calm that belied her racing heart, she stared him down. She took a breath when he replaced the cigarette back in the package.

He sat back in his chair and eyed her. "I don't *need* to be here. I don't have a problem."

The chart showed Walker had flunked out of the program twice in the last four years.

"Your criminal record indicates otherwise. Let's start the assessment. I already have your past history, so we can just pick up —"

"Are you married, honey?" He tilted his head and pushed his sweatshirt sleeves up his forearms, exposing tattoos.

"Please address me as Dr. Stone."

"Well, I didn't mean to ruffle your feathers." He winked.

Her antisocial meter swung to a seven on a one-to-ten scale. *Much higher and he'll hit serial killer range.*

"How much are you drinking now?" Charlie gripped her pen, poised to take notes.

Walker grinned, exposing nicotine-yellowed teeth. "Just a couple during the day." He tilted his head again, letting his black shark eyes roam the room before his gaze dropped to Charlie's chest.

She felt her shoulders stiffen. Her autonomic nervous system seemed to be jumping into overdrive. "You know the drill, Mr. Walker. How many is a couple?"

"Hey, it's just a case, besides it's beer. I'm not drinking the hard stuff or smoking dope. What's wrong with having a beer?" His voice lowered an octave as he abandoned the slouch to lean forward, gripping the arms of his chair.

Working to maintain her external calm, she took a breath and asked, "When was your last drink?"

"Yesterday." He rubbed his unshaven chin. She could hear the rasp of his stiff whiskers.

"I can smell the alcohol on your breath. If you're telling the truth, then we need to set up an immediate medical examination for you."

His eyes widened, and he sat back in the chair. "Why's that?"

"If you drank yesterday and you smell of alcohol now, it means your liver is so damaged that it can't metabolize the alcohol, so it's backing up into your system." Charlie flipped to the next page of the paperwork.

"I drank an hour ago. I don't need to see no damn doctor." He resumed his slouch.

"Thank you for *finally* being honest. Are you still a daily drinker?"

He grunted and shrugged one shoulder.

"With your drinking history and the amount you consume, it wouldn't hurt to get a check-up. In fact, you may need inpatient detox."

"*Inpatient detox!*" Wild-eyed, he sat straight in the chair.

Charlie matched his posture. "Yes, to go cold turkey, after drinking so much for such a long time, could cause a dangerous rise in blood pressure, D.T.'s, seizures, or even death." Sensing danger, she felt her entire body tense like an exercise band.

Walker stood, placed his hands palm down on the desk, and leaned over. With a deep rumbling voice, he yelled, "I don't need detox. I don't need this damn program. I don't have a problem!"

"Mr. Walker, I suggest you take your seat and lower your voice. You are court-ordered to complete this program or any program I deem appropriate. If you don't complete it, you *will* go to jail."

He loomed closer. Alcohol fumes and body odor assaulted Charlie's olfactory system. His face was as crimson as the jersey he wore. He sneered, one corner of his mouth lifted, "I can do ninety days in jail on my head. You bitch, I oughta —"

Charlie sprang to her feet.

With raised brows, Walker stepped back out of range.

She removed a knuckle stun gun from the open drawer and flicked it on. Giving him the look Marti called her "Don't mess with me, asshole" expression, she placed a hand on her hip. "*You* need to know that Judge Hinklesmith considers the staff of this program to be an extension of him. If you touch me, it will be as if you assaulted the judge. He'll make ninety days look like a vacation. This assessment is over. I'll inform your probation officer that you have refused treatment. Leave my office, NOW!"

Walker appeared to be considering his options. His eyes flicked to the stun gun. Shrugging his shoulders, he winked at her again, and turned to leave.

Weak-kneed, stomach churning, Charlie white-knuckled the handle and opened the door, grateful for the setup of her office. The stun gun remained gripped in her hand.

Walker snarled the word, "Cunt," as he steam-rolled past her.

He came to an abrupt halt in the hallway. Max and three other clinicians stood there ready to intervene if needed.

Max stepped forward with a hard, squinty glare. "Hello, Mark, I see you're back. I'll escort you off the premises, so you don't get lost."

Walker mumbled, "I don't want to be here anyway."

"He needs to call a cab or someone to drive him. He's been drinking." Charlie stepped into the doorway and leaned against the jamb.

Walker whirled to give Charlie a venomous look, his cheeks blotching red. "I ain't drunk. I don't need nobody to drive me."

Charlie took a step back in case he planned to take a swing at her.

Max moved toward him. "Watch your mouth, Mark."

Walker held up his hands, turned on his heels, and stomped toward the lobby. Max followed him.

Typical domestic violence perp, Charlie thought. *He's cocky with women, but he backs down when a man confronts him.* She released a pent-up breath and turned off the stun gun. She didn't want to fry her neurons by accident.

She assured the remaining staff that she was unharmed and then shooed them back to their posts.

Marti came barreling down the hall with a determined, tight-lipped expression. Marching past Charlie, she pulled her into her office, closed the door, and wrapped Charlie in a hug. Charlie began to tremble and broke into tears.

Marti rubbed circles on her back. "It's just the aftershock of adrenaline, let it go, Charlie."

Marti had X-ray eyes. She saw past all Charlie's defenses, down to the splintered pieces of her psyche, and still loved her as a friend.

After a few moments, Charlie regained her composure, snatched a tissue with a shaking hand, and swiped under her eyes.

A bang on the door caused them both to jump. Charlie opened the door. There stood Max, her boss, a white knight in wrinkled, mismatched clothing.

"Thanks for being there, Max."

"That's my job. I made sure Walker left and didn't cause any mischief in the parking lot." With a devious twinkle in his eye, he continued, "I also called the police and reported that a drunk driver just left our parking lot in a dark green Chevy, and I gave them his license plate number. He should have let us call him a cab."

Charlie and Marti looked at each other and laughed.

"I want to discuss this in detail with you after lunch. I plan to call his probation officer and Judge Hinklesmith; you know I play golf with him every Saturday."

Charlie closed the door and sank into her chair with a sigh. She felt as if her life force was dribbling from her body and pooling under her chair.

"Max is having way too much fun with this," said Marti. She waved her hand in front of her face. "Whew! It smells like he hasn't had a bath in a month, and instead tried to pickle himself in beer."

"True, but the guy brought it on himself. My antisocial meter hovered at a seven."

"If I remember correctly, your scale tops out at a ten. Walker's also an alcoholic bully, who doesn't see that he has a problem and needs help," said Marti.

"Also true, but Marti, we can only do what we can. I can't shovel recovery down his throat and make him swallow AA. Nellie called him a mini-series."

"Oh! He's one of *those* repeat performers. I thought he looked familiar."

"On the bright side, I'm awake now." Charlie attempted a smile but didn't quite pull it off.

"Good, I need to go back to work."

"Thanks for the hug, Marti, it's just what I needed."

"You did good, girl." Marti gave her a thumbs-up and walked out the door.

Charlie aimed toward the restrooms. *Being threatened by a large Neanderthal does strange things to a lady's bladder.*

The doors to the group room across the hall sprang open, and patients streamed into the hallway. Some made a beeline for the restrooms. Others shuffled toward the smoking area. The once-quiet hallway echoed with loud banter and laughter.

Janice Knight blocked her path and whispered, "Dr. Stone, can I talk to you for a minute?" She kept glancing down the hallway as if she expected to see the devil himself.

"Sure, let's pop in here." Charlie gestured Janice into her office, begging her bladder to hold on.

Janice skulked into Charlie's office and stood out of sight behind the door, wringing her hands.

Charlie closed the door. "What's wrong, Janice? You look petrified."

"Is *he* going to be in this program? If he is, I need to transfer somewhere else. I can't be here with *him*," Janice blurted, trembling. Tears welled in her eyes.

"What're you talking about?"

"Mark Walker," she whispered the name as if he would hear her. "I saw him come out of your office, and go out the front door with Max behind him. I thought he saw me and that was why he was so angry. Then I realized something else happened, and he didn't notice me."

Charlie crossed her arms. "Janice, why are you so afraid of him?"

"He nearly killed me."

"What?" Charlie walked behind her desk and sank into her chair.

"I met him at the Night Owl. He was the sexy, bad-boy type. You know, mysterious."

Charlie found nothing sexy or mysterious about Mark Walker. *Maybe dangerous and stinky.*

"We went out a couple of times, and then he got drunk one night and nearly beat me to death. I escaped to my car and hid at my girlfriend's house that night."

Charlie handed her a tissue. "Did you report this to the police?"

"Hell no, if I did, he'd kill me for sure. Anytime I see him in a club, I leave. He said I was *his* and nobody else could have me." Janice quivered with her arms wrapped tight like she was cold.

"I can't reveal confidential patient information, Janice. Just trust me when I say there is no reason for you to leave this program."

"Are you sure?" Janice nudged the tissue under her lower lashes to avoid smearing her mascara. It was too late; she looked like a depressed raccoon.

"I'm sure." Charlie stood and walked over to open the door. "You might want to check your makeup before you go back to the group."

Janice threw her arms around Charlie, "Thanks, Doc." Then she backed away, face red with embarrassment. She walked out the door with her head down and disappeared.

Holding her stomach, Charlie took mincing steps toward the employee restroom.

CHAPTER 16 - THE SECOND VICTIM

Charlie put down "Hard Latitudes," by Baron R. Birtcher, to get ready for bed.

Her mobile phone jangled the pithy tune assigned to Ryan Roberts.

"We have another murder, Charlie. It's the same M.O. as Harper's." His voice sounded grim.

A jolt of adrenaline drove sleepiness from her body. "Do you need me?"

"Get a pen. I'll give you the address."

Spanky raised her head, her ears twitching as Charlie raced to the kitchen drawer to grab a pen and paper. "Okay."

"The address is 2446 Philips Drive."

Charlie flashed back to the last murder scene and felt queasy. "I'm on my way."

****

Parking behind a police cruiser, Charlie crawled out of her green Honda. She locked her purse in the trunk and picked her way up the driveway in the dark. Following the procedure, she stopped to sign in with the officer manning the post.

"Hello, Officer Dennison, I haven't seen you since the last murder."

"Hi Doc, did you tell your uncle, George, I said hello?"

"I saw him Friday night. He plans to call you," Charlie scribbled her name on the sheet, along with her check-in time. "Where's your no-neck buddy?"

"Jackson?" Dennison shook his head and shifted his feet. "He's inside rubber-necking."

Great. Charlie walked up the sidewalk toward the front door but hesitated when a large man wearing a Tyvek suit raced out of it. With his head down and his hand over his unmasked mouth, he staggered into the bushes and started retching. It sounded like he was vomiting up a liver or maybe a gallbladder, based on the horrendous sounds coming from the tall azaleas.

The stench drifting from the open door made her queasy. Her stomach churned, as she pulled out a tissue and used it to cover her nose and mouth as she entered.

Ryan walked in her direction holding the suit, and an open container of vapor rub.

"What have we got?" Her voice sounded nasal, due to her best effort to avoid breathing through her nose.

"A forty-five-year-old white male named David Street." He plopped the small bottle of vapor rub in her hand. "Put some under your nose before you pull up your mask, it helps."

The pungent odor was a welcome relief from the stench of putrefaction. Smearing a generous amount above her lip, she closed the jar and returned it to Ryan.

"Thanks."

Next, he handed her the protective gear and gloves. Charlie steadied herself on his shoulder to slip the booties over her shoes, and then followed him as she pulled up her mask.

The foyer opened into a small living room on the right. In the middle stood a table covered in papers and banker's boxes. A tech was preparing them as possible evidence.

She followed Ryan into a den that was a converted garage, with a large television front and center, flanked by built-in bookcases. After a quick glance, she caught up with Ryan, who paused in the kitchen.

"Harvest Gold appliances, was that the sixties or seventies?" asked Charlie.

Ryan shrugged. "I just know they're old. The body's this way."

They walked down a long hallway toward the master bedroom. She heard a buzzing sound. A fly whizzed past her ear as a flash of light bounced off the walls of the hall.

"Jason has already started the crime scene photos." Ryan glanced at her. "Are you ready for this?"

Charlie lifted her chin and nodded. The buzzing sound grew louder as she approached the room. Another fly zipped past her as Ryan stepped aside to let her enter.

The stench almost knocked her back out the door.

"Holy shit!" She couldn't believe the intensity of the smell. There were flies everywhere.

'Shit' seems to be your go-to response, Doc."

Eyes watering, she said, "I work with living people, remember? The worst case of B.O. doesn't smell this bad."

Ryan chuckled. "That's true. The longer you're here, the less you smell it. Oh, I forgot, you're Dr. Bloodhound."

Charlie rolled her eyes. The repartee offered a reprieve from the gruesome scene before them. *Dark humor*, thought Charlie, *the coping mechanism of those who deal with death.*

Maggots crawled over the mutilated body. What was left of the man's face was moving. Maggots were creeping in and out of his gaping mouth and falling to the bed where he lay naked and spread-eagled. Flies beat against the windows, seeking escape.

Bile rose in her throat, and she gagged, covering her masked mouth with her hand.

"Don't upchuck on my crime scene," warned Joe Sparks, giving her a beady-eyed glare.

A camera flash gave the whole scene a ghoulish, horror movie quality.

Her stomach contents zoomed like a rollercoaster, threatening to shoot up her esophagus any second. She closed her eyes and

73

fought for control over her stomach and emotions. "No wonder that big cop ran out the door puking," she gasped.

Ryan said, "You mean Jackson, the uniform that gave you a hard time at the last murder scene."

Charlie blurted, "That was Officer No-Neck barfing his guts out in the bushes out front?" Her hand flew to her mask-covered mouth. *Oh shoot, I shouldn't have said that.*

"Woohoo! This shrink is starting to grow on me. I'll have to make sure Jackson is feeling better." Joe's eyes smiled at Charlie over his mask.

Charlie almost felt sorry for Jackson. He would take a ribbing about this for a long time. Closing her eyes, she composed herself. *I need to focus if I want to help catch this killer.*

The bedroom furnishings were sparse. Another big-screen television dominated the wall opposite the bed. Neat stacks of porn magazines sat on the chest-of-drawers. The top magazine depicted a slender, blonde woman with breasts much too large and perky to be natural. *I wonder if porn is connected to these murders?*

With reluctance, Charlie steeled herself to look at the body.

Again, most of the damage centered on the face and genitals. "This is bad, worse than the first if that's possible. Did the killer castrate him?" asked Charlie.

"Yeah, just like before." Ryan grimaced. "He also ejaculated, and he's wearing a condom."

The condom half-covered the bloody pulp of his penis, which was crawling with maggots.

"I wonder if that's the same brand of condom? Is the killer supplying hers or using the victims'?"

"That's a good question," said Joe, with a surprised rise of his brow.

Jason spoke up over the din of the buzzing insects. "I'm through in here. I'll go shoot the rest of the house."

"Good, bag the condom, Mike." Joe nodded to a young tech, turned his back and started talking to a member of the finger-printing crew.

"Gross!" Mike scrunched his face as he pulled the condom free of the bloody pulp of flesh with tweezers. Maggots flew in all directions as he jiggled the condom to rid it of its inhabitants.

Charlie gawked as he struggled to get the bloody condom into an evidence bag. She had no plans to move any closer and risk squishing, falling on, or touching any of those slimy, white creatures.

She turned to Ryan. "Was this victim handcuffed too?"

"Yep," said Ryan. "He has the same marks on his wrists."

"Do you know how long he's been dead?"

"It takes twenty-three hours for eggs to hatch into maggots in warm temperatures. Possibly one to three days, but the M.E. will have to check for the stages of their development," said Ryan.

A fresh pang of nausea washed over Charlie.

"It's only been two weeks since the last murder," said Joe.

Charlie nodded, averting her gaze from the squirming blobs. "That qualifies as a cooling off period. I agree with you, Joe; these murders are close in proximity. This shows a strong compulsion to kill. How did the flies get in the house to lay eggs?"

"There was a window cracked open in the den." Joe rolled his shoulders and stretched. "Female blowflies are attracted to the smell of blood from as far as a mile away."

Charlie swatted away several flies that buzz-bombed her with her gloved hand. "There are so many of them."

"They can lay as many as two hundred to five hundred eggs," said Joe.

Charlie turned to look at Joe. "I didn't know you were an expert on female blow flies."

Mike mumbled, "Don't make his head any bigger."

"I heard that," said Joe.

Charlie continued to swat at the swarming flies while moving toward the opposite wall to avoid the bed and maggots. Blood splattered the walls, and the white sheets were stained brown with the victim's once-vital fluids.

She pointed at the wall. "Does this splatter pattern mean the killer stood over there, on the right side of the bed again?"

"Yes, it's the same type of blood splatter pattern," said Ryan. "You see this section here, where it's like an arc?" Ryan leaned over, pointing to a specific spot. "That's spray from the knife cuts."

"Speaking of knives, was the murder weapon in the dishwasher at John Harper's house?"

"None of his knives matched the wound pattern. There were serrated steak knives, but the knife used to castrate him wasn't serrated," said Ryan.

The dark carpet was free of stains, but maggots dropped from the bed onto the floor. Charlie quivered at the thought of stepping on one and feeling that squelch beneath her paper booties. She pointed down. "The killer scrubbed the carpet to remove the blood."

Ryan moved to stand next to her. "Yep, we noticed that, too."

A crime scene tech walked in lugging a portable ultraviolet light. After he had plugged it in, he directed it toward the victim and the carpet. The previously invisible bloodstains on the carpet fluoresced, making the murder scene even more grisly.

"There are footprints! That looks like a ladies' sneaker. It's smeared from scrubbing, but I can tell she has small feet like mine," said Charlie. She placed her foot next to the print. They were the same size. "It's a size five."

Joe walked over to look, frowned; and gave Charlie an inscrutable look.

"You're right," said Ryan. "We may have just got our first big break. Too bad it's smeared. We might have been able to trace the tread pattern. On the bright side, carpet holds the shape better than hardwood floors."

"Can I check the rest of the house if I don't touch anything?" asked Charlie. She was holding her stomach with one hand.

"Sure," said Ryan. "Watch where you walk."

Everything was neat and in its place. There was a light coat of dust on the furniture, about what Charlie would expect after three of four days. The bathroom and kitchen were spotless. There were no towels on the racks in either bathroom. The dishwasher light glowed green, signaling a completed wash cycle. She was standing in front of the pantry door, debating whether she should open it, when Ryan walked into the kitchen.

"Ryan, the killer washed the dishes. There are also no towels in the bathrooms." She stepped aside as Ryan walked toward the pantry door.

Opening it, Ryan said, "Ahhh, the vacuum's still here, so the perp hasn't discovered that mistake yet."

Charlie wandered back into the den. Full of what appeared to be hand-me-downs, the den had a shabby, eclectic appearance. The only new furnishings were the leather recliner and flat-screen TV.

Ryan said, "The coroner is here, and we're ready to move the body. Joe suggested we go get coffee and discuss the case so that you can go off the clock."

Charlie clutched her hands in front of her. "I could use some fresh air and a cup of decaf."

"We'll take off as soon as they remove the body. Let me check with everyone to see if they want me to bring back anything."

****

Camera flashes and bright video lights blinded Charlie the moment she and Ryan stepped past the crime scene tape. The media swarmed them. Reporters shot questions rat-a-tat-tat at Ryan.

"No comment. No comment. No comment."

Taking Charlie's arm, he propelled her through the journalists and media correspondents. A local television reporter who'd interviewed Charlie a week earlier locked gazes with her. She saw his gaze drop to the laminated badge with the H.P.D. logo, hanging around her neck.

The reporter stuck a microphone in her face. "Dr. Stone, are you consulting on these murders? What can you tell us about them?"

"No comment," Charlie said, as she brushed past and strode to her car. Once inside, she slammed the door and locked it. She drove to the end of the street and waited at the stop sign. Ryan pulled around her, and she followed him.

CHAPTER 17 - COPING

Charlie warmed her hands on the steaming cup of coffee. After what she'd witnessed, the bright lights in the all-night diner made her feel safe.

"You handled that media situation well. All official comments to the press come from the department's spokesperson," said Ryan.

"Thanks," said Charlie. "I was given some guidelines for handling the press during my recent orientation."

"Are you all right?" His blue eyes softened with a concerned look.

"Do you ever get used to seeing all this carnage, Ryan? I don't think I could do your job full-time." Charlie shook her head and ran her hand through her hair.

He stared into the depths of his cup for a moment.

"Not all our cases are this bad, but you never get used to it. It's an assault on your system every time." He looked deep into her eyes. "You learn to turn off part of yourself, so you don't take it home and see it in your dreams. If you don't learn that skill, you burn out early. The worst part is the way I now see the human race. All the death and violence makes me sometimes wonder what makes humans so damn evil."

Charlie rolled her shoulders, trying to release some of the stiffness. "I think humans are both good and evil. Some are just sicker than others. I understand what you're saying. As a therapist, I hear people's subterranean thoughts and darkest secrets. I do my best to leave the trauma at my office, but I can't remove myself to the extent that I don't feel for my patients. This is different, somehow. I guess I just haven't adjusted to the visual impact and the smell of this situation yet. When people describe the horrors of what has been done to them, I only have to contend with my own inner visions of what they describe. Those are bad enough."

"What's making this so hard for you, compared to what you do already?" asked Ryan.

"This is so real, gory, and multi-sensory. I haven't succeeded yet in turning off the pictures in my head from these murders. I'm not sleeping well, and I'm having nightmares."

"Hey, Joe and I are affected by this case, too. I've had a few sleepless nights myself. Uh, don't tell Joe I told you that." Ryan grinned and winked.

"Your secret is safe with me." Charlie managed a low-wattage smile.

"You're doing pretty well so far," Ryan leaned forward, a smile tugging the corners of his mouth. "You haven't barfed or fainted yet! That's better than Jackson. I heard he was in the bushes throwing up until all he could do was dry heave."

"Hey, I thought I would be out there hurling my popcorn with him." *Dark humor* thought Charlie.

Ryan nodded and put down his cup. Charlie saw respect and attraction in his eyes. She was experiencing similar feelings toward him. She wondered if perhaps sharing trauma bonded people to each other.

The image of David Street flashed before her eyes like a transparency placed over Ryan and the diner, jerking her back to the scene of the murder. She shivered, shaking her head to dispel the image.

"Ryan, we may have a serial killer at work here. I could be wrong — I sure hope so." She ticked off the criteria on her fingers. "The FBI definition of a serial killer is one or more offenders, with two or more murdered victims. The incidents should be separate events, at different times. This is called a cooling off period. These murders were two weeks apart. The key will be if there is any connection between the two victims. During my training, we were advised to encourage law enforcement to check ViCAP for similar cases."

"*If* this is a serial killer, do you think Harper was the first?" asked Ryan.

"Hard to say. We're living in a mobile society."

Ryan shook his head. "That's a disturbing thought."

"The difficulty I'm having with profiling this case is that almost everything points to a female. The sex, the condoms, the choice of porn preferred by the victims, and now, the small footprints. Castration could fit a female profile."

"So what's the hang-up?" Ryan gulped some coffee, winced, and blew on the cup's contents.

"Bludgeoning is the M.O. of a male. Female serial killers are also a small minority compared to males, and they tend to use poison or smother people," said Charlie.

"Have there been many female serial killers?" Ryan eyed a guy covered with tattoos who walked in and slouched on a stool at the counter.

Charlie followed his gaze. "Maybe a dozen in the U.S., when you look back through history. The motives for killing are different for men and women. I think most females kill for monetary gain or to escape an unpleasant situation. Males seem to be more violent and are involved in most of the cases involving sexual compulsions. However, there were the cases of Gwendolyn Graham and Cathy Wood. As a team, they killed people in nursing homes in the eighties, and their crimes showed sexual cruelty."

"I can see that males would use more physical violence," said Ryan. "What about the hooker who was killing all those men in Florida?"

"Aileen Wuornos did break the pattern by shooting her male johns. She claimed the men raped her. She claimed a long history of sexual abuse from early childhood."

He nodded, emptied his cup and glanced at his watch.

"Ryan, as more information comes available, profiles can change. I ran this past Marti, and she's suggested that I not worry about the statistics and trends so much. I want to rework the profile and see if I can give you more information."

"That sounds reasonable," said Ryan.

"Since this victim was more mangled than the last one, the killer may be under more stress."

"I sure hope you're wrong, Charlie."

"Me too. Have you checked out the violent sex offenders in this area?"

"We have; no one matches our M.O."

"Damn. Maybe the forensics will give us more clues." Charlie folded and refolded the paper from the straw that rested in her water glass.

"Don't assume that because you see it on TV, the state can afford to own all that equipment. We do the best we can with what we have."

"I'll be curious to know if our latest victim was legally intoxicated. The stench was so bad! Heck, I couldn't smell anything but death and vapor rub. I'm putting these clothes in the washer the minute I get home." Charlie scrunched her face. "I can still smell it."

"Good idea. I always undress in the garage after working a scene and put my clothes directly in the washer. I always change into different shoes at the scene of a murder and never wear them inside. You want to be careful not to spread contaminants into your house. This suit will go to the cleaners tomorrow."

The image of Ryan undressing in his garage brought a saucy smile to Charlie's face.

"What?" Ryan pushed back from the table, cocking a brow.

"Oh, nothing." Her face felt hot. Embarrassed, she shifted in her seat. "That reminds me, I didn't see a car. How did he get home?"

"Good to see you were paying attention."

"I try, but all the blood, gore, and maggots are distracting."

"Let's not forget the stench." Ryan scrunched his nose.

"Oh, I won't be forgetting that anytime soon." Charlie shook her head with emphasis. "Any suggestion for how to get this smell out of my nose?"

"Do you have a neti pot?"

Her brows rose. "I do. Never thought of that."

Ryan glanced back at the tattooed guy at the counter. "If our killer picked David Street up in a bar, then his car would either still be there or towed. Joe and I will canvass the clubs and see if there have been any abandoned vehicles. We can run him in the system to find out the make, model, and tag number."

"I'll give you a call when I rework the profile."

"I'll contact you when we have the autopsy and forensic results."

"Good." Charlie glanced at her watch. "I need to go home and let Spanky outside."

"Who's Spanky?"

"She's my seven-month-old beagle puppy. I need to install a doggie door. I'm away too long sometimes for her to hold it. Thank goodness for puppy pads."

"I could do that for you. I'm Mr. Handy." Ryan wiggled his eyebrows and winked. "I put one in for my sister a few months back."

"I just might take you up on that. These early morning wake-up calls are killing me."

Ryan walked Charlie to her car and opened the door.

"Goodnight, Ryan." She slid into the seat.

"You be careful driving home, Doc."

"How long do you think it will be before everyone finishes and you get to go home?" He looked so tired.

"It'll be a long time yet. Nice that you're concerned." He smiled as if pleased by the thought. "I've got to go back in and get coffee for the guys."

He placed his hand on her shoulder, gave it a quick squeeze, and then closed her door. Her shoulder tingled. As she drove, pondering what to include in the psychological profile, she suspected sleep would elude her again tonight.

CHAPTER 18 - THE GUM REBELLION

Charlie entered the lobby and spotted Melissa Major reading a paperback book. Charlie noticed that Melissa's grooming had improved since the last session. She had on a clean pair of jeans and a fitted tee shirt. With a fresh-scrubbed face and her hair pulled up in a scrunchy, Melissa's natural beauty glowed without need of adornment.

"Hi Melissa, it's time for your appointment."

Once they were seated and comfortable in the office, Charlie said, "You look nice today. No paint."

"Thanks, Dr. Stone." Melissa scanned Charlie from top to bottom and offered Charlie a wicked little grin. "I've been catching some flak from the people in my group about you."

Charlie's eyebrows shot up. "Me?"

"They want to know if we're sisters." Melissa smirked as she leaned back in her chair.

"Sisters! You're a brunette, and I'm blonde. What makes them think we're sisters?"

"Hell if I know, they say we favor each other, that we have the same build."

Charlie sat back and looked at Melissa from a new perspective. She could see they both had oval faces, with similar facial features and body types. *I guess I could pass for her older sister. Wow.* Feeling awkward, she decided to get the session back on track.

"How are you doing in the program?"

Melissa shifted in her seat. "I'm doing fine. The man who did group last night …"

"Jonathon?"

"Yeah, he talked about that THIQ stuff and how addiction is a disease."

"That's an important topic. Research shows that in addicts and alcoholics, a small part of the body detoxification process produces a buildup of tetrahydroisoquinoline in the brain. You can see why they shortened the name to THIQ."

Charlie and Melissa both laughed.

"Researchers believe that an addict's genes tell the body to make the THIQ. The more you drink or use, the more the THIQ builds up in your brain. That's why they say in AA, 'Once an alcoholic, always an alcoholic.' This means you can never drink or use drugs again, without the same problems developing."

"You're saying *if* I'm an alcoholic, that I can never drink again, right? What about reefer?" Melissa sat up straighter, a look of alarm on her face. "Reefer's different, right?"

"I'm afraid not. You reported on your paperwork that you have four blood relatives, besides your father, who have addiction problems. You appear to be genetically predisposed to addiction by your father's genes."

Melissa nodded agreement. She reached into her purse and produced a pack of gum.

"You triggered your genetic predisposition when you started using alcohol and drugs, so now you're prone to become addicted to *anything* that is addictive. It will be easy for you to develop a cross addiction and change your drug of choice. Do you understand?"

Melissa nodded her head, yes, but Charlie wasn't sure she believed her.

Melissa offered gum to Charlie. "But I quit all those years, what about that?"

Charlie accepted a piece and unwrapped it. "When you stopped drinking and using drugs, you also stopped the progression of your addiction. When you started using again, you triggered the THIQ in your brain and picked up where you left off." She popped the gum in her mouth.

"Oh." Melissa's brows pulled together. She selected a piece of gum and dropped the remainder in the purse on the floor by her chair.

"Are you enjoying AA?" Charlie settled back in her chair, trying to set a more relaxed tone.

"It's okay. I'm not as bad off as those other folks." Melissa unwrapped the gum, put it in her mouth and began chewing.

Charlie rubbed the back of her neck. "We all like to think we're different and our problems aren't as bad as other peoples'. That rationalization makes us feel better, but keeps us stuck."

Melissa rolled her eyes, sighed, and crossed her arms.

"Melissa, you have too much potential to stay stuck. You need to remember that you have three convictions for DUI and a history of alcohol-related memory blackouts. You're awaiting trial for a felony under Alabama's new DUI law. I would call that a problem — a serious one. I want you to take advantage of every means of support to get better. Do you have a sponsor yet?"

"No, I really think I can handle this on my own." Melissa raised her chin and compressed her lips, the glint in her eye warning Charlie against challenging her. Belying her show of bravado, her foot was beginning to bob.

Charlie leaned forward to establish eye contact. "This is a serious and deadly disease, and you're going to need *all* the help you can get. Melissa, you *deserve* all the help you can get. Don't deny yourself. Remember, it's a requirement of the program."

"How do I get one?" she conceded, with another sigh. She looked at the paper wrapper from the gum.

Charlie dared her to start folding it with a look. "Ask the chairperson at your AA meeting to help you choose a temporary sponsor, or ask someone who you admire at the meetings. They should have at least a year or two of recovery experience. Your sponsor will support you through your recovery program. I recommend same-sex sponsorship, unless you have a same-sex orientation."

"Why's that?" Melissa wadded the paper and tossed it into the trashcan by the door.

"To discourage 'thirteenth stepping.'"

Melissa's brows went up. "What's that?"

"When sex becomes the goal, instead of recovery," said Charlie. "A sponsor will also help you work the Twelve Steps. Get one this week."

Melissa slumped in the chair and began twirling her hair. "This program has a lot of requirements," she said, pouting.

Charlie suggested, "Let's discuss your family."

Melissa wiggled in her seat, eyes shifting from side to side.

"What do you want to know?" Her tone held a hint of unease.

"Were you raised by both parents?"

"For a while. My mother died when I was twelve. My father raised us until he died when I was seventeen. They're both buried at Huntsville Memory Gardens. Then my aunt in Colorado took us in and raised us."

Hmmm, age twelve was when she had her first drink, Charlie recalled. The connection was obvious. *The death of a parent can be a strong trigger to self-medicate.*

"When did you move back to Huntsville?"

"I dunno, a few months ago." Melissa looked down and fiddled with the edge of her shirt.

"How did your mother and father die?"

A crease formed between Melissa's brows, and her dark eyes hardened. "Are you reporting all this to my C.R.O.?"

"No, your C.R.O. only wants to know your attendance, general progress, and if you relapse," said Charlie. "I'm asking these questions so I can help you get better."

"Oh…well, okay. My mother died of cancer."

"I'm sad to hear that. My mom died of cancer too. What kind of cancer did your mom have?"

"It started in her ovaries and spread to her pancreas. What kind of cancer did your mom have?"

"Lung cancer," said Charlie.

"Smoker?"

"Yeah, she smoked herself to death." Charlie shifted in her seat.

Melissa looked down. "I bet you miss her. I miss my mom all the time." Her eyes were misting.

"I miss mine all the time, too. Sometimes I feel orphaned. How about you?"

"Yep, orphaned — that's a good way to describe it. The doctors said that my mom's cancer had already metastasized when they found it." Melissa reported this with the same emotional detachment that Charlie had seen in many walking wounded.

Charlie eased back into her chair. "Tell me about your mom," she invited.

Melissa's body relaxed a bit. "She was always home with us and kept a clean house. She would bake great cookies and read stories to us, and we played games. Her chocolate chip cookies were the best." She smiled at the memory, a far away expression softening her gaze.

"Those sound like good memories."

"I look just like her except for my dad's dark eyes and hair. Everyone said she was a beautiful woman. My mom was blonde, like you."

"Was there any verbal or physical abuse in your home?" Charlie asked, watching Melissa's face for a reaction.

"She never hit us. Dad did all the spanking. She'd scream at us sometimes because we were always making a mess."

Charlie jotted a few notes in her chart. "Did your mother drink or use drugs?"

With a contemptuous tone, Melissa replied, "No. Dad was the family drunk."

Charlie noted in the chart, *Melissa sees her Mom as the good parent and her Dad as the bad one.*

"How did your parents get along?" Charlie knew this one question often revealed a great deal about family dynamics.

"Dad worked long hours and different shifts. They argued most of the time about him messing up the house."

"Sounds like my parents," Charlie commented. "How did your family handle your mother's death?"

Melissa's eyes welled with tears. "My sister and I were devastated. We felt abandoned because Mom was always there for us. We had to take over the responsibilities of the house. That's when Dad started drinking more." She shrank into her seat and hugged herself.

Charlie saw a small frightened child, rather than an adult woman. She'd finally hit some form of emotion other than anger.

"How did your father die?" Melissa asked, trying to change the subject.

"Lung cancer, same as my mom. He was a smoker, too. He stopped, that's why he outlived her by ten years." Charlie rolled her pen between her fingers. "How did your dad die?"

Melissa's lips curved in a smug little smile. "His car was hit by a train."

Charlie shivered. *That was a creepy smile.* She made a note about this odd reaction in the chart.

Charlie put down her pen and folded her hands. "You've had a great deal of tragedy and loss in your life. I'm sorry you lost your parents so young. It must be hard for you."

"It was terrible! Mom became sicker and sicker. There was no one to help, so my sister and I had to take care of everything that summer." At this point, Melissa looked like she'd failed at an assigned task. "My world changed after her death." Her shoulders slumped.

"How did it change?" Charlie asked the question with a soft, gentle tone.

"We had different lives after mom died." She shrugged her shoulders in a defeated manner, her head down. "That was the way it was."

"So, you have one sister." Charlie jotted a note in her chart.

Melissa nodded and twirled her hair around her finger.

"Are you close?"

"Yes, but we're different. She's better with…people than I am." Her head was still lowered.

"You sound like you admire her." Charlie tilted her head to better see Melissa's expression.

"I admire the way she adapts, but she lets people take advantage of her sometimes. She gives in, gets weak. If people take advantage of me, they pay." Melissa lifted her head and shot Charlie a lethal glare. It was an exclamation mark at the end of her sentence.

Taking a deep breath, Charlie asked, "How do they pay?"

"That depends on who they are, and what they do. I don't want to talk about this anymore." She sat back in her chair, her arms crossed. It was clear the subject was closed.

"Tell me about your dad. What was he like when he was drinking?" Charlie asked this as softly as she could and still be heard.

"He was a cop," Melissa answered, flipping her hand as if this answered the question.

"Did he also use drugs?"

"No drugs, he just drank. He was a cop." Melissa held her hands palms up, as a means of explanation.

"What was it like living with your father after your mother's death?"

Melissa hugged herself again, her jaws tight. More tears welled in her eyes. A single tear escaped the corner of her left eye and coursed down her cheek.

Something tells me he abused her. Maybe I can get her to open up and admit it. "Did your father abuse you?"

Melissa jerked her chin up. "I don't…besides; my time's up."

Charlie sensed a will of titanium. She pushed her box of tissues toward Melissa, who refused to acknowledge their presence.

"Yes, but before we finish, it sounds like you've been in survival mode ever since your mother died. I would like for you to someday be able to put the past and your anger behind you. Learn to live with joy, instead of just survive. You deserve something better."

Melissa chomped savagely on her gum. "There's nothing wrong with surviving."

Charlie shrugged and picked up her pen. "I didn't say there was. I only want something better for you. Let's finish by discussing your goals for the program."

Melissa's shoulders relaxed into a slump. "I want to be able to control my drinking and stop having nightmares." She appeared to be grateful for the change of subject.

"We don't have much time today, so we'll discuss your nightmares during our next session. I want us to have plenty of time to examine them. Regarding your other goal, I will say this. In my experience, controlled drinking is not an option for addicted people. I hope that as you go through the program, you'll come to understand this important point."

Charlie stopped, waiting for a reaction. She received none. Melissa sat as steadfast as a brick wall. It was time to ask the necessary question.

"Have you been drinking or using any drugs since you've been in the program?"

"No." Melissa dropped her gaze and shifted in her seat. She was twirling her hair again.

Charlie leaned forward in her chair, causing it to squeak. "My gut tells me this may not be true."

"Honest!" She shifted in her seat again but managed to look Charlie in the eye.

After about three minutes of silence, Melissa broke, "Oh, all right! I drank this weekend."

"What nights did you drink and how much?" Charlie asked, pressing the advantage.

"Saturday," she replied. "I had a couple of beers."

"What constitutes a couple?"

Melissa confessed with a downward cast of her eyes, tucking her chin. "I don't know how much. I guess I blacked out."

"Yet on Monday you reported you were clean and sober in the group. This is a program of honesty, Melissa. To improve your life and to have a quality recovery, you must get honest with yourself and others. You need to report and discuss your relapse, and apologize for being dishonest with your group tonight."

Melissa's eyes blazed. "Shit!"

"If you can't maintain your sobriety, we may need to refer you to an inpatient treatment program."

"I can do it outpatient, just give me a second chance," Melissa pleaded, eyes now wide with alarm.

"I've seen other patients turn their lives around at this point. Melissa, you can, too. I'm sending you home with some Step One homework."

"What's that?"

"Step One of the Twelve Steps is 'We admitted we were powerless over alcohol...that our lives have become unmanageable.'"

"Oh, that!"

"If you have problems between now and our next appointment, feel free to contact me."

Charlie escorted Melissa to Kathy and scheduled an appointment for the next week.

As Charlie turned back to go to her office, she could hear Melissa chanting, "Shit! Shit! Shit!" all the way out the door.

CHAPTER 19 - MAX AND THE CHICKEN DANCE

Marti stopped at the doorway to Charlie's office. "Was that your client who was chanting 'shit' on her the way out?"

"Yep, Melissa Major."

Marti cocked her head like a bird. "What's the problem?"

"I suspect she's pissed at me, or maybe herself. She relapsed this weekend, so the team will have to staff that issue on Friday." Charlie slammed her chart shut.

"Darn, I thought she was doing better." Marti leaned against the doorframe and crossed her arms.

"Me too." Charlie felt like she could collapse inward, from exhaustion and disappointment.

"Want to do lunch?" Marti had that look, the one Charlie knew oh so well. Marti had a food craving.

"Sure, you know me, I'm an eating machine. What are you in the mood to eat?"

With a sly smile, Marti said, "Hot wings."

"I'm game!"

They were en route to the restaurant when Marti asked, "How's the case going?"

"I guess you heard on television there's been another murder. I'm meeting with Joe and Ryan this afternoon to do a briefing and give my updated profile. If you have time before I go, I want you to look over it."

"Sure."

Charlie stomped the accelerator to pass a poke-along who insisted on driving in the left lane.

Marti pulled on her shoulder harness, trying to adjust it. "I heard both of the victims were beaten to death."

"It was the same M.O., only worse." Charlie caught her up on the latest details.

"Yuck! Murder, blood, and maggots, my favorite pre-lunch conversation."

"Sorry, but you asked." Charlie shrugged and offered a brief apologetic look.

Marti sighed as she shook her head. "Huntsville has such a low crime rate compared to other parts of the country. It seems strange to have something this horrible happen here."

"True. What frustrates me is that it takes so long to get the reports back from the state lab. That information is vital. The state budget cuts aren't helping matters." Charlie stopped for a light and glanced at Marti.

"Bureaucracies are always tedious. So how is Detective Hot Stuff?" Marti yanked on her seatbelt again. "I hate these things."

"Hot as ever." Charlie smiled and pulled into the parking lot of Hot Wings Plus, one of their favorite restaurants.

After they had been seated at a booth near the window, Charlie lowered her voice and asked, "Do you think I look like Melissa? She said some of the group members asked if we were sisters."

Marti squinted and tilted her head. "I can see that. Of course, your coloring is different, but your features and basic body build are similar." She fluffed her hair a bit. "I want to hear all about Detective Hot Stuff."

"He has blue eyes that twinkle when he teases me, and he wears Polo cologne." Charlie winked. "You know what Polo does to me."

Marti laughed. "I remember the time you followed some guy who was wearing Polo cologne all through that department store. He thought you were stalking him."

"Well you didn't help, following me and cackling like a hyena." They both chuckled.

"This Detective Hot Stuff sounds like a real hunk," Marti teased.

Charlie looked up from the menu in time to catch Marti scanning the room, taking in the wealth of male diners. *I agree, Marti,* she thought. *Hot wings and men — what a combination.*

"All right, I'll admit it," she said aloud. "Ryan's the first interesting male I've met since the divorce. We seem to click. He gets my sense of humor. Too bad he's a cop, and I'm working a case with him."

"He can't be your standard cop, or you wouldn't be so attracted." Marti pulled hand sanitizer from her purse and squirted some in both of their hands.

"Well, he's different from his partner, thank goodness. There's this strong magnetism or chemistry between us. My attraction to this guy is like nothing I've ever felt with anyone before." Charlie leaned across the table and whispered, "He makes me tingle."

Marti's laugh tinkled like wind chimes. "He what?"

Charlie leaned closer. "Every time he touches me, I feel a tingling sensation."

"Not a shock, like static electricity?"

"No, a tingle. Has anyone ever made you feel like that?"

"No. I'm jealous. Every lady deserves a little tingle in her life." Marti rested her elbow on the table and propped her chin in her hand. "I've been worried about you, Charlie, you've been emotionally detached for too long. So what're you going to do about Detective Tingle?"

"To be truthful," Charlie looked to make sure no one was eavesdropping, "he scares the bejeezus out of me. I could fall for this guy."

I can't believe I just admitted that. Charlie sat back in the booth as a waiter hustled over and set glasses of ice water on the table. Desperate to change the subject, she leaned forward again. "Did you hear what Max did last Friday while you were away on vacation?"

"No. What did that man do *this* time? I'm only letting you change the subject because I'm curious."

"Two ladies from one of the local churches came to ask if a clinician could come talk about Methamphetamine abuse to one of their Sunday school classes. You know how casual we dress on Fridays. Max was dressed to play golf after the staff meeting. He was in plaid Bermuda shorts and a white tee shirt. Both looked like they'd been in the dryer for a week."

Marti shook her head. "I know Max is a savvy businessman and all, but if the fashion police catch him, they'll lock him away in a deep, dank dungeon."

"He won't win any fashion awards, that's for sure. It was an intense staff meeting. Two of our patients relapsed, so we had to make decisions about the consequences. To make it worse, all of us women were premenstrual and snarky. Max was running his hand through his hair like he does when he gets uptight."

Marti nodded, grinning. "Yeah, he tends to do that."

"So his hair was standing up like the feathers on a rooster's head." Charlie spread her fingers and held them over her head and wiggled them. "I believe Max thought he should lighten things up a bit during the break, to reduce the tension. He came around the corner into the view of the church ladies, doing a funky chicken dance."

Marti's eyes grew wide as she reached for her glass of water.

"He strutted around with those pale bowlegs of his, wagging his elbows up and down like wings. Max chicken-walked a few yards down the hall, raised his head and let loose a loud crow like a rooster. When he lowered his head, he looked at me and grinned. I pointed at our guests. When he spotted the two church ladies dressed in their Sunday Finest, he froze like a deep freeze chicken. After a second or so, he had thawed a bit, and ran around the corner and back down the hall."

Marti choked on her water and started coughing.

"One of the church ladies, eyes big as Frisbees, said to Kathy, 'Was that one of your patients? Is he on that Meth stuff?'"

Marti's eyes began to water as she continued to cough.

"Kathy gave them a big ole smile. 'Oh no, that was our program director.' "

Marti's face was half-buried in her napkin. The part that was visible was a mottled shade of pink.

"The church ladies left without another word. I laughed so hard I almost got sick."

Marti had both hands over her mouth as tears streamed down her cheeks.

"I…would love…to have seen that," Marti gasped between giggles. She blotted her face and took some deep breaths. "It's those moments that keep me in this business. I just love Max as a boss — he's such a hoot."

Charlie nodded. "He's a great boss, but I wouldn't want to be married to him."

"Me neither."

Charlie cocked her head, sat back in the booth and grinned. "I thought you should know about this since you'll hear about it on Sunday."

"What do you mean?"

"Those ladies were from *your* church and mentioned that they were members of *your* Sunday school class."

"Oh my God!" Marti's head dropped to the table. Bang. Bang. Bang.

"Can I take your order, ladies?" the waiter asked, winking at Charlie. He looked down at Marti, who was still face down on the table, and mouthed to Charlie, "Is she okay?"

His name tag read "Brent."

Charlie smiled and let her gaze travel over him, absorbing all his maleness. Unlike Ryan, who was more masculine, Brent had little-boy charm. "She'll be just fine, Brent, after she has some unsweet iced tea. I'll have the buffalo wing special. Hot. And some sweet tea."

Marti raised her head. "I'll have the same."

After Brent had left with their orders, Marti said, "I wonder what he's like in bed? Did you see his legs and that cute butt in those khaki shorts?"

"Well, you just took the thought right out of my head." Charlie ran her hand up and down her water glass. *I know I'm love-starved if hot wings and cute waiters have me craving sex.* But the idea of another relationship still scared her. "I'm sure he'd be great, but I saw *trouble* tattooed on his forehead."

The hostess was seating a group of men in suits at a nearby table. Marti was smoothing the paper napkin in her lap and eyeing them.

"You ever wonder what Detective Tingle is like in bed?"

"Every single day since I met him."

Marti nodded toward the table of men. "What do you think about them?"

Charlie scrunched her face. "Lawyers."

Taking a second glance, Marti said, "Are you sure?"

"Look at the suits and shoes. I recognize the one seated on the end."

"Too bad." Marti looked disappointed. "The one with the red tie is cute."

"When I first moved here from Birmingham, Huntsville seemed like a city of opposites. Urban and rural, technical and blue collar, military and civilian." Charlie held both hands palms up as if weighing each choice.

"It wasn't always like this. Redstone Arsenal, NASA, and all these defense contractors have morphed it into a more sophisticated city," said Marti. "It's grown a lot since I moved here from New Mexico."

"I'm not surprised. Six-figure incomes attract more entertainment options." Charlie pulled her hair back in a scrunchy.

"That's why Huntsville attracts all these physicists, computer geeks, engineers, and —"

"Attorneys." Charlie tilted her head toward the well-dressed group across the aisle. "Lawyers feed off of prosperity like leeches."

"Here comes the food." Marti rubbed her hands together with anticipation.

Brent placed baskets of steaming hot wings drenched in hot sauce, with mounds of salty fries and crisp celery sticks, in front of them. Conversation stopped for a while as Charlie and Marti gave the wings the attention they deserved.

After a period of messy indulgence, Marti wiped sauce from her lips. "Charlie, are these cases still bothering you?"

Charlie wiped her hands and added the napkin to the growing pile on the table. "I'm still dreaming about them if that's what you mean. When I have quiet moments, I get this gut feeling that if I don't do something soon, another person will die."

"Sounds like the beginnings of post-traumatic stress to me." Marti wiped her hands and pointed at Charlie. "Girl, you need to rip that Master of the Universe patch off your sleeve. You're not a homicide detective. You're the consultant. If you don't get over this Wonder Woman crap soon, I'm going to buy you a cape."

"I know…it's just that I can't shake this feeling."

Marti grinned as she waggled her eyebrows. "If you'd loosen up and give Detective Polo Cologne a ride, it might cure your nightmares."

Giggling, Charlie said, "Thanks for making me laugh. You always know just what I need. Ryan would get a kick out of all these names you have for him. I admit my love life isn't great right now. However, this," she held up a wing saturated with hot sauce, "is a chance for an oral orgasm." She took a large bite, smearing sauce around her lips.

"Hear, hear!" Marti agreed. They settled into the comfortable silence of good friends and tasty food.

CHAPTER 20 - THE BRIEFING

"Some of you are wondering why I asked you to be in this briefing." Captain Strouper raked his gaze over the six detectives seated around the oval conference table located in the middle of the rectangular conference room. "I know this is Sparks and Roberts's case. The rest of you are here because we may need to develop a task force in the future.

"I've asked Dr. Stone, our new psychology consultant, to do this briefing. She'll distribute a profile she's prepared and will explain it. If you have any questions, don't be shy about asking them."

Charlie walked to the front of the conference room and swallowed to push what felt like a ping-pong ball back down her throat. She stood in front of a lectern placed to the right of a large whiteboard. Her black suit, sporting a white collar and cuffs, felt hot and confining. Grasping the lectern for support, she faced the room full of men: Captain Strouper, Joe, Ryan, and the four other detectives she'd just met, and whose names she didn't remember.

Willing her hand to not tremble, she took a sip of water, unhinging her tongue from the roof of her mouth.

Until her arrival twenty minutes earlier, she'd expected to do a casual briefing with Ryan and Joe. She tried to imagine that she was talking to one of the treatment groups at work and not a room full of skeptical police detectives.

"Um, thank you, Captain, for allowing me this opportunity."

Silent stares. Squaring her shoulders, Charlie opened her notes.

"Has this department ever handled a serial killer case before?"

Captain Strouper shifted his lanky frame. "This is our first one."

"In that case, I'm going to give you a little more information about serial killers. Everything you see in the movies isn't true."

Joe spoke up. "You sure this is a serial killer, Doc?" He was sitting with his legs extended and crossed at the ankle, with his fingers laced over his belly.

"Good question, Joe. According to the FBI and other experts, this case qualifies. There are four criteria. You have one or more perpetrators. There have been *at least* two murders with similar M.O.s. The crimes occurred in different locations, and there was a psychological cooling off period, in this case, two weeks. That meets all the criteria."

Charlie noticed several nodding heads. Her hands stopped shaking. The jitters passed, and she was in her element.

"Despite the theatrical portrayal of serial killers as demented loners, most of them have families and jobs. This camouflage of normalcy is why they are sometimes overlooked by law enforcement."

A black detective with a shaved head said, "I thought they were transient, moving around all the time to avoid detection."

"Serial killers, like most of us, like to have an anchor point like homes or offices. They have comfort zones they kill in, so they stick to basic geographical areas. They may relocate if things get too hot."

"So they don't move around?" He ran his hand across his shaved head.

"You're partially correct. There are a few transient serial killers that follow the interstates or railways. These people can be the homeless, migrant workers, truck drivers or those in the military. The principles still apply. A serial killer who drives an eighteen-wheeler will use his truck as an anchor point and the interstate routes as killing zones."

Several of the detectives were taking notes. Not Joe, who now had his arms crossed and his eyes narrowed.

Ryan asked, "How many serial killings are there a year?"

"Only one percent of murders in the United States are serial killings."

There was a rumble of discussions.

"I thought there would be more than that," said a mustached detective sitting toward the back.

"It would seem so, but this is because the media sensationalize these murders. Some experts believe that only twenty serial killers are operating nationwide, and they estimate these killers account for about 200 victims a year. Now think about your homicides. This is your first serial case, but how many murders do you work in the projects?"

Their heads were bobbing in agreement. Everyone in the room was giving her their full attention, except Joe. He sat like a statue.

Charlie paused and swept the room with a steady gaze. "New information came to light right before this briefing. The ViCAP search came up negative, is that correct?"

The FBI's Violent Criminal Apprehension Program maintains the largest investigative storehouse of major violent crime cases in the U.S.

"That's correct." Ryan turned in his seat so all could hear. "There are no cases involving our M.O. I used the search words murder, bludgeoning, blunt object, castration, knife, sexual activity, and several others."

Charlie scanned the faces of her audience and took a second to gather her thoughts before she turned to another page in her notes.

"Let's enter the mind of our unsub and discuss the profile. The killer is a Caucasian female. We know this because of the DNA left on the victims' bodies and the condoms. The victims were both heterosexual males.

"Based on FBI statistics, the unsub is most likely between the ages of twenty-five to forty-five. A waitress who saw our possible unsub with John Harper described her as attractive, busty, with long dark hair and a height of about five-foot-six or seven. She was well groomed. The witness didn't see her face, and the bartender still hasn't been located. She's most likely single since she's targeting nightclubs. She'll be employed and is lower-middle to middle class."

Charlie paused as the detectives scribbled notes. Turning another page, she glanced at her notes and took a deep breath.

"I believe we have a neophyte serial killer. Why the killer started stalking in Huntsville is unclear." She took a sip of water.

Joe stood and walked toward the coffee pot at the back of the room. Charlie saw Captain Strouper stare after him, a frown on his face.

"Doc, what makes a serial killer? Are they are born that way?" asked a rotund detective in the rear.

"I honestly think a few of them are born hard-wired to kill. I know of a case involving a five-year-old boy. He tried to set the cat on fire, pushed a sibling in front of an approaching car, and was caught trying to drown a puppy in the bathtub. His violent behavior started at age two."

A wave of grumbling spread over the group as the detectives exchanged glances. She understood why this disturbed them. *It's hard to believe a child could be a killer.*

When it was quiet, she continued. "My theory is *most* serial killers are made. As infants, some psychopaths fail to bond with their mothers; therefore, they have no bond to humans in general. Without that connection, it makes it easier to kill without remorse.

As young children they may fail to develop coping skills, using violence instead. Other contributors to the problem are neglect and abuse, especially when violence and sex are combined in the abuse."

A wave of murmurs passed around the table. Joe had his back to her, fussing over his coffee.

"There are other complicating factors, like addiction, which can be a trigger to increase aggression and lower inhibitions, making it easier to commit a crime. You've seen that in many of your cases."

Charlie noticed several of the detectives nodding agreement, including Captain Strouper.

"Then there is brain trauma. A person with a severe head injury can develop personality changes and become violent."

"The pro football player defense," said the mustached detective. He glanced around to see who got the joke as everyone chuckled.

Joe ambled back to his seat in the front.

Waiting for quiet so she could continue, Charlie eyed two detectives in the back who were whispering to each other. One of them looked up and nudged his buddy to stop talking.

"The experts have identified eight motivators for serial killings: anger, power and control, thrill, sex, mental illness, criminal enterprise, financial gain and ideology. Our unsub has five of them."

Several detectives picked up their pens, ready to write. Ryan gave her an encouraging smile. All eyes were riveted on her. Almost all, Joe was peering into his coffee cup.

Charlie walked to the board and wrote *Motivators*. "The first motivator is anger, bordering on rage. However, it's a focused rage. The targets appear to be middle-aged, alcoholic men. Both victims had dark hair. These men had porn in their homes and were known womanizers. As you know, they were beaten and castrated. Most of the damage was to the face and the genitals."

Several of the men grimaced.

"I believe there are five factors affecting our killer's choice of targets: opportunity, middle-aged dark-haired men, alcoholism, womanizing, and porn."

Charlie paused for questions while she wrote them on the board in black. Joe seemed to be paying attention.

"Beating a person's face beyond recognition is a practical or psychological compulsion to destroy that person's identity. To obliterate them. In this case, it was psychological, since the victims were left in their homes and their wallets with I.D. were nearby. That also rules out the motive of killing for financial gain, since there was no indication of theft."

A couple of the men nodded. One whispered to his neighbor. Captain Strouper extended his long legs and crossed his ankles.

"Our killer's second motive is the combination of power and control. Being able to lure these victims to their own homes, a place where they would feel safe, made this killer feel powerful. This also allowed her privacy and plenty of time with her victims, while reducing exposure to potential witnesses."

"Where does the sex come into play?" asked Joe. Nervous laughter rounded the table.

"Joe, this killer felt empowered by making these guys want her. She would see them as weakened by their desires. She chose men who were intoxicated, therefore easier to restrain, and she even controlled the transportation. This allowed her to avoid possible police interference, by not letting these drunk guys drive. Both victims had DUI's, didn't they, Joe?"

"Yes, several each." Joe sat straighter, adjusting his blazer.

"By driving her vehicle, she also assured she would have a means of escape and a place to conceal her weapons. Sometime during their sexual encounter, the killer handcuffed the men to their beds, thereby immobilizing them — more control. The bodies weren't positioned, just left after the cuffs were removed. No effort was made to cover the bodies, so there was no show of remorse. This killer used every form of control possible to feel powerful and safe and to avoid detection. That included removing all the towels used in the cleanup." Pausing, Charlie checked to make sure there were no questions.

Joe cleared his throat. "We never did find those towels. We haven't found the murder weapons either."

Captain Strouper rubbed his chin, a pensive expression on his face.

Charlie continued, "The third motivator of our killer is the thrill. I believe this killer gets a thrill while stalking her prey. Her hunting grounds are clubs that attract her target population. The beating and torture provide an additional thrill."

The men sat, riveted by Charlie's every word.

"This takes us to our fourth motivation, sex. Our killer is a sexual sadist."

The detectives started mumbling again, participating in side conversations.

Charlie raised her hands to quiet the group. "The unsub is driven to kill to fulfill her sexual needs and desires. I suspect violence and sex got mixed, maybe from sexual abuse while she was growing up. Our case shows overt and covert sexual contact in the crime scene. Not all cases do."

Ryan raised his hand. "Would you explain that, please?"

"Our unsub had *overt sex* with our victims, who ejaculated and were wearing condoms. Sometimes the sexual thrill doesn't require actual sexual contact. Torture, control, or the act of killing itself, is sexually stimulating to the perp. In this case, the killer was sexually excited by the fear and pain of the victim. That is covert and is why this unsub is both overt and covert. Most of the blows were delivered with precision while the victim was alive. We know this from the blood splatter."

"Dead people don't bleed," Joe grumbled. He sprawled again in his chair. His hands rested with laced fingers across his tie: the very one Charlie had cleaned at their first meeting. It seemed like a century ago.

"That's right, Joe. These men were still alive when she beat them and castrated them. I believe the severe killing blows to the face and genitals occurred after the castration, so the unsub could enjoy the victim's pain for as long as possible before he bled out."

All the men were quiet. Their faces scrunched like they smelled something unpleasant.

Charlie rubbed little circles on her stomach with her left hand. She felt a little indisposed, too. Developing a profile involved more than compiling the evidence, supporting facts, and information from similar cases. She had to empathically place herself in the mind of the killer. Every time she did, she felt the need to take a long, hot shower. *I could use a shower right now,* she thought with a touch of weariness.

"Let's look at our killer's final motivator — mental illness. The unsub is too organized and careful to have a severe psychosis."

"Whoa! You lost me, Doc, with all that psychobabble crap. What does psychosis mean?" asked Joe.

Captain Strouper rubbed his jaw and squinted at Joe.

"Sorry about that," Charlie replied. "Psychosis means the person's thoughts and perceptions aren't based in reality, that they are having hallucinations or delusions."

Joe gathered himself to sit forward like he was going to complain again. Charlie raised a hand. "Auditory hallucinations are when the person hears sounds or voices that aren't there. Sometimes these voices tell people to hurt themselves or others."

Charlie paused for questions. Someone was tapping a pen on the table toward the back of the room.

Okay, no questions so far. "Visual hallucinations occur when people see things that aren't there, like spiders crawling all over them."

Several of the men shivered.

I don't blame them, Charlie thought. *I'm not fond of spiders myself.* Aloud, she said, "Delusions are beliefs that have no basis in reality. I once had a psychotic patient who believed the devil resided in our local psychiatric unit, so when I talked to her about going to the hospital, she attacked me. She thought I was trying to send her to the devil. Did I explain that well enough?"

Joe muttered, "I'd try to kill you, too if I thought you were sending me to hell." That drew a few chuckles. Ryan nudged him with his elbow.

Charlie continued, "Our unsub does *not* suffer from psychosis. I do believe the killer has a mental illness, namely Obsessive Compulsive Disorder, commonly called OCD. The cleanup at the crime scenes was obsessive. Objects were straightened and lined with the edges of the furniture. Magazines were sorted and stacked in a precise manner."

The mustached detective asked, "Do all serial killers have this OCD?"

"Yes, to some degree. OCD is like anything else; it varies in the type of symptomology. Please don't misunderstand me; the majority of people who suffer from OCD are *not* killers. The typical OCD patient obsessively cleans, counts things, has rituals that make them feel better, gets a thought stuck in their heads or hoards things."

Charlie took a breath and continued. "Those who are killers will be obsessed with their victims and their crimes. They will feel a compulsion to kill again and again, and may take souvenirs and clip articles about the cases."

Charlie paused to let that information settle into their brains. She needed their full attention for the next revelation. "There are two new developments that indicate that the killer is escalating and experimenting. Ryan, can you brief us on this part?"

With a grim set to his jaw, Ryan stood at his place at the conference table and picked up his notes. His hair was mussed from running his hands through it. "I just received David Street's autopsy before this briefing. Street's body had more broken bones than Harper's. Also, a small splinter of wood was found inside Street's anus. He was sodomized. Harper's body showed no evidence of sodomy." Ryan exchanged glances with Captain Strouper, who shifted in his seat to sit upright. Gesturing to Charlie to continue, Ryan sat.

The room was quiet. It seemed everyone was digesting these new developments and they weren't settling well, based on everyone's pale faces.

"Thank you, Ryan. I believe the woman who committed these murders was sexually abused, raped, and maybe sodomized. That past abuse involved elements of violence combined with sex. I think she's taking a form of symbolic vengeance on dark-haired, middle-aged, alcoholic men, who may remind her of her abuser. This unsub may have been placed in foster care or with relatives at some point in her life, due to the abuse in her home."

Charlie paused to down some more water. "To summarize, the unsub is Caucasian, twenty-five to forty-five years old, attractive, brunette, lower-middle to middle class, and employed. Her targets are middle-aged, male alcoholics who are womanizers. Her hunting grounds are nightclubs that attract her target population, and the kill zones are the victims' homes. While this part of the profile isn't clear to me yet, the killer could have an accomplice, someone who is helping with the murders and the time-consuming cleanup. This woman is intelligent, cunning and deadly."

Charlie stopped and cleared her throat. The men were scribbling notes.

"The experts say that the more serial killer's avoid capture, the stronger and smarter they feel. They begin to feel omniscient like they can't be caught."

"Ten feet tall and bullet proof," said Ryan.

"That's right, Ryan, This is when they start to make mistakes and cut corners. It's a myth that serial killers want to be caught. They don't. They believe that law enforcement *can't catch them.*"

Several of the detectives grumbled under their breaths. A few were scowling.

"Yes, gentlemen, our killer will become arrogant, and that arrogance will help you catch her. Ryan, will you pass around the copies of the profile, please? Any questions?"

CHAPTER 21 - I SHOULD DECLINE

After the briefing, several of the detectives surrounded Charlie, asking questions. As the last detective left the briefing room, Ryan sidled up to Charlie and nudged her with his elbow. "That was an interesting profile."

"Thanks, I hope I didn't put in too much psychobabble. I wasn't expecting to do a formal briefing."

"Do you still need a doggie door installed? I have all the tools and could drop by on Saturday to do it."

"I should decline, but I need that doggie door. Spanky's tired of hopping from one paw to the other, waiting for me to get home." She shrugged. "Against my better judgment, I'll say yes."

Ryan laughed, his eyes crinkling. "What time do you want me to show?"

"About ten, if that's good for you. I still have to buy the door."

"Be sure and buy one big enough for when she gets older," Ryan advised. "My sister bought one that was too small and we had to exchange it. I could come with you and help you pick it out."

Charlie smiled. "I think I can pick out a dog door, but thanks for offering. I've been researching them for the past week."

He nodded. "I'll see you Saturday at ten."

"I live in Madison County. Do you want my address?"

Ryan grinned. "I'm a detective. I know where you live. While I'm working on the door, I'll update you on any new developments that may occur between now and then. Maybe you'll make me a sandwich for lunch?" He headed for the door.

"Maybe…goodbye." She waved, checked her watch, and then sprinted to the exit.

CHAPTER 22 - THE TRUTH REVEALED

Charlie ushered Janice into her office, noticing with approval that Janice was wearing lavender scrubs instead of seductive clothing.

"Thanks for reassuring me about Mark the other day, Doc," Janice said as she sat down. "He scares the crap out of me."

"Do you want to talk about it?" Charlie settled into her chair.

Janice's brows drew together. She looked down and started playing with her necklace. "I saw you on TV, on the news."

"Oh, you saw that interview I gave about methamphetamines?" Charlie smiled; excited to think someone had seen the interview.

"No, I mean at the murder scene. Are you involved in those cases?"

"I'm a part-time consultant for the H.P.D." Charlie sat back in her chair. "Why do you ask?"

Janice glanced at the closed door, leaned closer and lowered her voice. "I'm afraid that Mark killed those two men and that it was my fault."

A blade of ice sliced down Charlie's spine. She shivered and leaned toward Janice, using the same near-whisper. "Why do you say that?"

"I told you that Mark tried to kill me." Janice trembled and hugged herself, tears welling in her eyes. "Mark got real drunk that night and accused me of being with another man. He told me he'd kill any man he caught fucking me. He threw me against a wall and choked me." Janice stopped mid-explanation and began hyperventilating, one hand covering her throat and the other clutching the arm of her chair. Her chocolate eyes had gone huge in her too-white face.

"Take slow deep breaths," Charlie advised.

After sucking in several shaky breaths, Janice reached for a tissue from the box on the corner of the desk and blotted the sheen from her face. "I kneed him in the groin and managed to get away, but he grabbed me by my shirt, pulled me back, and punched me in the face. I saw stars for a moment. I was afraid he'd broken my nose. There was blood gushing everywhere. Lucky for me, I fell near the coffee table, where I'd sat my purse. I could see him coming for me. I swear, Doc, I saw murder in his eyes. I reached into my bag for my keys and felt my stun gun, so I grabbed it. When he leaned over to grab me, I zapped him. The son-of-a-bitch fell on top of me. I managed to squirm out from under him. When I got free, I grabbed my stuff and ran like my panties were in flames."

Charlie now understood Mark's reaction to her stun gun. "I wish you'd called the police."

"I was too scared. Those men who were murdered..." Janice's hand hovered near her throat. "It's my fault." She wept, face in her hands.

Charlie eased the tissue box closer.

"Why are their murders your fault, Janice?"

Janice sobbed louder. Unsure what to think, Charlie sat silent and let Janice regain her composure.

When Janice had calmed somewhat, Charlie repeated, "Janice, why do you think you're responsible for those two men's deaths?"

"I slept with John Harper and David Street. Mark saw me with both of them. Whenever I saw him in a club, I'd leave, but I'm sure he saw us leave together. Shortly after, both of them were murdered. The news said they were beaten to death. What should I do?"

Charlie pushed back her chair and rubbed her temples, contemplating the situation, while Janice wept into a tissue.

"Janice, since I'm your therapist and consulting on these murder cases, I think our center director, Max, needs to advise you as to what to do. He can be objective." Charlie rose and headed to the door.

"Okay. That sorta makes sense." Janice dabbed under her lashes with another tissue.

"Stay here. I'll be right back." Charlie closed the door and had to steady herself for a moment against the wall. She looked toward

Max's office and saw with relief that the door was open. She walked to it and tapped on the doorframe.

"Hi Charlie, you're just the person I wanted to see. Come in and close the door," said Max. He was frowning, his bushy brows bristling.

Uh, oh. When Max frowned, it was never good. Heart pounding in her chest, Charlie sat and gripped the arms of the chair. *I know that look. Somebody's screwed up big time. I hope it wasn't me.* Mind racing, she tried to recall any of her misdeeds.

"I've been listening to the chit-chat outside my window, and it concerns your patient, Janice." Max leaned forward, rested his forearms on his desk, and clasped his hands.

The smoking area was located near Max's office window. Max closed his door and blinds, did paperwork, and listened. He knew which therapists the patients respected and who bragged about a weekend relapse.

"What about her?" Charlie's throat felt dry.

"Ever since she's entered the program, she's the hot topic in the smoking area. Yesterday, I heard someone boasting that Janice had sex with him in one of our restrooms."

"Oh, great!" Charlie groaned. "It's possible; I'll ask her about it. Right now we have a more pressing issue to handle regarding Janice."

The untamed brows inched toward Max's hairline, "Something tells me I'm not going to like this."

****

Fifteen minutes later, Max agreed to discuss the matter with Janice and escorted her to his office. Max tapped on Charlie's door thirty minutes after he took Janice to his office

"Make the call, she's willing to talk," he said.

Charlie called Ryan. Max leaned in her door while Charlie explained why she thought Ryan should talk to Janice. Charlie ended the call and turned to Max. "Detective Ryan Roberts will be here in fifteen minutes."

"I think under the circumstances you need to let me handle this interview. I'll get Janice to schedule another appointment with you tomorrow about the alleged sex-in-the-bathroom incident."

"Thanks, Max. Do I need to transfer her case?"

"Let's wait and see how this pans out. You're the only therapist on staff who deals with sexual addictions." Max straightened and left.

Charlie scooted down to Marti's office and slid into a chair across from her desk. Marti looked up, and stopped writing, her eyes going wide.

"What's up, Charlie? You look pale."

"There's good news and bad news."

Marti leaned back in her chair and steepled her fingers, her elbows resting on the armrests. "Give me the bad news first."

"Janice thinks her former lover, Mark Walker, may have killed the men in the murder cases," said Charlie.

"Whoa! That's the guy who threatened you in your office, right? The one Nell called a mini-series?" Marti sat forward.

Charlie explained the details. "That's not all. Max heard someone bragging about having sex with Janice in one of the restrooms in the building."

Marti took a sip of her hot tea. The scent of jasmine filled the room. "That girl gets around. Most of the guys in the program are salivating over her. Heck, there are even a couple of women interested in Janice."

Charlie gave a resigned sigh. "This, of course, will come up in the staff meeting on Friday. I get to confront her about it tomorrow."

Marti shook her head and took another sip.

"Ryan will be here to talk to Max and Janice in about ten minutes." Charlie waited for Marti's reaction.

Marti plopped down her tea and sat erect. "Detective Hottie — here?"

"I thought he was Detective Polo Cologne or was it, Detective Tingle?" Charlie teased.

Marti closed the chart she was working on with a resounding smack and put it in a file drawer. Grabbing her mug of tea, she rose to her feet.

Charlie blinked. "Where're you going?"

"I'm going to the front office. I want an up-close and personal view of Detective Tingle. In fact, I want to shake his hand, to see if I tingle, too." Marti winked.

"Good grief." Charlie looked at the ceiling, praying for Divine intervention. Heaving herself out of the chair, she headed down the hall to hide in her office.

After completing all her group therapy notes, Charlie ambled down the hallway to the break room for a jolt of liquid energy from the coffee urn. Through the doorway, she saw Marti and Max laughing and hesitated. *What's going on?* She entered the break room, glanced to her right, and ground to a stop.

"Hi Charlie, good to see you again." Ryan shook her hand, holding it a beat longer than necessary. The tingle eased up her forearm, warming her.

"Hi Ryan, appreciate you coming."

"I'm going back to the precinct to discuss this with Joe. Your patient will be in tomorrow to make a statement. We'll probably pick up Mr. Walker for questioning. Max has made it clear we need to respect your ethical and legal boundaries regarding both patients." Ryan looked from Max to Charlie.

Charlie glanced over at Marti, whose eyes were dancing with mirth. *I'll hear about this later. I wonder what new nickname she'll stick on Ryan, next?*

Max was looking back and forth from Charlie to Ryan, his caterpillar brows forming a V. *Oh great. That's his speculative expression.*

"Well, uh, I have a patient waiting," she said feeling awkward. "Thanks again for coming, Ryan."

"No problem, this may be the break we need. I'll see you Saturday to install that doggie door."

Charlie barreled through the door as if she had on gasoline panties and someone had just lit a match.

CHAPTER 23 - DISTRACTION

With a wry expression, Ryan escorted Janice Knight onto the elevator. "This way, please." When the doors opened on the second floor, he gestured her through the doorway to the bullpen. They would have to walk the length of the room to reach the interrogation room. He thought *This should be interesting.*

The rectangular room had rows of metal desks lined up facing the doorway, with a central aisle between them. A raucous environment of ringing phones, slamming desk drawers, and boisterous conversations filled the space.

The moment the detectives became aware of Janice's presence, all eyes were on her. The large room became as quiet as an empty cathedral.

Ryan pointed. "We're going to that room at the other end of the aisle."

She walked the aisle between the desks like a model on a runway. Ryan noticed Joe standing slack-jawed behind his desk, his gaze tracking Janice's long legs and swaying hips.

When Ryan reached his partner, he said, "Close your mouth and come on in."

At last, they were in the interrogation room. Ryan waved his hand to indicate where Janice should sit. As he closed the door, he heard the normal din of police work begin.

Ryan and Joe chose chairs across the table from her. After performing the pre-interview ritual, Ryan asked, "If you would prefer to have an attorney present, we can reschedule this for another time."

"I'm fine."

Ryan pulled the yellow legal pad close and plucked the pen from his shirt pocket. He noticed Janice eyeing his left hand. She blasted a seductive smile his way, hot enough to singe his eyebrows.

He'd found Janice attractive during his talk with her yesterday when she was wearing scrubs. Today, she'd fluffed her dark hair, wore a low cut top with a short skirt, and looked ready to hit the nightclub circuit. *It's too early for this unless she's a hooker. Damn, the woman's a hard on at first sight.* "Janice, I know we discussed this the other day, but we need to go over your story again, in more detail."

Janice nodded and shifted to pull her skirt down. She crossed her arms and rested them on the table. She leaned over as if to share a secret.

No bra thought Ryan. The interview scene in the movie, *Basic Instinct*, flitted across Ryan's mind. He dragged his gaze from her large boobs to her face and made himself focus on the task at hand. *I'll start her at the beginning and work up to Walker.* "How did you meet John Harper?" he asked.

"At the Night Owl. He loved that place."

"How long did the two of you date?"

"Only about a month. Things were going really well, that is until his granddaughter's birthday party." She paused, scowling.

Ryan gave her a nod to continue.

She shifted, reached in her bag for a bottle of water, and downed a third of it before complying. "His granddaughter's party was at his daughter's house on a Saturday afternoon. We had a date the Friday night before. He was telling some of his friends about the present he'd bought her. I came back from the ladies' room just in time to hear him describe the swing set." Janice sat back in the chair and crossed her arms. "That was the first I'd heard about the party. I was pissed. John said he would talk to his daughter and get me invited."

"Did Harper talk to his daughter?" asked Ryan.

"He never invited me." Lower lip protruding, she continued. "I showed up anyway."

"What happened?" asked Ryan.

Her chin lifted. "His daughter answered the door and asked me what I wanted. I told her I was John's girlfriend and was there for the party. She told me I hadn't been invited." She tossed her head. "I went right on in past her. She had no business disrespecting me that way."

Janice stopped and drank more water. The plastic bottle crackled under the force of her grip.

"Then John's ex-wife ran into the living room and started screaming at me to leave. She was calling me names like slut and whore and threatening to hit me. I was about ready to deck the bitch. About then John came in from the backyard with another guy and two kids. John grabbed me and forced me out the door. I managed to wring my arm out of his grasp on the sidewalk. We had a big fight. I got in my car and left. That was the last time I saw him alive."

Ryan remembered Sherry Harper mentioning that a woman named Janice had come uninvited at her granddaughter's birthday party.

Clearing his throat, Joe said, "Doesn't sound like a way to treat a lady."

"Thank you. John bruised my arm." She pointed to an area on her right bicep. "That wasn't the first time he was an asshole."

"Did he treat anyone else that way?" Joe ran a finger inside his collar and yanked.

"Pretty much everybody. John had this, *I'm Mr. Radio,* attitude, like his shit didn't stink. Oh, he was a charmer when he wanted to get you in bed, but when he was drinking, he would say mean things."

Ryan glanced over at Joe, who was staring at Janice with his jaw unhinged. He kicked Joe's ankle under the table, suppressing a grin when he jumped.

"When did Mark Walker see you with Harper?" asked Ryan.

"The night I found out about the party. I didn't see Mark come in the club, or I would have left *immediately*. John and I were dancing to a slow song. I looked over his shoulder and saw Mark sitting on a stool, giving me that same crazy look he had on his face the night he beat me. I insisted we leave because I knew Mark would get drunk and start a fight."

"How did David Street come into the picture?" asked Ryan.

"John and David used to be best friends and drinking buddies. John told me once that after he had divorced, David moved in on his ex, Sherry. They got into a fight about Sherry and were both arrested for D and D."

There was a gleam in Janice's eyes as she recounted the events.

"David claimed that he'd always had a soft spot for Sherry. I don't know why — she's such a bitch. Anyway, David knew he'd never have a chance with her unless he stopped drinking. He went to AA and turned his life around for a while. They hooked up and went on this cruise together." She was animated now, waving her hands for emphasis.

"The story circulating in the bars is that David relapsed on the cruise, so Sherry dumped him." A vicious grin spread across her face. "He must have got shit-faced drunk because he never knew what he did to make her break up with him."

Ryan shrugged. "So how did you two hook up?"

"After the breakup, David hit the clubs again. I ran into him and felt sorry for him. We had something in common, both rejected by the bitch. We were out one night, and Mark showed up. He caught us making out at a corner table. I told David I needed to leave, so we did."

Ryan and Joe passed a glance between them. Ryan asked, "Were the two of you still dating when he was killed?"

She shook her head. "We only dated a couple of weeks. I walked in a club one night and caught him squeezing the ass of some slut on the dance floor. I was pissed! I snatched that little bitch by her red hair. David shoved me down on the floor, right there in front of everybody!"

Eyes blazing, chest heaving, Janice gripped the edge of the table. Ryan noticed that Joe was watching every rise and fall of her chest.

After she had calmed down, Ryan said, "Janice, tell us about the incident with Walker."

Janice recounted the scene. They made her go through the whole story again. Ryan made a note that both accounts were consistent with what she'd told him in Max Haumper's office.

Toward the end of the interview, Joe asked Janice, "Do you have an alibi for the times of the two murders?"

She twisted the cap on her bottle on and off as she looked at Ryan, and then Joe. "No. I was home alone, high on Oxycodone. You're not going to tell my therapist, are you?"

CHAPTER 24 - WHO IS THE PRIME SUSPECT?

Ryan leaned a shoulder on the doorframe of the interrogation room and observed as Joe escorted Janice out of the building. It was like watching a wave in the stands of a football game. The guys stood in silent awe, grinning like fools, and then sat, resuming their tasks after she passed. *That woman is like a lust fairy. When she passes, every dick rises and salutes.*

Once Joe returned, Ryan noticed that he seemed to need a few minutes to regain his equilibrium. When he joined Ryan at the coffee pot, he poured a mug full, and they headed toward the conference room.

"Sounds like we need to bring Walker in for questioning." Joe took a tentative sip of the black sludge in his cup and winced.

Ryan frowned down at the dark brew in his cup. "With his rap sheet, he looks good for the deed, but he doesn't match Charlie's profile, and we know there was a woman there."

"Doc did say there might be an accomplice," Joe reminded him. "It won't hurt anything to bring him in and check his alibis."

"Fine by me, I don't mind rattling his cage a little. I don't like guys who beat up women. Did I tell you he tried to get rough with Charlie in her office?" Ryan mastered an unexpected surge of anger.

"Doc?" Joe looked surprised. "What happened?"

"I saw Walker's probation officer at the courthouse yesterday afternoon. She told me Charlie backed him down with a stun gun." Ryan grinned before downing some coffee. He grimaced. "What century did they make this shit?"

Joe laughed and shook his head before shoving away his cup. He picked up his legal pad, squinting. "In my mind, if it's not Sherry Harper, then Janice is our prime suspect. Both meet the physical description, were involved with both of the vics, and had nasty breakups with each of them. Janice may be framing Walker to throw us off."

"I agree. Let's run it by the Captain." Ryan placed both palms flat on the table and rose.

Joe stood, bowed, and extended an open palm toward the door. "Lead the way."

"By the way, remind me to call Charlie's boss when we get out of the Captain's office."

"Why?"

"I promised him I wouldn't place Charlie in an unethical position. He needs to know that Janice is now a suspect so he can transfer her case to another therapist."

"Huh," Joe grunted.

CHAPTER 25 - CONFRONTATION

Charlie took in Janice's skimpy outfit and wondered how the interview had gone at the police department.

"Is Detective Roberts single? I noticed he wasn't wearing a ring." Janice placed her purse on the floor next to her chair.

Charlie's gut twisted. She rubbed her stomach and did her best to maintain a calm face, even as she felt her smile flat-line. "Why do you ask, Janice?"

"No reason, I was just wondering." Janice fingered an oval pendant she was wearing and smiled.

Charlie flipped open her chart. "Have you had time to think about the information I gave you regarding sexual addiction?"

"Um, well, I thought I was here because of my forged prescription."

"You are, but you do realize you have two addictions — opiates and sex, right?"

"So I like sex. What's the big deal? It doesn't mean I'd go fuck anyone, anywhere. I'm not a slut, you know!" Her eyes glittered with anger as she reached into her bag for a water bottle. She chugged half its contents, replaced the top, and banged it down on Charlie's desk.

Charlie sighed. "I wasn't implying you are anything, Janice." Without another word, she settled back in her chair and studied Janice, watching the other woman's increasing discomfort as the silence grew.

"This is a program of honesty, Janice. Is there something you need to tell me?"

"I don't know. What've you heard?"

"What do you think I've heard?"

Red-faced, Janice blurted, "I didn't mean to relapse, honest, I didn't. I was upset about John, and then David was murdered. When he offered me the pills, I didn't think."

Charlie sat erect, grasping the arms of her chair. "Who gave you the pills?"

Janice's lower lip protruded into a pout. "I don't want to tell you. He's gonna know I snitched on him."

Charlie sat back in her chair and waited for Janice to reveal her source. She watched a battle of emotions cross her face as she struggled with the decision.

Panic won. "Am I going to get thrown out of the program?"

"I don't make those decisions," Charlie told her. "The team will make that decision during tomorrow's staff meeting. It's likely you'll be asked to start over at week one of the program."

"Oh…but I won't be kicked out?" Janice still sat tense, holding the arms of her chair.

"No guarantees. Who gave you the pills?"

"Kevin Humster." She grabbed the water and guzzled.

"Did he give them to you or sell them to you?"

Janice looked down, wringing her hands in her lap. "He sorta sold them to me."

Charlie arched a brow. "How did you pay for them?"

Janice's face blushed puce. "I had sex with him."

"Did it happen in one of the bathrooms here at the treatment center?"

Janice's mouth gaped. "How did you know?"

Charlie shrugged. "Men like to brag, and rumors spread like ants on chocolate cake." Charlie leaned forward and looked Janice in the eye. "We can't have our patients participating in sexual relations on our premises. We have an obligation for our facilities to be a safe place to work on recovery. I can't believe you and Kevin are buying and selling drugs at the treatment center. That's not fair to the patients who are trying to create a new life and work a strong recovery program."

"Oh God, what now?" Janice tightened her grip on the bottle, causing it to partially collapse.

Charlie eyed the bottle, the noise annoying her. "In addition to your three AA meetings, you are now required to attend one Sex Anonymous meeting a week."

There was a rap at Charlie's door.

"Excuse me, Janice." Charlie cracked the door and saw Max looking stern, his hair sticking up in front. *Uh-oh, something has happened.*

"I need to speak to you and Janice." Max stepped in and closed the door. He ran his hand through his hair and cleared his throat.

"Janice, I've discussed your situation with my boss. We believe your case needs to be transferred to Marti Hathoway, since Dr. Stone's consulting position with the police department is causing a conflict of interest. We would like for you to meet with your new therapist on Monday if you can arrange an appointment."

"But…but I like Dr. Stone."

"I'm glad to hear that, Janice. Due to the circumstances, I can't allow Dr. Stone to continue as your therapist. This is my decision, not hers." Max tightened his jaw and crossed his arms.

Charlie sat back in her chair, stunned. She took a moment to gather her thoughts. "In that case, you'll learn the treatment staff's decision from your new therapist, not me. I'll give you a drug screen that you must take today. If you refuse to take it, you run the risk of dismissal from the program. Let's go down the hall now and see if Ms. Hathoway is busy."

"I had her in group once. She seemed nice." Janice reached for her bottle and purse.

"She's a great therapist. I think you two will work well together." Charlie hesitated and added, "I'm sorry about this, Janice. I never thought there would be a conflict of interest when I accepted this consulting position."

CHAPTER 26 - WHERE WAS I?

Charlie opened her eyes to see Spanky looking down at her, paws planted on her chest.

"What are you, an alarm clock? This isn't the Eastern Time zone. You're an hour off." She pushed Spanky from her chest and felt for her comforter.

She wasn't in bed! She was on the floor in the living room. With a groan, she rolled over, crawled to the couch and dragged herself onto it. *Good grief, I feel as though I've been run over by an asphalt-tamping machine. I remember waking from a nightmare at 1 a.m., but how did I get in here?*

Spanky whined and pushed her nose under Charlie's hand. She grunted as she stood and shuffled to the back door to let Spanky outside.

Over coffee and a bagel, Charlie considered her situation. *I wonder if I was sleepwalking?*

Charlie opened the door again. Spanky ran from the other side of the fenced yard, barreling toward the entrance. Charlie eased aside and watched the dog sail over the two steps. Landing in a sprawl on the slick tile floor, Spanky slid several feet into a large peace plant. The pup yipped as it plopped on top of her with a rustle, obscuring all but her nose.

Charlie laughed so hard her stomach hurt. Spanky crawled from under the plant and shook the potting soil off her coat. Trotting to Charlie, she pushed her nose into her outstretched hand.

"Are you okay, Spanky Doodle? You've got to learn speed control and braking. You're driving like a drunk teenager."

Spanky gave herself one more vigorous shake, shimmying from stem to stern, before burying her mouth in the food bowl. Charlie righted the plant and grabbed a broom and dustpan to sweep up the mess.

It was Friday and her day off. She was grateful she wasn't at the staff meeting to vote on Janice's fate in the program. *I feel bad enough that I had to transfer her case.* After putting her dishes in the sink, she grabbed her duster. *I'd better spiff up the house a bit. Ryan will be here tomorrow to install the dog door.*

CHAPTER 27 - RYAN THE TOOL MAN

After a final stir on her famous chicken salad, Charlie reached for the plastic wrap and covered the bowl. Easing aside a pitcher of sweet tea, she placed it in the fridge. She eyed her clean house and breathed a contented sigh.

Curious about Spanky's whereabouts, she searched until she spotted her, taking a morning snooze in a pool of light that spilled from the bedroom window.

The doorbell chimed. She rushed from the bedroom to open the door.

There stood Ryan, holding a wicked-looking reciprocating saw and a toolbox. "Hi, are we ready to install a dog door?"

"Waroof! Waroof!" Spanky dashed from the bedroom, claws digging in the beige carpet for traction. The Beagle gained momentum as she approached the invading stranger.

"No, Spanky, stop!" Charlie stood rooted to the spot with dread.

Spanky reached the hardwood floor of the foyer. Seeing her opponent up close, she straightened her front legs to put on the brakes, but instead rammed into Ryan's shins and flipped tail over head. With a yip, she scrambled to her feet and shot like a rocket back to the bedroom.

Charlie stood, both hands over her mouth, round-eyed, looking at Ryan. Her ex would have been cursing and pitching a fit by now.

Throwing back his head, Ryan roared a deep belly laugh. Charlie chuckled with him.

Still laughing, Ryan bent over and put down his tools. "That's … quite a … watch dog … you've got there, Charlie." He rested his hands on his knees as he struggled to regain his breath.

"She hasn't grown into her feet yet, or her brakes."

"So I saw. Is she okay?" Ryan looked up from his bent position.

"Spanky, sweetie. It's okay. You can come out."

Charlie walked into the bedroom. Spanky was nowhere in sight. Charlie got down on knees and elbows and peered under her bed. There in the shadowed recesses lay Spanky, nose between her paws.

"Come on sweetie. It's safe." Charlie patted the carpet at the edge of the bed.

One paw in front of the other, Spanky eased from under the bed. Charlie gathered her trembling puppy into her arms and checked her for injuries, crooning to her the whole time. Satisfied Spanky was all right; she kissed her pup on the top of her head.

"Is she okay?" Ryan stood leaning into the room with his hands braced on both sides of the doorframe.

"I think so. Have you been standing there all this time?"

"Oh, yeah." His grin was mischievous.

Charlie climbed to her feet. Holding Spanky in one arm, she planted a fist on her hip. "You were looking at my ass, weren't you?"

The grin widened. "Well, it was sticking up there, in plain sight."

"Out!" Charlie pointed. "Get out of my bedroom."

Ryan held up his hands and backed out of the room. Carrying Spanky, Charlie whisked out of the room and slammed her bedroom door.

Ryan assembled his tools and unpacked the directions for the door installation. Spanky sniffed each one and provided tail-wagging efforts toward project supervision.

"You may need to put her back in the bedroom. The saw is loud, and we don't want her to get hurt," said Ryan.

"Good idea. She's a busybody."

Charlie scooped the pup in her arms and deposited her in the bedroom with a rawhide bone to keep her occupied. When Charlie returned, Ryan was already tracing the pattern onto the door. They worked side by side in silence.

"You seem to anticipate just what I need," Ryan commented. "What are you, the queen of home projects?"

"I was always my dad's little helper."

"Do your parents live around here?"

"They're both deceased," Charlie looked down and fiddled with a slot head screwdriver.

"Oh, I'm sorry to hear that. Any brothers or sisters?"

"Just one brother, he lives in New York. I don't see him very often. What about you?"

"My parents and two sisters live in Birmingham. My older brother lives in Savannah, Georgia."

The conversation came to a halt as Ryan struggled to cut the holes in the metal door on both sides, using the reciprocating saw. He slid the dog door into place. It fit.

Grinning, he got to his feet and gestured with both hands, as though he was presenting door number one on Let's Make a Deal. "Perfect fit. You can let Spanky out now. I'm through with the saw. I just need to insert the screws."

Charlie released Spanky from the bedroom while Ryan finished the door. Project completed, Charlie vacuumed up the mess, while Ryan gathered his tools and returned them to the trunk of his car.

It was almost noon. When Ryan returned to the house, Charlie asked, "Would you like a chicken salad sandwich?"

"I love chicken salad. I'll go wash my hands," Ryan nodded toward the guest bathroom in the hall.

Spanky followed Ryan with a wagging tail and lolling tongue. When he closed the door, she plopped down, whining. Charlie walked over, gathered her puppy into her arms, carried her to the back door, and placed her on the porch. "Go do your business, Spanky, you can adore your new friend later."

After washing her hands, she assembled the sandwiches, grabbed a bag of chips, and poured sweet tea.

They sat at the small table near a bay of windows, next to the kitchen. Ryan grabbed half a sandwich and took a bite. Reaching for a chip, Charlie watched for his reaction.

"Mmmmm." He rolled his eyes toward heaven. "I love the grapes and pecans. Is that dill I taste?"

Charlie's jaw dropped. "You know about dill? Do you cook?"

"A guy can't live off fast food forever. You look surprised."

"You just seem like such a … manly man."

Ryan chuckled. "Oh, so I can't be a manly man and know about dill, huh? Are you stereotyping me, Dr. Stone?"

Charlie laughed, too. "Guilty, sorry about that."

Ryan shifted to a serious mode. "I called Max and informed him that Janice Knight is now a person of interest."

Charlie put down her glass of tea and sat back in her chair. "So that's why her case was transferred to Marti."

"I need to update you on our interview with Janice." Ryan placed his sandwich on the plate. "She filled in quite a few gaps in this case and brought to light some connections. Guess who escorted Sherry Harper on her cruise?"

"Who? It didn't seem like she would go on a cruise alone." Charlie picked up her tea and took a sip.

Ryan smiled as he delivered his bombshell. "David Street."

Choking on her tea, Charlie grabbed her napkin and covered her mouth. Eyes watering, she rasped, "Our second murder victim?"

"One and the same. We checked with the cruise line. Janice was telling the truth about Sherry Harper having an affair with him. Harper and Street were drinking buddies until Street joined AA and hooked up with Sherry," said Ryan.

"This throws her to the top of our suspect list. I can see the motive for killing her alcoholic ex-husband, but what would be her reason for killing David?"

"They were vacationing with another couple. David relapsed on the last night of the cruise. Sherry and her friends left the casino and spotted David doing a little dirty dancing with another woman in one of the lounges. There was a big row." Ryan crunched a chip.

"Then she's our main suspect. What if David helped her kill John, and then she killed him, so that he couldn't tell. Maybe she felt wronged by both men who were unfaithful and killed them both. Wait, what about Mark Walker, is he still a suspect? Does he fit in here anywhere?"

Ryan held up his finger as he swallowed a bite of sandwich and washed it down with tea.

"We pulled him in for questioning. Based on what Janice told us, he looked good for the murders. Joe and I thought maybe he was an accomplice. It turns out he had alibis for both. He was in jail for DUI during the first one and shacked up with his latest girlfriend for the second one."

"Bless her little heart," said Charlie. "I hope he doesn't beat her to death someday."

"His P.O. told me he's looking to have a long stay in our penal bread and breakfast, thanks to you." Ryan popped another chip in his mouth.

"Me?" Charlie's sandwich paused midair. "I wasn't responsible for his DUI."

"She told me he threatened you in your office. You didn't mention anything about that situation." Ryan gave her a serious look.

Charlie gave him her sweetest smile. "Remember that little conversation we had about H.I.P.A.A., ten-thousand-dollar fines, loss of a license to practice, and confidentiality?"

"Huh," said Ryan. He picked up the remaining half of his sandwich and pushed some escaping chicken salad back in the bread with his finger.

"You still haven't explained why Janice is a person of interest in this case?" Charlie took a large bite of her sandwich and chewed.

"She was dating both vics, and both break-ups were adversarial." He swallowed some tea. "She's still holding a grudge."

Charlie considered this a moment while she chewed. "I hate to say it, but she does fit the profile. I could see her luring a guy to his home. I have a hard time thinking of any of my patients as being a killer, except for Mark Walker. When do you plan to interrogate Sherry Harper?"

"As soon as we find her. She isn't answering her phone, and she isn't at her house."

"That's suspicious. Sherry just returned home, and she's left again?" Charlie finished her sandwich and wiped her hands on a napkin.

"Appears so."

Charlie rose from her seat. "Time for dessert." She found the container she'd filled with fresh-baked cookies and offered it to Ryan. The smell of chocolate and vanilla drifted in the air, making her mouth water.

His face brightened like a little boys. "Yum, chocolate chip cookies are my favorite. These are still warm. I would never have pegged you for a domestic goddess."

"Are you stereotyping me, Detective Roberts?"

Ryan chuckled. "Darn, you caught me." He decimated half a cookie in one bite and chewed, looking like a chipmunk.

Charlie gathered the dirty dishes. "You should taste my pot roast. It's so falling-apart tender you can't slice it." Charlie placed the dishes in the sink and returned to her seat.

"You'll have to invite me over sometime, so I can try it." Ryan pinned Charlie to her chair with his intense gaze.

Charlie felt like a bunny in a trap. *Oh no, he wants an invitation, what do I say?* To buy time, she reached for her glass of tea. She took a sip, and all the ice shifted in the glass, smashing her in the face and causing the tea to splash down her shirt.

"Oh," Charlie gasped. She sat down her glass and dabbed at the tea on her blouse. An ice cube shimmied down her cleavage, causing her to shiver.

Ryan grinned. "Vicious ice."

Charlie swiveled in her chair so Ryan couldn't see her reach down the front of her shirt. When she turned back around with the wayward ice dripping in her hand, her face burned with embarrassment.

Ryan's eyes crinkled with mirth.

"I'm curious, what made you decide to be a forensic profiler and a consultant for the department?" Ryan's gaze returned to the cookies.

"Jennifer." Charlie looked at her hands, clasped on the table.

"Who's Jennifer?" Ryan reached for another cookie.

"She was murdered in September of last year — up at the park."

"Wait. Are you talking about Jennifer Mendanza? The girl found on one of the hiking trails?"

Charlie ran her hand up and down her sweating glass of iced tea. She looked up and nodded, tears dotting her lower lashes.

"She was such a great kid, and that monster murdered her. It's been over six months now." Charlie sat back in her chair. "I check on her family from time to time. Jennifer's mom is still so depressed she's like a zombie. Her dad's drinking way too much, and her brother's flunking out of his senior year. Jennifer deserves justice, and her family deserves closure. I keep thinking that Jennifer's killer is still out there, looking for his next victim." Charlie shivered. "Is Jennifer one of your cases?"

"No, but I'll let the guys running her case know that you're interested and available to consult." Ryan swallowed his cookie and wiped his mouth. "I heard Johnson and Mastin talking after the briefing the other day. They were impressed with your profile."

"Which ones were they? I'm terrible with names."

Johnson's the black guy with the shaved head and Mastin is the one with the mustache."

"I was hoping my first case to profile would be Jennifer's. I never suspected this mess would land in my lap."

Spanky pushed her way through the doggie door and shook herself from nose to tail.

"Smart dog," Ryan commented. "We had to teach my sister's dog to use the door."

Charlie and Ryan cleaned up lunch dishes together, working as a team.

"Did you check to see if Sherry Harper is staying with her daughter, Debbie?"

"No, do you want to run by there with me?" Ryan dried a glass and sat it on the counter.

"Let me change my shoes and my blouse."

Charlie ran into her bedroom and made short work of changing. When she returned to the living room, Ryan pulled his phone from his pocket and told Siri to call his partner's mobile number.

"Hey Joe, you wanna run by Sherry Harper's daughter's house? Yeah, Debbie. Okay, bye."

Cocking her head to the left, Charlie placed a hand on her hip. "Welllll…."

"Let's saddle up. Joe will meet us there," said Ryan.

Charlie kissed her sleeping pup on the head, locked the door, and followed Ryan to his car.

CHAPTER 28 - CHARLIE SAVES THE DAY

Charlie settled into the Crown Victoria's passenger seat and fumbled with the seatbelt. "How are we going to handle this?"

"We'll wait until Joe arrives so that we have back-up. You'll stay in the car until I signal you to come in. If she's there, we'll take her back to the precinct. If she's not, I want you to come in and help with Debbie. She seemed to like you."

Joe pulled up five minutes after they did. Ryan and Joe left their cars and met on the sidewalk. Charlie lowered her window so she could hear their conversation.

Joe squinted as he peered through Ryan's windshield. "Is that Doc in your car? What's she doing here?"

"I asked her to come. Debbie relates well to her, so she might help us get some information."

"Huh." Joe ran his hand over his chin.

Ryan shook his head, "Come on, Joe, let's get this over with; it's Saturday."

"Tell me about it. Sarah's chewing my ass because she wants to go shopping. I don't know what's worse, working on Saturday, or shopping."

Charlie watched them ring the doorbell and show their badges. They pulled open an outer glass door and went inside the house. After about ten minutes, Ryan stuck his head out the door, and she joined him on the porch.

"Her mother's not here. She claims she went to visit a sister. She won't tell us how to contact her. Joe's threatening Debbie with charges of interfering with an investigation." Ryan raked his hand through his hair and gave her a pleading look.

He held the door open for Charlie. She left the bright outdoors and entered a dim living room that smelled of popcorn. It took a minute for her eyes to adjust.

Joe stood still as plaster of Paris near the fireplace, with his arms crossed, glaring at Debbie Brown. Debbie sat on a beige sofa opposite the fireplace, crying. A tall man with blond curls stood behind Debbie with his hands on her shoulders, scowling at Joe. Two small children squealed and ran around the sofa and coffee table in the small room.

Charlie walked to the sofa, sat down, and patted Debbie's arm. "Hi Debbie, do you remember me, Dr. Stone?"

Debbie looked at her and nodded.

"Are these your children?" Charlie smiled as she watched the circling youngsters.

"That's Jimmy, and this is Carolyn." Debbie sniffled and hiccupped, her chin trembling.

Carolyn stopped running, crawled into Charlie's lap, and began twirling Charlie's long blond hair.

"Hi, Carolyn. My, but you're a cutie. How old are you?"

Carolyn held up five fingers and offered a smile that highlighted a missing front tooth.

Jimmy grinned as he crawled onto the sofa next to Charlie. "I'm six!"

"Six! So, you're the big brother. I bet you take good care of your little sister."

Jimmy nodded his head up and down in an exaggerated way.

Charlie looked out the window. She could see a swing set sitting in the middle of the fenced backyard.

"I need to talk to your mommy for a few minutes," she told Jimmy. "Do you think you could take Carolyn outside to swing?

It's so warm outside. She would need a big brother to watch out for her. Could you do that?" She tilted her head and smiled.

Jimmy nodded his head and grabbed Carolyn's hand.

"Come on, Carolyn, I'll push you on the swing." Carolyn looked back at Charlie as Jimmy dragged her out the door, then it slammed closed behind them.

Joe stopped glaring and relaxed his stance. Charlie grabbed some tissues from a box on the table and handed them to Debbie.

Debbie wiped her eyes and looked at Charlie. "Every time you see me, I'm crying."

"Every time you see me, I'm handing you tissues. Is this your husband?"

Debbie nodded, "Frank, this is Dr. Stone. She's the lady who gave me the name of the children's therapist." Frank nodded his appreciation but kept his eye on Joe.

"Debbie, your mother's friend has been murdered, just like your dad. We need to find her to talk to her. We need to clear her alibi and find out if she knows who would want to kill these two men. I'm also concerned about her safety."

Debbie's eyes widened with alarm. "Is my mother in danger?"

"I hope not, but she had an intimate involvement with two murder victims, and we don't know who is doing this yet."

"I guess that *could* be true." Her eyes dropped to the tissues she twisted in her lap.

"These detectives want to question her at the precinct where it's safe. Based on what she tells us, we'll better be able to determine the level of danger."

Debbie pulled her phone from her pocket and tapped in her mother's number.

"Mom, the police are here. Yeah, they need to talk to you at the precinct. I don't know, I'll ask." Debbie placed her hand over the receiver, "Does she need to call her attorney?"

Charlie nodded. She slid a glance over toward Joe, who scowled.

"Call him. Uh huh. I'll ask. What time do you want her to meet you there?"

Ryan answered, "Three o'clock."

After returning to Ryan's car, Charlie buckled in and looked at Ryan. He looked pleased if the grin on his face was any indication.

"You handled that well. It was chaos in there. Joe and Frank were yelling at each other, Debbie was sobbing, and the kids were cranked into high gear. You walk in, everybody loves you, and Sherry Harper is coming in for questioning. Great work," he said.

"Thanks. I noticed Joe never said a word to me," Charlie donned her sunglasses as Joe dropped into the driver's seat of his car. The car leaned to the left.

Ryan shrugged. "That's Joe."

Charlie laughed. "Yeah, I know; he's a real teddy bear. Do I get to sit in on the interrogation, or am I behind the one-way mirror?"

"For now, you're behind the one-way mirror, sorry."

"Just for the record, I'm praying that Sherry Harper is innocent." Charlie rummaged in her purse for her lipstick.

Ryan looked at Charlie, his brow creased. "Why?"

She flipped down the vanity mirror and applied the lipstick before answering. "Debbie just lost her dad. The last thing she needs is a high-profile murder case with her mom as the accused. That would disrupt her and her family's life." She capped the tube and returned it to her purse. "You never told me, did Debbie and Frank have an alibi for the time of the murder?"

"They're clear."

"Two fewer suspects." With a smile, she released the mirror. It went back in place with a pop.

CHAPTER 29 - PICTURE OF PROPRIETY

Charlie and Ryan stood chatting in the small room behind the one-way mirror. Ryan lounged against the wall as he told her about a former case. When Captain Strouper entered the room, he stood erect, like a soldier.

The captain nodded to Charlie. "Nice to see you again, Dr. Stone."

"Thank you, sir."

Ryan straightened his tie. "We're almost ready to start the interrogation."

"Good, I think I'll sit in if that's all right with you." The captain looked around in search of a chair.

Muttering that he needed to find Joe, Ryan left the room.

Charlie sat in a metal foldout chair the captain set near the mirror for her. He set up another one next to hers and settled his long, lanky frame into it.

Rubbing his chin, Strouper arched a brow at her. "Is Sparks giving you a hard time?"

Somewhat taken aback, Charlie shifted in her chair to look at him, "Why do you ask?"

He shrugged his coat hanger shoulders. "He was in my office the other day on a rant about something, and your name came up."

"Does he hate women or just psychologists? Captain, I think I could stand on my head twirling flaming batons, and it wouldn't impress Lieutenant Sparks."

The captain chuckled, but neither confirmed nor denied Charlie's statement. "I spoke with Roberts. He seems very pleased with your work."

Charlie nodded. "Thanks, that's good to know."

"Don't take Joe personal — he's dedicated," Strouper said. "He and I go back a long way. He's a hell of a cop and solid as a rock. He's just old school. Years ago, Joe had a perp walk on one of his cases because the chain of evidence was compromised. The killer committed another murder a month later during a robbery." Strouper paused for a second. "After this case is resolved, I'd like to discuss extending your services into other areas in the department, if you're interested. We're considering a Sexual Assault Task Force."

"Thanks, Captain. I'm interested in hearing what you have in mind. About Joe, I deal with alcoholics, addicts, criminals, and mental health patients. I think I'm equipped to deal with Joe Sparks."

A slow grin spread across the captain's face. "I'm sure you are."

Ryan and Joe ushered Sherry Harper and her attorney into the interrogation room and sat them where they would face the one-way mirror. Dressed in black pants and a dusty rose sweater topped with a string of pearls, Sherry was the perfect picture of propriety.

Her attorney looked as if he'd just left the golf course in a lime green shirt with khaki pants. "I'm Blaine Stephens, Ms. Harper's attorney. I have instructed my client to answer no questions unless I approve them. What's this all about?"

"Let me start the recorder." Ryan performed the recorded interview ritual and nodded to Joe.

"We have two murdered men. Your client was married to one and involved, until recently, with the other. Both these murders have the same M.O., so you can see why your client is a person of interest," said Joe with his grumbling voice.

"I didn't murder anyone." Sherry sat forward in her seat, her brow furrowed. Blaine placed a hand on her wrist and gave her a stern look. She sat back and dropped her eyes to her hands.

Joe continued, "We find it interesting that you traveled to Tennessee after David Street's murder. Do you have an alibi for the time of his death?"

"What was the time of death?" asked Blaine.

"Late Saturday or early Sunday one week ago." Joe placed his forearms on the table.

Blaine nodded to Sherry. Tears brimmed in her eyes.

"I was with my friend Betty that Saturday night. I slept in late, so I didn't attend church Sunday morning. I met my daughter and her family for Sunday lunch at the Mexican restaurant near her home."

"Where did you go on Saturday night?" Ryan looked up from the note he was scribbling.

"We went to several clubs. Betty convinced me that I needed to drown my sorrows and have a good time."

Ryan jotted down a few notations and looked at Sherry. "We'd like Betty's last name and contact information to verify your alibi."

Sherry rummaged through her purse and pulled out her phone. Once she had the entry, she passed the phone to Joe so he could copy the information. When he finished, he handed the phone back.

"Is this Betty the same person who was on the cruise with you?" asked Joe.

"No."

Joe leaned forward. "Was anyone else with you on the night in question?"

Sherry rummaged once again in her purse. She pulled out a wadded tissue and dabbed at her eyes. "No, it was a girl's night out."

Ryan shifted in his seat. "Can anyone at any of these clubs verify you were there?"

Touching her pearls with her hand, Sherry answered, "I didn't see anyone I knew. I had a bit too much to drink. Betty drove me home. I don't go to clubs much."

"Did you or Betty use a credit card?" asked Joe. He tapped his pen on the legal pad in front of him.

Sherry's gaze was riveted to the pen. The corners of her mouth pulled down as if she was annoyed. "No, we both paid with cash." Moisture dotted her upper lip.

"What clubs did you go to that night?" asked Ryan.

"Three or four, I don't remember the names." After dabbing her upper lip with the tissue, Sherry pulled a folded paper from her bag and began fanning herself.

Joe leaned forward and sneered. "Oh come on, Sherry, surely you remember the names of some of those clubs. What time did you start partying?"

Sherry leaned away from Joe and closer to her attorney. She worked her pearls between her thumb and index finger. "Nine o'clock. We began at The Roustabout."

"That's interesting." Joe held her gaze. "We found Street's car abandoned at the Roustabout."

"That's it," said Blaine. "Unless my client is in danger or you plan to charge her with a crime, we're leaving."

Ryan sat tall in his chair. "We have two men, both murdered in a brutal fashion. If you didn't kill them, we can't rule out that someone connected to you did."

"Is Dr. Stone here?" Sherry's lips thinned. "Debbie said I should talk to Dr. Stone." Her chin firmed with determination.

Joe shook his head and frowned. He ran his finger around the inside of his collar and stretched his neck.

Ryan stood. "Would you excuse us a minute?"

Chairs scraped as Ryan and Joe pushed them back and walked out the door. They opened the door to the room where Charlie and Captain Strouper were seated. Unfolding his lean frame, the captain gestured for everyone to exit. They reconvened in the empty conference room and closed the door.

Captain Strouper leaned against a wall and crossed his ankles and arms. "What do you want to do?"

Joe's face turned crimson. "I'm against sending her in there. This is police business, and she doesn't know what the hell she's doing."

Turning his gaze toward Ryan, the captain nodded his head. "What do you think, Ryan?"

"Charlie deals with criminals every day, Captain. She knows what she's doing. Besides, Sherry Harper and her daughter, Debbie, trust Charlie. They may tell her things they wouldn't tell us."

Everyone looked at Captain Strouper. Charlie stood to the side with her arms crossed and a hip cocked.

"Dr. Stone, are you willing to go in and see what you can find out?" asked Captain Strouper.

Charlie stood straight. "Yes, I'll try."

Rubbing his hand over his short gray hair, Joe grumbled, "Well, hell." He looked angry enough to stroke-out as he turned, opened the door, and slammed it behind him.

Frowning, Captain Strouper pushed himself away from the wall. "Dr. Stone, it's time to stand on your head and twirl flaming batons."

Charlie laughed.

Looking confused, Ryan shook his head and followed them out of the room.

Charlie introduced herself as a consultant for the department and shook Sherry's hand first, then her attorney's. Using a neutral strategy, she sat in a chair at the end of the table, aligning herself between Sherry and Joe.

"My daughter trusts you," said Sherry. "The therapist you recommended for my grandchildren has helped them deal with John's death,"

Charlie offered a gentle smile. "Debbie and I have an unusual relationship so far. She cries, and I hand her tissues. I met your grandchildren today. They're sweet kids. I'm glad the therapy is working out."

Sherry smiled, her shoulders lowering to a relaxed state. "They are my pride and joy."

"Sherry, you seemed frightened earlier. Has someone threatened you?" asked Charlie.

Fingering her pearls, Sherry pressed her lips together.

During her training as an intern, Charlie had learned about the power of silence. She used that power now. Blaine sighed, fingering the phone peeking over the front pocket of his shirt. Joe had his chin in his hand. His complexion now looked mottled.

At last, Sherry spoke. "The threat wasn't against me, but John and David were threatened." She looked at Blaine. He nodded assent. Charlie waited for her to continue.

"Betty and I became friends a year before John asked for a divorce. I'd caught him with several women by then. Betty was my sounding board. She helped me get through the divorce."

"A friend is helpful during hard times like a divorce." Charlie nodded for her to continue.

"She never liked David — said he was just like John. I didn't believe it. John never went to AA to get sober, David did. I thought we'd get married. I should never have insisted on that cruise." Sherry looked down at her hands. "The minute we were on board they were pushing alcoholic beverages. I guess it was too much for David because he relapsed." Sherry looked at Charlie with glistening eyes.

"I was so angry, I threw all his stuff out of the stateroom and flew back without him. Every time I cried or complained about John or David, Betty would say, 'They deserve to have their balls cut off and stuffed down their throats.' " Sherry's hand covered her throat.

"When Debbie picked me up at the airport, she only told me that John was beaten to death. My grandchildren were in the car, so we didn't discuss the murder. Then after I arrived at home, she didn't have time to tell me much before the police brought me in for questioning. After I had left here, I asked Debbie about John's murder. She told me about the castration. Imagine Debbie finding her father in that condition. I just couldn't believe that Betty would do something like that. I needed to get away, to think. I went to my sister's house. I didn't want to be alone."

"Your behavior says that you do think Betty is capable of what she threatened," said Charlie.

"It's just so weird, people are murdered all the time, but the castration …"

Charlie folded her hands in front of her on the table. "How many times did Betty tell you this about John and David?"

Sherry clutched her purse against her chest. "Every time I complained. That was often about John and just recently with David. When I talked to her on the phone the other day, and I told her what happened, she said, 'They got what they deserved.' After talking to Debbie today, I wondered if Betty might see me as a threat."

Charlie nodded. "Possibly so, if she killed these two men. Betty may have seen them as competition or a threat, in which case she may interpret your talking to the police as an act of betrayal." Charlie paused for a beat. "If you don't tell us what you know, you'll be withholding vital information to solve the case. That would be a betrayal of your daughter and obstruction of justice. This is one of those damned if you do, and damned if you don't situations."

"My allegiance is to my daughter," said Sherry.

Charlie leaned forward. "Sherry, I need you to try to remember where you went that night."

Wrinkling her brow, Sherry rubbed her forehead with her fingers.

"I just can't remember. Everything was so fuzzy. I only had two drinks. I don't know why they knocked me for such a loop."

Roofies thought Charlie.

"What did you drink?" asked Ryan.

"Margaritas."

Charlie tilted her head. "How did you feel the next morning?"

"Hung over with a whopper of a headache. I was still so drowsy that it didn't feel safe to drive, that's why I missed church." Sherry's hand moved to cover her stomach. "I didn't eat much for lunch, the smell of the Mexican food made my stomach turn."

Ryan looked up from his legal pad. "Could you describe Betty?"

"She's thirty-five with long brown hair and real cute. She never liked John, because he made a pass at her while we were married. Are you bringing Betty in for questioning?" asked Sherry, looking at Charlie.

"I don't make those decisions, Detective Roberts and Lieutenant Sparks do." Charlie nodded toward the two men.

Ryan requested a DNA sample from Sherry.

The attorney looked at Sherry and shook his head no. "Let me discuss this further with my client."

Sherry left with her attorney. She was warned not to leave the state, again. Charlie suggested she stay with her daughter if she didn't feel safe being alone.

After Sherry and her attorney left, Captain Strouper joined Joe, Ryan, and Charlie around the interrogation table.

Charlie said, "It's plausible that someone slipped Rohypnol into Sherry's drink. Since the powder form is odorless and tasteless, she'd know it was there. It affects the memory and leaves people feeling *very* hung-over. It leaves the system within twenty-four hours."

Joe scowled. "Do you believe that crap?" He slammed his pen down on top of his legal pad. "She got drunk and was hung-over."

Strouper spoke up. "We don't have enough information to make any determinations yet." He rubbed his chin. "Dr. Stone, good work in there. You can go home and enjoy your Saturday."

"Thanks, Captain."

Joe wiped his face with his hand. "Now I have to take Sarah shopping."

Charlie stood and gathered her purse."I'll go shopping with Sarah. I've been anxious to meet her," she offered.

"Oh no, you might give her ideas. That woman is hard enough to handle now. She's got it in her head that she wants to be the part-time secretary at our church." Joe shook his head and grunted.

Captain Strouper shook his head at Joe. Smiling at Charlie, he nodded and walked off.

CHAPTER 30 - HUNTER OR HUNTED

The Nightscape was dim and crowded. The Huntress was disappointed to see that it catered more to the thirty-something crowd. Dynamic in a low-cut blouse and a flowing skirt, she strolled toward the bar with a loose-hipped sway, feeling the skirt swirl around her legs with each step. Her hair was trying to stick to her neck, so she lifted the mass of dark curls off her shoulders. The breeze from the rotating ceiling fans cooled her neck, but not her need. Her gaze roamed the room as she searched for her usual prey.

A dark-haired man with penetrating eyes caught her attention. She stopped, letting her gaze wander up and down his lean body. Tall, with perfect posture, he radiated a confidence that she seldom saw in men. He eased between the tables with the sensual grace of a panther. The air between them sizzled as they locked gazes.

Transfixed, the Huntress rubbed her arms in an attempt to dispel the chill that draped her. Aware of her increased heart rate, she shut her eyes to compose her mind. *Go away. I'm on a mission.* She took in a breath, letting her lungs expand, and opened her eyes. *Please let him be a mere illusion, let him be gone.*

He was still there, staring at her. This kind of man was dangerous, at least for her. She felt her resolve begin to weaken as the very air crackled between them. This man wasn't her prey. He was a distraction — a detour from her plans.

His gaze never left her face as he weaved his way through the crowd. This man didn't need a few drinks to build his courage. He appeared to be as comfortable in his sexuality as she was in hers.

"Would you like to dance?" He smiled and reached out to her. She felt an irresistible pull to be with him.

"Yesss," she sighed the word, unable to wrench her gaze from his. She dropped her purse under a nearby table.

He wrapped warm fingers around hers. The contact seemed to burn as he led the Huntress to the dance floor. The fast song ended, and Marvin Gaye's *Let's Get It On* began playing. When their bodies touched, an incredible chemistry sparked, igniting into an instant passion. Bodies merged and hands roamed as they swayed to the music.

"I'm Carlos. My buddy runs this club. I know a place near his office where we can have some privacy," he whispered in her ear. He kissed her neck, and she pressed against him moaning.

When the song ended, he guided her past the restrooms and turned left down a hallway. He parted some curtains and led her to a dimly lit, secluded alcove. He pulled her close and ran his hand up her thigh.

"I want you. Right here. Right now." Carlos ground his pelvis against her body.

"Yes," she breathed before he covered her mouth with his.

He pulled her blouse over her head and dropped to his knees in front of her. Burrowing his face in her breasts, he squeezed one in each hand. He closed his warm mouth over her nipples, circling each one with his tongue. Seizing one of the turgid peaks between his teeth, he nipped her. Writhing, the Huntress cried out.

She ran her hands through his hair and over his broad shoulders. Reaching behind her, she unzipped her skirt, letting it fall in a pool of fabric around her feet.

Carlos stood and backed away as he pulled his shirt over his head, tossing it to the floor. A fringe of hair fell over his brow, making him appear savage and dangerous. He braided his fingers in her hair, roughly yanking her close. She skimmed her hand across the hair on his chest. His heart pounded beneath her palm. Reaching down, she loosened his belt and unzipped his pants. They dropped around his ankles. Stepping out of them, he kicked them to the side. She slid her hand over his smooth shaft and squeezed. He turned her to face the wall and placed her hands against it, rubbing against her.

No! The Huntress stiffened, struggling to breathe as terror roared through her. Pulling her hips toward him, he kicked her feet apart to provide him complete access to her body.

Panic raced along the pathways of her nerves, holding her rigid with fear. Her pulse pounded in her ears. She felt like she was smothering. "Can't breathe…stop! Not…this way!" she gasped.

She tried to run. Carlos wrenched her arm behind her back. She cried out in pain.

"It's any way I want it, Babe." He shoved her back against the wall and penetrated her.

She was no longer the Huntress. She was thirteen. Alone. Helpless. In her mind, once again a sex slave to her father.

****

She could hear her sister beating on the locked door, trying to save her, as she stood naked in her bedroom in front of her father.

He squeezed the nipple of her budding breast. She retreated, covering her chest with her arms.

"Stop running, Baby Girl. You know what can happen if you get me mad. Daddy wants to teach you how to play takedown, like the show on television. You should know by now I always get what I want. If you keep fighting me, I'll have to hurt you."

Tears slid down her cheeks. "I don't want to play, Daddy. Please don't make me do it."

The banging became more frantic. *If I can only get to the door.* She tried to run. He caught her arm, pulling it up behind her back. Squeaking with pain, she still tried to escape.

Leaning down, he whispered in her ear, "Do you want me to break it again?"

She slumped and shook her head.

"Then get your hands on the wall," he said, pointing to the area he had prepared.

Trembling, she stepped up on the box he had placed on the floor near the wall.

"Now spread your feet," he said. He kicked her feet further apart and began frisking her, probing her developing body. Tears leaked from her closed eyes. She heard the dreaded sound of his zipper.

"You've been a bad girl. You must be punished. Tell me that you've been bad and deserve to be punished, Baby Girl."

She hung her head, her tears dripping on the box. The thought of having to put his dick in her mouth again filled her with dread.

"Dammit, I said tell me you want me to punish you." He yanked her head back by the hair.

"I was bad, Daddy. I deserve to be punished because I was so bad. Please don't hurt me."

She heard her sister yanking on the door handle and screaming, but her sister couldn't save her. No one could.

He pulled her hips back. She screamed and then whimpered with pain at each thrust. Blood dripped down to the white painted surface of the wooden box, her innocence gone forever.

****

Trapped in the memory, she felt her spirit leave her body. It floated to the ceiling in the hallway, and she watched with detachment as Carlos thrust into her again and again and again. Tears rimmed her lower lashes, but she felt nothing because she wasn't there.

After he had finished, Carlos leaned against her, pinning her to the wall. Somehow the Huntress was back in her body. She heard him panting in her ear, knew the unwanted heat of him as his sweat trickled between them, tracing a path down her spine. She clung to the wall when he pushed away from her. She heard him pull up his pants, heard the jangle of his belt buckle and the zip of his fly as he closed it. Tears spilled down her cheeks, blurring her vision.

He turned her to face him.

Numb, hovering between the past and the present, she stood submissive, as she had so many times in her childhood. Through the haze of tears, she thought she saw her dad's face. *Please, Daddy, no more.* She shook her head. Carlos's face swam into focus, and she remembered where she was.

"Thanks, Babe, you were great. Love those titties." Reaching over, he pinched her right nipple. "We'll have to do that again sometime." Winking, he tucked his shirt into his pants and walked through the curtain, back into the club.

The threat was gone. Shame flooded her body. Sliding down the wall, she curled into a ball and wept until she was empty of tears and drained of emotion. Feeling like death walking, she fumbled her way into her clothing and found her way to the ladies' room, where she locked herself in a stall and with precision placed the tissue on the seat. Holding her face in her hands, she attempted to expel his sperm from her body.

She shook, just as she had as a child after her father had finished raping her.

Gaining some measure of control, the Huntress returned. With a hand on each side of the stall, she steadied herself. Her head aching and her stomach roiling, she turned and flushed away the seed of her tormenter. She pushed out of the stall, relieved that the bathroom was empty.

The image in the mirror above the sink showed hair that was awry, black streaks of mascara, and lipstick slashing her cheek like a wound. The Huntress washed her face and ran her fingers through her hair. Desperate to leave, she exited the bathroom and searched among the tables to find where she'd dropped her purse. She spied Carlos on the other side of the club, talking to another woman. Anger boiled in her stomach. *I'll kill you someday.* Like a general retreating to fight another day, she left the club.

She reached her car and retched, spewing her shame onto the black asphalt. With a trembling hand, she wiped her mouth. Tonight she was the prey, not the hunter.

It'll be different next time.

CHAPTER 31 - NIGHTMARES

Charlie cried out in her sleep.

Blind with panic, arms thrust in front of her, Charlie blundered down a dim hallway lined with doors. At last, she slowed and bent at the waist breathing in ragged spurts, her hand to her chest. Heart throbbing, she licked the salty sweat from her upper lip.

A door on her left creaked ajar. Inhaling courage deep into her lungs, she exhaled her fear and slipped into the room.

A scream echoed off the dark green walls. It took Charlie a moment to realize the scream was hers.

A man was handcuffed and bleeding on a bed. She sprinted to him. He was alive. She searched the top of the table next to the bed for keys. None.

Snatching the drawer from the table, she turned it upside down on the brown hardwood floor and sifted the objects through her fingers. Nothing seemed useful to open the cuffs.

She crawled back to the bed and clawed her way up. She straddled the naked man and grabbed the cuffs' chains, the shiny metal digging into her palms. Tears and sweat dripped onto the man's bare chest as she jerked and tugged with all her might.

Her efforts to pull him free were useless. Grasping the top of the headboard, she rested her brow on her forearm and wept. She looked up. The mirror above the headboard reflected her haunted eyes. She was naked.

****

Charlie jerked awake to the familiar darkness of her bedroom. Shaking with convulsive sobs, she sat up and threw off the covers.

When Spanky jumped on the bed, Charlie pulled her close to cuddle her. Using several tissues, she wiped her eyes and blew her nose. Now shivering, she settled under the comforter and hugged Spanky to her chest, gaining comfort from her warmth.

"I have to figure this out, Spanky. Is there some clue that I've missed? It's Saturday night. God, please don't let anyone else die."

CHAPTER 32 - DENIAL

Melissa sat across from Charlie, clutching her Step One homework.

Charlie smiled at Melissa. "I see you did your homework. Let's see what you wrote."

Melissa handed her the papers with obvious reluctance. Charlie took them and scanned them. After a moment, she looked back up at Melissa. "Remember, Melissa, Step One of the Twelve Step Program of Alcoholics Anonymous is designed to help you to understand the different ways your life was out of control."

Melissa set a bottle of water on the edge of Charlie's desk. She didn't comment.

"You've written that you put your life and the lives of others in danger by drinking and driving." Charlie laid the papers down.

"But no one was ever hurt." Melissa shifted in her seat and started twirling her hair.

Charlie sighed. *I've heard that rationalization so many times.* "Melissa, if someone took a loaded gun and under the influence of alcohol or drugs started firing it around people, would you consider that dangerous?"

"Well, yeah." Melissa grabbed the bottle of water.

"If the person managed not to shoot anyone, was it still dangerous?"

"Sure, he could've shot someone." She grimaced as she tried to twist off the cap.

"Melissa, I want you to consider a car to be a four-thousand-pound weapon. You drove it in an altered state and were lucky enough not to hit anyone."

Charlie sat back to let that settle into Melissa's brain. Her pensive expression alerted Charlie that the analogy hit home.

The cap came loose, and water squirted out of the bottle, wetting Melissa's jeans. "Shit, it looks like I pissed myself."

Charlie rolled her eyes and sighed again. She wanted to bang her head on the desk but resisted. Instead, she picked up the homework. "Is that all you could think of to report about the dangers of your alcohol and drug use?" She gave Melissa a *get real* look. *This is like trying to break through her denial and minimization with a hammer and a chisel.*

Melissa looked down and wiped at her jeans. "That's the only thing I could think of at the time."

"Have you ever ridden in a car with someone under the influence?"

"Several times on girls' night out. We had a few close calls." Melissa began telling stories of near arrests, fights, and near collisions, growing more animated with each story. After describing several narrow escapes, she went still and compressed her lips, as if to stop any further exposure of wrongdoing.

I do believe I made my point, Charlie thought, as she scribbled notes in the therapy chart. "Melissa, have you worked while under the influence or hung-over?"

She looked up at the ceiling as if the answer was printed there. "I only did that once or twice."

"Were you aware you could have an accident, which could affect you or your coworkers?"

"I never thought about it that way before." Melissa laughed. "I remember once I was working as a cook and I burned my arm because I was so hung-over." She pulled up her sleeve to reveal a two-inch-long scar on her forearm.

Charlie leaned forward to inspect the scar. "Do you realize you were smiling and laughing while describing a painful burn?"

"No, um, I didn't mean to do that. It hurt at the time."

"Despite the pain, you continued to use. That is what Twelve Step programs mean by the insanity of addiction." Charlie was still examining Melissa's scar.

Melissa yanked down her sleeve and crossed her arms.

Charlie looked at Melissa's homework again. *She has an above-average intelligence and several years of college, yet she still doesn't have a steady career.* "So, how many jobs have you had since you relapsed?" she asked.

Melissa twirled her hair. "Five."

"How did you lose them?"

Melissa shrugged. "Different reasons. Most of the time it was because I was late to work. Then there was the time I failed a drug screen. I was managing an apartment complex. You know how that works; they don't pay you much, but you get a free apartment.

They fired me and kicked me out of the apartment, so I wound up homeless and jobless on the same day. That was a pretty sucky day."

"Wow, it sure was. Are you still painting apartments?"

Melissa nodded. "Yeah, that's working out."

Charlie frowned as she read. "Your Financial Step One reveals two thousand dollars in alcohol- and drug-related expenses since you relapsed." She looked at Melissa and arched a brow.

"That's hard to believe." Melissa shook her head. "That may be true. Yeah, I've had some problems, but I'm not an alcoholic or addict. I can quit anytime I want. I did it once so I can do it again." She raised her chin.

Charlie smiled. "Yes, you did, and I'm proud of you for that. But addiction is a sneaky disease. Like a monster, it waits for you to let down your guard. Then it pounces. Before you know it, addiction has you in its clutches again. Melissa, the essence of Step One in AA or NA is accepting you are out of control and your life has become unmanageable. You need to work on acceptance, but don't get discouraged. For some people, Step One is the hardest step." Charlie put down the homework and clasped her hands.

Melissa crossed her arms and pasted on a defiant expression.

It's time to change gears. "You made a statement during the last session that you make people pay when they mess with you. What did you mean by that statement?" Charlie leaned back in her chair.

Wide-eyed, Melissa sat up straight. "I wasn't threatening you or anything. I was just ... blowing off steam. I know you're just doing your job."

"Yes, I'm doing my best to help you and the others who come through this program." Charlie gave her a stern look. "Melissa, I won't tolerate threats, veiled or otherwise."

Melissa's eyes widened. "I'm sorry, I was upset that day." She pouted a moment, then asked, "Why do you work here, anyway?"

"What do you mean?" Charlie sat back in her chair.

Melissa leaned forward, a curious expression on her face. "Why do you keep trying to save us? Why bother? It can't pay that much." She locked her gaze on Charlie.

"I'm attempting to stop people from killing themselves with addictive substances." *Like my parents.*

"Why do you care?" Melissa scooted to the edge of her seat and placed both hands on Charlie's desk.

"I just do." *Because I failed my parents and they both died from smoking.* Charlie paused a second. "I believe I can help people save themselves." *If I try hard enough.*

Melissa leaned closer still, her dark eyes gleaming. "What if they don't want to be saved?"

"If people don't *choose* to change their destructive behaviors, they will eventually bring about their demise."

Melissa sat back, closed her eyes, and appeared to ruminate on that thought.

When she opened them again, Charlie said, "Now that we have that issue settled, tell me about your nightmares." She leaned forward, rested her elbow on the desk and cupped her chin in her hand.

Thrown by the change in subject, Melissa sat back in her chair and stuttered, "I ... I have them several times a month."

"Do you remember the subject matter of the nightmares, and is it the same one each time?" Charlie was always interested in her patient's dreams since they often revealed some of their unconscious issues.

"I remember parts of it, but I always wake up before I die." Melissa shivered, despite the warmth of the room. "I'm not ready to talk about them yet, maybe next time."

"All right, just remember I'm here to help, and I may be able to help you stop those dreams." Charlie glanced at the clock on the back wall. *The hour's up, and she needs to get back to work.*

Melissa left clutching more homework. While she made a return appointment, Charlie slipped out the staff entrance to her car. She raised the trunk lid and shoved her emergency box out of the way, looking for her journal.

The front door of the building slammed. Charlie peeked around the trunk lid in time to see Melissa stomping out of the building.

Melissa passed in front of Charlie's car grumbling. "What makes her think I'll tell her my secrets? They're none of her business. Just because she says she wants to help me, doesn't mean I trust her."

Charlie heard a car door slam.

CHAPTER 33 - SLEEP WALKING?

The door was open, so Charlie tapped on the doorframe to Marti's office. "Hi, do you have a minute to talk?"

Marti was sitting at her desk, writing in a chart. She looked up. Running her gaze up and down Charlie, she frowned. "Has there been another murder this weekend?"

Charlie closed the door and slid into the chair on the other side of Marti's desk. "Only in my nightmare." She ran her hands through her hair and looked at Marti, seeking some form of wisdom.

Marti closed her chart and put down her pen. Then she rose, moved around her desk to give Charlie a much-needed hug, and sat in the chair next to her.

Charlie recounted the terrifying dream. "This is the scary part; several times I've woken up somewhere other than my bed. I don't know how I got there."

Marti picked up her pen and tapped it against her lips. "How long has this been going on?"

"Since I became so sleep-deprived. I guess losing an hour or two every night becomes cumulative." Charlie yawned.

"Were you a sleepwalker as a kid?"

"As a matter of fact, I was. My mom told me I got up one night, walked into the hall closet and closed the door behind me. When she opened it, I was facing the coats, having a conversation."

"What did she do?"

"She led me back to bed. My dad was a sleepwalker too."

Marti's brows drew together into her concerned look. "I think you need to see your doctor."

"I did —"

Marti raised a hand and interrupted, "Make another appointment. You may need a sleep study. The stress and insomnia could be triggering you to sleepwalk. As to your nightmare, the message seems pretty clear. You feel that if you can reach some insight, these murders will stop. If you don't, more men will die. I'll remind you again; you're only a consultant on these cases. You're not the police detective hired to solve them." Marti reached for her cup of tea and took a sip. "You do the same thing with your patients, Charlie. You can't control the world."

Charlie rubbed her temples. "I know, but what if I'm missing something that makes a big difference?"

Marti drained her cup. "Maybe you are, maybe you aren't, but it seems to me that the biggest hindrance to these cases is the system. Aren't y'all still waiting on some of the forensics from both murders?" She put her cup down with authority, as though to emphasize her point.

"You're right. I'm a small part of this investigation. There's still something about these cases that's bothering me."

"There are lots of things about these cases that's bothering *me*, and it's not my job," said Marti.

Charlie stood and stretched her arms over her head. She felt better and more focused. Marti always had that effect on her. "Thanks for listening. I've got to go back to work."

"Anytime," said Marti, with her gentle smile. She straightened and snapped her fingers. "I know, maybe you need to get out in nature more. Hiking always calms you. You're off this afternoon.

Take Spanky for a walk at Monte Sano State Park. It'll do you both some good."

"That's a wonderful idea. Spanky will love it. I can take the trail to the overlook."

CHAPTER 34 - THE SET UP

Ryan saw Spanky first. The pup was dancing about and baying, tail slashing the air. Waroof, waroof!

As he walked through the sun-dappled shade toward Spanky, the pup bounded toward him, her leash dragging behind. He caught the leash on Spanky's second excited circle around him and dropped to one knee, chuckling. Spanky rewarded him with sloppy puppy kisses.

"Hey, girl." Picking up the wriggling puppy, he scratched behind her ears.

Charlie sat on a nearby bench, gaping at Ryan. The north Alabama mountains provided a beautiful backdrop of multiple shades of spring greens.

A beautiful scene — a lovely woman, thought Ryan. "I didn't know you liked to hike." He grinned at Charlie's upturned face. "I'll have to thank Marti for the tipoff."

"It's one of my sanity savers." Charlie paused and furrowed her brow. "What do you mean by 'thank Marti'? Did she call you?"

He placed Spanky on her feet and handed the leash to Charlie. "Marti told me you wanted me to meet you up here, at the overlook."

Charlie's face flushed pink. "I'm going to kill her."

"Then I'll have to arrest you." Ryan's grin widened. "Sounds like a set-up to me."

Charlie smiled back. "Since you're here, would you like to join me for a snack?"

"Don't mind if I do." Ryan swiped leaves off the bench. She scooted over to offer him more room.

Charlie rummaged through her pack. "This is a perfect place for a snack. It's so tranquil. Spanky loves to walk on the trails. Her sniffer has been in overdrive."

"Nice view too," said Ryan, looking at her.

Spanky pranced in place and snuffled the air, whining, as Charlie pulled dog biscuits from the pack. After Charlie had poured water into Spanky's small hiking bowl, she offered her a treat. The pup scarfed it down.

"How can you even taste that, you silly dog?" Charlie scolded. She cleaned her hands with a sanitary wipe and offered one to him, which he accepted.

After wiping his hands, he looked around for a trash container. Finding none, he placed the wipe in his fanny pack. They both pulled their water bottles from their packs and slaked their thirst.

"Chocolate?" Charlie waved a bar of dark chocolate with caramel and sea salt.

Smiling, he took the chocolate and offered some of his mixed nuts.

"A virtual feast," said Ryan, balancing his goodies on the napkin Charlie had given him.

He watched as she nibbled dainty bites of her chocolate. *She eats like a cat*, he thought. She appeared to be savoring the flavor, extending the oral pleasure of its dark silky texture for as long as possible. Just watching her eat was arousing him more than he'd have believed possible. *Does she approach sex that way?*

He shoved his allotment of chocolate into his mouth, chewed, and swallowed.

They looked at each other and smiled. Her eyes were grey-blue, like the ocean on a cloudy day. His gaze strayed to her chocolate. *Will she let me have the rest?*

She moved it away from him.

I guess not. "You like to make things last, don't you?"

"Yes, savoring life is a lesson I learned several years ago while watching my mother die." Charlie lowered her eyes and took another nibble.

"I suppose watching someone die could change the way a person does things." Placing his arm on the back of the bench, he shifted to see her face. "How did your mom die?"

Charlie appeared to contemplate her answer while she admired the mountain view. "Suicide by tar and nicotine. It still makes me angry. I understand tobacco companies lied about the lethal effects of smoking, but she didn't stop after she learned the truth."

"Cancer? Heart attack?" His thumb rubbed her shoulder. *Her shirt feels so soft.*

"Lung cancer." She popped the last morsel of chocolate into her mouth and crushed the wrapper with a loud crackle.

Ryan grimaced. "That's a hard way to go, gives a person plenty of time to think."

She shoved the trash into a pocket of her pack. "My mom was full of remorse about many things. She regretted all the missed opportunities and small things in her life that were there all along, but that she never noticed until near the end. I don't want to die that way — missing opportunities." Charlie shifted the pack to the ground by her feet.

"What about your dad?" Ryan shifted his arm to be able to cup her shoulder.

"Ten years later, lung cancer stole him, too. He quit after Mom's death, but by then the damage was done. I called him Mr. Silver Lining. He was one of the most positive and joyful people I've ever known in my life. He never lost his zest to learn new things and his child-like love of play."

"I wish I had a chance to know him." Ryan smiled.

She smiled back, her eyes sparkling in the light. "Dad would approve of you."

Ryan gave her shoulder a squeeze. "You're a lot like your dad, upbeat despite a hard job."

She raised her hand, and Ryan saw smears of chocolate on two fingers. She began licking them clean, one finger at a time. Ryan felt his penis harden as he watched each finger slide in and out of her mouth. He shifted on the bench.

Whimper.

For an instant, Ryan thought the sound had oozed from his mouth. He looked down at the prancing pup as she whimpered again. "Spanky is giving you one of those 'I'm going to faint if you don't give me a dog biscuit' looks."

The pup shifted on her haunches, emitting a desperate whine, and licked her chops.

"Okay Sweetie, you can have just one more." Charlie gave the pup her treat and packed away the water bowl and snacks.

"You mind if I hike along?" asked Ryan. *Say yes.*

"I just thought before you appeared, that hiking alone wasn't such a good idea. I thought about Jennifer and her death here on the mountain."

"I told Jefferson and Hodge that you have an interest in that case. Have they called you yet?"

Charlie shook her head.

Ryan felt a surge of testosterone. He wanted to protect this woman, to keep her safe. He wanted *her*. Uncomfortable with the intensity of his emotions, he changed the subject. Chuckling, he pointed at the pup dancing at the end of her leash.

"Spanky would protect you."

Charlie giggled. "Like she did at my house, right before she hid under the bed."

"I'll never forget her slamming on the brakes and flipping when she ran into me."

They both laughed as they reached down and scratched the wiggling puppy. The pup's tongue lolled, and she squeezed her eyes shut.

Charlie shouldered her pack. Ryan strolled down the trail with her in companionable silence. The leaves overhead rustled like wind chimes in the strengthening breeze.

The trail narrowed, and Ryan let Charlie lead. As he followed her, his eyes strayed to her curvy ass. He walked entranced, watching it swish from side to side. Arousal kicked in again.

Charlie came to an abrupt stop. Focused on her ass, he didn't notice until he collided with her.

He looked over her shoulder, eyeing the drop-off. Then he eased around her and with one smooth motion stepped off the three-foot descent.

Charlie fisted her hands on her hips. "What are you, part mountain goat?"

Ryan chuckled. He reached up and placed his hands on her waist, marveling that he could almost circle it. He eased her down to the trail in front of him.

Spanky leaped down. Off balance, Charlie steadied herself by placing her hands against his chest.

Her touch jolted him with desire. He pulled her close and kissed her, sparking heat that spread through his body and headed south. Charlie seemed to melt against him and ran her free hand through his hair. She was making little moans of pleasure.

He slid his hands under her shirt, groaning as he felt the warm silkiness of her skin.

Spanky shot into the underbrush in full bay, chasing a squirrel.

Charlie pushed against him and backed away, her cheeks rosy and a dazed look in her eyes. His gaze locked on her heaving chest.

He ran a hand through his hair. "That was —"

"Electrifying?" Charlie held a hand over her chest, as though she was trying to hold her heart inside her ribcage.

The squirrel had scampered up a tree. Ryan could hear it chattering at Spanky, who kept leaping, trying to climb the trunk.

Still pink-cheeked, Charlie rushed into the underbrush to retrieve her.

Ryan ran a hand down his face. "Damn," he muttered, under his breath. *Just when things were starting to get interesting.*

CHAPTER 35 - HOT OR NOT

It was one of those gray days that dulled the hues of spring and blurred the edges of reality. Charlie felt as monochromatic as the day. Her father had always called days like today, "bluepy."

Since several of her patients had called and canceled, it was an ideal day to catch up on the never-ending flow of paperwork. Charlie had slogged through all her group notes and was considering a cup of coffee when Marti stopped in her office and suggested lunch.

"Where do you want to eat?" Charlie already knew the answer. On days like today, Marti always wanted Mexican food.

"Mexican would be good. I need some heat, spice, and comfort." Marti smiled and did a Cha-cha step in place. "From the looks of you, you could use a little comfort, too."

"We tend to eat Mexican on rainy days. Do you think we're self-medicating?"

"Who cares if we are?" Marti flipped her hand. "Let's go."

Charlie used caution as she steered her car around another accident. A hunking Suburban had tried to drive over the top of a Miata. It looked as if the vehicles were mating, like a Great Dane and a Chihuahua. Of course, everyone had to inch by and "rubber-neck," even if it didn't affect their lane of traffic.

"Why is it that people won't slow down in the rain or snow to prevent an accident, but they will creep and crawl to look at one?" asked Charlie.

"Because they're idiots, that's why." Marti shook her head as she gazed out the rain-streaked side window. The wipers beat a mind-numbing rhythm trying to clear the pounding rain.

At the restaurant, Charlie remembered why they came here during inclement weather. The cheerful, gaudy atmosphere lifted her spirits.

A waiter took their order and brought salsa, chips, and their tea. Marti took a deep swallow of her iced tea and winced at the taste.

As she stirred in a packet of artificial sweetener, she asked with a sly grin, "How are things going with Detective Hottie?"

Charlie felt her face burn. "Umm, fine."

Marti's eyes narrowed to a speculative squint. She arched a brow and began tapping her index finger on the table.

Charlie snatched a chip and dipped it in the salsa, drizzling salsa across the table on the way to her mouth.

Marti's brow was still up.

Charlie wiped up the spill with her napkin.

"What's happened?" asked Marti.

"What do you mean? Nothing's happened." Charlie hesitated. "Well...."

"Well, what?" Marti's mouth formed an O and snapped shut. "Oh my God, you had sex with Detective Hottie."

"No!" Charlie looked around to see if any of the other diners heard. "It was just a kiss."

"*Just a kiss?* Back up, when did this happen?" Marti scooted forward in her seat.

Squaring her shoulders, Charlie decided to go on the offensive. "It's your fault. 'Go for a hike, Charlie. Get into nature.' Well, I got into nature, and then *you* sent Ryan out to meet me."

Marti flitted her hand in the air as if performing magic. "One of my better ideas." Her grin was mischievous.

"Spanky and I stopped to have a snack at one of the overlooks, and there came Ryan, tromping down the trail. One thing led to another, and he kissed me." Charlie rubbed her throbbing temples, elbows propped on the table.

Marti leaned forward and gave her a conspiratorial wink. "How was it?"

Charlie looked up, embarrassment heating her cheeks. "It was 'clothes ripping' passionate. I thought he would electrocute me right then and there."

"Darn, girl. Sounds like a zing-dinger experience. What happened next?"

"I heard a noise. I thought someone was coming down the trail, and I froze. It was a damn squirrel. Spanky ran after it, so I ran after Spanky." Charlie dropped her head into her hands.

Marti reached over to pat Charlie's forearm. "Did y'all talk about it?"

"While I was trying to corral Spanky, I kept seeing flashes of Nathan standing in our bedroom with his pants down, getting a blow job from Eric." Charlie looked up. "What makes me think I can pick a decent guy after the Nathan fiasco?" Charlie sat straight. "I told him good-bye. I wasted no time driving away. He was still standing in the parking lot, watching me leave with this forlorn look on his face."

Marti shook her head. "The poor guy."

"What about me!" She used her hands to indicate her body. "Here I am, steaming with desire and too scared to do anything about it." Charlie's volume rose.

They both looked at each other with wide eyes and turned to see if nearby diners had heard Charlie's last comment.

Their food arrived seconds later, breaking the tension.

"What're you going to do?" Marti dispensed artificial sweetener into her new glass of tea.

"I don't know." Charlie looked down at her plate of steaming food. The spicy aroma was making her salivate.

"You've got to talk to him, tell him how you feel," Marti said, cutting her tamale into neat sections.

"You want me to phone Detective Buns of Steel and tell him that I want to rip off his clothes."

"How do you know he has buns of steel?"

"You saw him, it's obvious." Charlie picked up her fork and shoved rice in her mouth.

"You can pretend you don't have feelings or needs, but it doesn't keep you from having them." Marti bit into a salsa-laden chip.

"I know, I know. I hate it when you talk like a therapist. I've been trying to maintain some level of professional decorum. You know … the double standard. If Ryan sleeps with me, he's a hero and a stud. If I sleep with him, I'm a slut and got my position on my back." Charlie stabbed at her enchilada.

"Go on a date and see if this attraction is real or not." Marti waved the salsa-laden chip in her hand. Some salsa dropped off the chip and splattered down the front of her green blouse. She grabbed her napkin, dipped it into a glass of water, and dabbed at the stain.

Charlie laughed. "See what happens when you stick your nose into my business. What if we become a couple and then break up? He could make it difficult for me to work for the H.P.D."

Marti chuckled. "I overheard you telling one of your patients there are no guarantees in life or love. You have to take your chances like everyone else. If you want a guarantee, buy a washing machine."

Charlie thought about that while she munched a chip.

"I'm just gun shy since the divorce. I trusted Nathan. He not only vaporized that trust, he also broke my heart as he made a fool out of me. I don't want to be hurt like that again."

"Become a nun."

"What?" Charlie lowered her fork.

Marti waved her hand. "You were raised Catholic. Become a nun, be married to God, no worries."

"And no sex. I can't live without sex," said Charlie in a whispered hiss.

"You seem to be doing fine without it so far. How long has it been since you got a little nookie?"

Charlie focused on cutting her second enchilada into perfect slices. When she finished, she mumbled her answer. "Over a year."

Marti's eyes rounded. "Whoa! That long?"

"What should I do? I just left the guy standing in a parking lot with a woody and drove off."

Marti laughed again. "I'm not suggesting you strip him naked on the spot. Let things take a natural pace, but stop pretending it's strictly business. Because it isn't."

Charlie sighed and turned her attention to her refried beans, using her fork to hunt out hidden jalapeno peppers.

After a few minutes, Marti put down her fork and wiped her mouth. "Can I change the subject?"

"Sure."

"Are you still walking in your sleep?"

"Not since our last talk. I saw my doctor again. He thinks the sleeping pills he gave me were responsible for the sleepwalking. I quit taking them."

"Good, I've heard they can have that effect. Have some salsa and chips." Marti pushed the salsa bowl over the invisible centerline of the table into Charlie's dining territory. "Chips and salsa cure just about everything."

They both chuckled. Charlie dipped a chip, held it high and said, "Here's to courage."

"Hear, hear," said Marti.

CHAPTER 36 - BROKEN HEART

It was Friday night. The parking lot at the Broken Heart was full. A light rain was pattering on the Mustang. The Huntress noticed that the neon lights on the building reflected their patterns in the raindrops on the hood. As she stared at them, they swam out of focus.

I remember when I was sixteen and learned I could control men, instead of them always controlling me.

****

"Take your clothes off, Baby Girl, and come sit in my lap."

With a seductive bump and grind, she removed part of her clothes, imitating the stripper she'd watched in a movie that afternoon. Men put money in the stripper's G-string. She wanted money for some shoes she'd seen at the mall.

Dancing and gyrating, she asked, "Do you want to play lap dance?"

Her dad moved to the edge of his chair. He squinted at her, rubbing the stubble on his chin. Malice darkened his eyes, and his mouth was grim. "Where did you learn about lap dances, Baby Girl?"

"I watched one of your movies, so I could learn to play more games. Do you have money to stuff down my panties?" She jiggled her bare breasts.

Smirking, he yanked out his wallet. Pulling out several tens, he waved them in the air.

"Come here, Baby Girl, let's see how many you can earn."

****

A couple walked past the car, and the woman giggled. The dots of rain on the hood came into focus. The Huntress shook her head, as if to clear it, and got out of the Mustang.

Entering the club, the Huntress flashed a brief smile at the bouncer. Inside, she paused to watch the dancers. The computer-operated lighting system was making their movements appear disjointed. A haze of smoke diffused the bright lights, stinging her eyes.

Most of the tables were occupied.

The pressure — the need to kill — was building inside her like rising steam. The Huntress could still feel the humiliation of being used and discarded like trash. Anger boiled in her stomach and inched up her esophagus, making her want to puke. *Revenge burns to the core with satisfaction*, she thought. *I plan to have mine tonight.*

She prowled through the room, seeking prey. At last, she noticed a man sitting alone, at a table set back in the shadows. He appeared to be well on his way to intoxication. Empty glasses littered the table. In his late forties with hair graying at the temples; he looked to be the perfect victim.

"He will pay for what was done to me, he will pay," the Huntress murmured to herself as she headed toward him.

"Hi! All the tables are full, may I sit here?" The Huntress flashed a dazzling smile as she rested her hands on the table.

He looked up, eyes popping wide as if surprised. "Sure, little lady! Sit yourself on down!" He pulled out a chair for her. His demeanor brightened as if he'd won the lottery.

During their shouted conversation, she noticed how he focused on her breasts. She guessed he must be a titty man. *Daddy was a titty man.* She sensed his desire to touch her.

He bragged, "I'm still the top salesman on staff. Nobody sells more copy machines than ole Harve."

She knew the location of the copy company because she passed the store on the way to work. "How do you do that? I don't think I could ever sell anything." She snuggled against him.

"Well darlin', what you do is…." He slid his arm over her shoulder down to her breast and brushed his hand across her nipple, as he finished his discourse on sales techniques. The nipple hardened in response, exciting her. She reached up and unbuttoned two buttons to allow him access to her bare flesh.

"Darlin', you've got me hotter than a firecracker. Let's you and me leave this place."

"Let's go to your house." She ran her hand up and down his thigh.

"Darlin', I'm in town on business. My house is in Nashville. I'm one of the area supervisors," he bragged. He cupped one of her breasts. "But we can go back to my hotel room. I'm staying by the civic center."

Damn! Hotels have staff, thin walls, and too many witnesses. This fool's no use to me and no one else here is suitable. She looked at her watch. Not enough time to drive to another club, find another sucker, and have the time she would need to play. She shoved away from him, buttoned her blouse, and stood to leave.

"What're you doin', Darlin'?" He looked confused, mouth gaping open. "Aren't you comin' back to my room?"

"Hell, no!" Turning, she merged with the crowd.

"What the fuck!" he yelled.

She heard him and kept walking.

CHAPTER 37 - TO ASK OR NOT?

Ryan stared at his computer screen, tapping an envelope against his chin.

Joe came in the room with his usual coffee and doughnuts. "Is that your invitation to the policeman's ball?"

"Yeah, have you gotten yours yet?"

Joe put down his coffee on the corner of his desk, sloshing some over the top. "It's right here." He patted the breast pocket of his sports coat. "Sarah's been waiting for months for this event. It gives her an excuse to go out and spend my hard-earned money. She can't wear the same dress she wore last year because someone might remember it. Who makes up these rules, anyway?" He pulled a paper napkin from his pocket and dabbed at the coffee. "I think they should issue policemen's wives dress uniforms. It would cut out a lot of hassle and be cheaper to boot."

"All you're interested in is the cheaper part. Ladies, dressed up and sexy, are one of the best parts of the occasion. It's not the speeches." Ryan pushed away from his desk and stretched.

"Ain't that the truth?" said Joe. "Remember that hot little number George brought last year in that low-cut red dress? I've *never* seen a set like that on a woman in my entire life. Sarah didn't speak to me for a week after that night." Joe laughed and took a bite of his doughnut. The white sugar showered onto his navy pants. Swiping at them, he smeared the sugar across the right leg. "Damn!"

"You weren't laughing then," Ryan reminded him. "In fact, you were whining nonstop about being denied your conjugal rights after Sarah locked you out of the bedroom. I don't blame her, either. You spent the entire meal staring at the woman's tits and then offered to do 'mouth to breast resuscitation' when she choked on her chicken."

Joe gave a sheepish shrug. "It was a slip of the tongue." He took another bite, but this time leaned over the trash can.

"Charlie would call it a Freudian slip." Ryan got up to pour another cup of coffee.

"Freud had nothing to do with it. I was fully aware of my intentions. I just didn't mean to say it in front of Sarah." Joe moved papers aside to make room for the remainder of his doughnut. "Who're you taking this year?"

"Not sure." The chair squeaked as Ryan sat down. He sipped his coffee, testing the temperature.

"Sure you are, you want to take Doc. I have to admit, she sure is a looker, to be so smart." Joe took a large bite of his doughnut and chewed. Powdered sugar ringed his mouth.

"You don't have to be a bimbo to be attractive, Joe." Ryan shook his head. "I'd love to take Charlie, but she gave me one of those 'let's keep it strictly business' speeches when I invited her to join us for drinks for Brian's birthday."

"That's her professional side talking. You two can't keep your eyes off each other." Joe chuckled with a sly grin. "You know you want to do her."

Ryan looked up, praying for divine intervention. "I could have predicted you would say something like that."

"Are you telling me you aren't interested in beddin' that woman?"

"Sure, what guy wouldn't?" Ryan shrugged. "But Charlie's special." He glanced around to see if anyone else had heard him. After clearing his throat, he started rearranging papers on his desk.

"You have a bad case of it! You better go ahead and invite her, so we can get some work done. I'd hurry, a woman like her can get a date just like that." Joe snapped his fingers. He took another bite of his doughnut. Powdered sugar drifted into the garbage can.

Leaning back in his chair, Ryan cupped his hands behind his head and rested his right ankle on his left knee. "What do you mean, I have a bad case of it?"

"Love. When you can't get a woman off your mind, it's love. I've been watching. You talk about her all the time. Charlie said this...Charlie thinks that …."

"I don't talk about her *all* the time."

"I remember when I first met Sarah," said Joe. "I knew she was the one. I had to marry that woman so that I could concentrate on my work."

Ryan chuckled. "So that's how Sarah met her fate?"

He had to duck to avoid the last bite of Joe's doughnut.

"If you're smart, you'll just screw her, get it out of your system, and move on. Women are expensive. Besides, this one may be trouble."

"I can't believe I'm listening to a man whose wife wouldn't give him any for a week, because of his own stupidity."

Joe rubbed his hands over the trashcan to remove the sugar. Looking up, he held Ryan's gaze for a moment. "Something about her bothers me. I'll let you know when I figure it out."

CHAPTER 38 - THE INVITATION

"Good morning!" Charlie chimed, as she strolled through the lobby.

The lone occupant looked up with bleary eyes.

Charlie thought *Another newbie who partied hardy last night. I guess that's the best he can manage with a hangover. Bless his heart.*

"Good morning, Kathy!" She sang the greeting.

"Good morning, Charlie, you look chipper today."

"I feel chipper." Another weekend had passed with no reported murders.

169

After stopping at her bin to collect her charts, Charlie swept by her box to pick up her mail, memos, and messages. With her arms loaded, she sped toward her office.

As she was sifting through her mail, Charlie noticed an unusual envelope. She slit it open and pulled out an invitation to the Huntsville Police Department Ball and Award Ceremony at the civic center. The dress requirement was formal, and it was a dinner dance.

What should I wear? Better yet, who should escort me? Despite her general clumsiness, Charlie transformed into a graceful nymph on the dance floor. The idea of going with a non-dancer was most unappealing.

She had only dated a few men since her divorce, and none were promising prospects. James, an engineer, was okay, but he couldn't dance. Barry, who was a coach, would be bored.

Of course, there's…no, that's not an option, she thought as she remembered Ryan's kiss. Heat flushed over her. Snatching the invitation, she fanned her burning face.

The phone rang. Charlie put down the invitation and answered with a bright, "Dr. Stone."

"Hi….this is Ryan." His tone was hesitant.

"Do you have some news about the cases?" Her heart began to pound. "Please don't tell me there's been another murder." Her hand covered her mouth.

"There's one less drug dealer in town, but I'm pretty sure that's not what you meant. I'm calling because some of the forensics came back on the David Street case. The vaginal secretions match for both cases, which means the DNA matches. Now we can make comparisons with any suspects. The blood type should help too, AB negative."

"AB negative blood is very rare," said Charlie. "I know because I have that same blood type."

Ryan chuckled. "Aha! Where were you at the time of the murders?"

"I was at home in bed. You can ask Spanky." Charlie laughed as she picked up her invitation.

"Joe plans to talk to the D.A. about a court order to get a DNA sample from Sherry Harper."

"Is she still refusing to give one?" Charlie laid the invitation in the center of her desk blotter.

"She was willing, but her attorney is still advising against it," said Ryan.

A heavy silence fell.

"Um, Ryan...I'm sorry about the other day," Charlie said at last. "I don't know what came over me. I shouldn't have left you standing in the parking lot that way."

"No, it was my fault. I've wanted to kiss you since the first day I saw you. You were something, hands on your hips, ready to take on Jackson at that first murder scene. I guess my timing could've been better."

"I'm not sure there was a good time in this situation."

"While we're discussing this, have you received your invitation to the Policeman's Ball?"

"Yes, I just opened it." She picked up the card again and fanned herself with it.

"If you haven't already asked someone, I thought it would be appropriate for me to escort you."

Silence stretched as Charlie considered the invitation. *It would resolve the issue of who to invite.* She remembered Marti telling her, "If you want a guarantee, buy a washing machine."

"Charlie, are you still there?" His tone sounded concerned.

"I haven't had a chance," said Charlie.

"Great, my tactic worked." He sounded elated. "Will you go with me?"

"Do you dance?" She remembered too many miserable times with Nathan, watching others while she sat and tapped her foot to the music.

"You'll have to come to find out," he teased.

"All right, you may escort me to the ball, Prince Detective."

"Fantastic! I'll get together with you on the details later." He sounded like a giddy little boy.

Marti tapped on the door as Charlie placed the phone in the cradle. "Good morning!"

Charlie glanced up, holding the invitation.

Marti stopped mid-step. "What's wrong?" Her brows rose. "You look like a kid who's been caught with her hand in the proverbial cookie jar."

"*This* is what's wrong," Charlie showed her the invitation.

"You've been invited to the Policeman's Ball. Who's your date? Please don't tell me you asked that James guy." Marti cocked a hip and planted a hand on it.

"You'll be surprised to hear that Ryan Roberts called this morning and asked to escort me."

"I hope you said yes! You did say yes, didn't you?" Marti grabbed Charlie by the shoulders and looked as if she would shake her if she said no.

"I did, but now I'm having second thoughts." Charlie stood and started pacing the room.

"Why? This opportunity is just what the two of you need, a semi-business occasion to get together." Marti smiled, clapping her hands.

Charlie rubbed the back of her neck. "This could get complicated."

"The two of you are professional enough to handle this situation. Besides, it's not as if you're working with him on a day-to-day basis, in the same office. You're a consultant with the police department, not a direct employee."

"This guy is persistent, and I always wear down under persistence." Charlie ceased pacing and plopped into her chair.

Marti slid into a chair across from her. "Give him a chance. You aren't so fragile you can't afford to put your heart on the line again."

"I guess I'm overreacting. I need to take this 'One day at a time,' like they teach in AA." Charlie rose and started pacing again in front of the aquarium. The fish flitted along in hot pursuit, hoping to be fed.

Marti squinted at the calendar posted on the wall. "When is the Ball?"

"Two weeks from Friday." Charlie continued pacing.

"What're you going to wear?"

"Leave it to you to get down to the nitty-gritty. I'll pull something out of the closet." Charlie waved her hand in the air as if by magic, she could produce an outfit on the spot.

"I think you should wear that black and gold sequined dress with the bare-back." Marti twitched her eyebrows up and down.

Charlie stopped pacing and grinned. "If I wear that dress, Ryan will self-combust."

CHAPTER 39 - I'M FINE

Melissa slid into the chair in front of Charlie's desk and clutched its arms the way people do at a dentist's office.

"How's it going?" Charlie pulled her chart from the desk drawer.

"Fine."

Charlie gave her a mischievous smile. "Do you know what the acronym F.I.N.E. means in recovery language?"

Melissa took the bait. "No, what?"

"The clean version is Freaked-out, Insecure, Neurotic, and Emotionally unstable."

Melissa laughed and relaxed a bit. "That just about describes me. I can guess the original version."

Charlie took a moment to observe Melissa. *No red eyes or dark circles.*

"How was your weekend?"

"It was okay, but a little frustrating." Melissa shrugged her shoulders as if to say, *oh well.*

"How was it frustrating? You didn't relapse, did you?"

"No. Things just didn't go the way I expected, so I was frustrated." The taut set of Melissa's jaw made it clear she didn't intend to elaborate.

Charlie knew better than to push. "Welcome to my life. Things don't always go the way I planned, either." Charlie flipped open the chart and spied her reminder note to ask about Melissa's nightmares.

"I wanted to talk about your nightmares today. Do you have a recurrent theme, or are the dreams different?"

Melissa's shoulders tightened. Pulling her ponytail forward, she twirled it around her finger.

"Both, but most of the time a shadow man without a face is chasing me. I know if he catches me, he'll kill me. I run, trying to escape. Only, there's no escape." With a haunted look in her eyes, Melissa began to rock. "I always wake up just before he catches me. It's hard to fall back asleep after one of *those* dreams." She crossed her arms and shivered.

"I understand what you mean. Everyone has scary nightmares about being chased. Do you think this is about your Dad?"

"Maybe." Tears welled in her eyes. "I talked to my aunt the other day. She said I should try to let you help me."

"I'm willing to try if you'll let me."

Taking a deep, shuddering breath, Melissa began, "There were times I was afraid my dad would kill me. He used to beat me when he was drunk, always where it wouldn't show. Once he broke my arm. He broke my sister's arm, too, and gave her a concussion," Tears gone, her dark eyes glinted and hardened.

"Did you tell the doctor at the hospital what happened?"

"No, my dad threatened me, so I didn't tell. He told the doctor I fell down the stairs." She shrugged her shoulders as if that was typical for her family.

This wasn't the first time Charlie had heard of incidents like this from her patients. "Did the doctor believe him?"

"He gave him a funny look, but he didn't say anything." She shrugged again. "He didn't hit my sister as often after breaking her arm and giving her the concussion. She learned early to play up to him. I just told him to go to hell." Melissa looked uncomfortable and squirmed in her seat.

Charlie sensed she'd pushed Melissa far enough today. She closed her chart.

"Melissa, I'm sorry your dad went astray, and you and your sister paid the price for it." Charlie gentled her tone. "This was *not* your fault. He was the adult. It was his responsibility to love, cherish and protect y'all. What he did was wrong and abusive."

Melissa didn't respond. She was staring into space, her arms crossed.

"You still seem pretty angry about this. I forget, how long has your dad been dead?" Charlie was hoping for a response, but not the one she received.

Melissa shot out of her chair and shouted, "Not long enough!" Yanking open the door, she left without another word.

CHAPTER 40 - I KNOW WHERE YOU LIVE

It was Monday, and Ryan sat opposite Charlie in their usual booth at Mullins, nursing along his cup of coffee and discussing the latest developments in the case.

Ryan was a regular, so the staff without asking guided them to the same booth. Mabel, the steel-haired grandmother of four who always waited on them, had their order memorized. Being a creature of habit, Ryan had made Charlie a predictable part of his routine. He sensed this made her nervous.

"I still think we need to contact the FBI," said Charlie.

"If we conclude there's no connection between these two murder victims or there are more murders, we'll consider that option. For now, Joe is reluctant to bring in the Feds. Besides, you gave us a profile."

"I understand that. I just don't want to miss anything," Charlie blew a wisp of hair off her face.

"I understand your thinking on this. Believe me; I've been awake some nights wondering if I missed anything, too." Ryan wedged himself into his favorite position in the corner of the booth.

Charlie blew on her coffee to cool it. "For some reason that makes me feel better. You seem to handle all this so well." She glanced up at an elderly couple tottering past, holding hands.

Ryan grasped his cup. "Charlie, murder investigations are a new area for you. I've had more time to adjust, and I'm more familiar with the procedures and delays. Believe me, when I was a new detective, I worried and fretted my fair share."

Ryan paused to eye a construction worker who was ambling toward the register to pay. *I know why he's so familiar. I arrested him for DUI when I was a rookie. The guy was so soused, he took a swing at me and knocked himself on his ass.* Ryan smiled at the memory.

"That's true. You do have more experience. And I'll admit, patience has never been my virtue. Did you follow up with Sherry's friend Betty?"

"We did. Betty insisted both victims deserved what they got, but denied killing them. She had an alibi for Harper's time of death. She offered to take a polygraph and gave us a DNA sample."

"Did it match?"

"Nope. In my opinion, Sherry Harper was trying to put the focus on her friend Betty to take it off herself. We have Sherry's DNA sample now, but we haven't received the results from the lab yet. She's still our top suspect. Then there's Janice. She's our number two suspect. She's lawyered up, so we're still trying to get a DNA sample from her."

"I guess now it's a waiting game." Charlie sipped her coffee and added sugar.

"To change the subject, we should discuss arrangements for the Policeman's Ball," said Ryan.

Charlie shifted in her seat and grabbed her cup as if it would save her. "What time should I meet you at the civic center?"

Wise to her maneuver, he sat up straight. "No way, Charlie. I'll pick you up. Besides," he waggled his eyebrows and imitated Count Dracula's voice, "I know where you live."

Charlie tilted her head to the side and smiled."I don't mind meeting you. Then if you're tired after the Ball, your drive home won't be so far."

Ryan leaned forward to take her hand. "Why are you trying so hard to keep me at a distance?"

She jerked her hand away. "I just don't feel it's professional ...."

"Oh, come on," said Ryan. He pushed away from the table, feeling irritation build in his chest. *What's holding her back?*

Her full lips compressed into a thin line. "You're a guy. It's different for you. All the guys will pat you on the back. 'Way to go, Ryan.' I'm a woman. Those same guys are taking bets on when you'll screw me. I run the risk of losing their professional respect."

Ryan's ears burned as he remembered Joe discussing the bets the forensic techs were making about Charlie. He understood her point but knew there was more. *It's almost like she's afraid.*

"That's not all of it, and you know it." He raised his chin and crossed his arms.

Charlie looked down. She white-knuckled her ceramic mug as if it was the only thing keeping her afloat. Tears brimmed in her eyes, but he could see she was fighting for control.

Damn! I made her cry.

"Let's get out of here," he urged. He threw some bills on the table and led Charlie outside. He placed a protective arm around her as he walked her to his car. Helping Charlie into the front seat, he handed her his handkerchief. As he started the car, he turned and grinned at her. "By the way, it's okay to blow your nose in that handkerchief."

Charlie chuckled and honked into his hanky. Ryan felt relief flood over him. By the time he pulled to the curb at Big Spring Park, she had managed to compose herself.

Leading Charlie to a secluded bench under a weeping willow, he eased her next to him and tenderly draped his arm around her shoulders. He felt his need to protect her swell inside his chest.

Big Spring Park was pleasant this time of year. The large duck pond loaded with decorative Koi was a favorite spot for walkers, a picnic lunch, or for children to feed the ducks and fish. Ryan could see the fountain from where they sat.

"Charlie, I care about you, and I have no intention of hurting you." He eased a lock of hair behind her ear, wanting to see her face.

She looked him in the eyes. "I'm sure most people start a relationship with the best intentions. People get hurt. It just happens. I'm not very good at relationships."

Confused, Ryan wrinkled his brow. "Why do you say that?"

"They never last. The relationship starts out promising. The man thinks I'm great. The honeymoon phase ends, then the guy becomes distant. He treats me like a shabby piece of furniture to be walked around and used until he replaces me. At least, that's what happened in my marriage."

"Any man who treated you like furniture is a fool. If you were —"

"If I were your woman, you wouldn't treat me that way," interrupted Charlie. "I've heard it all before. Maybe the old phrase 'Familiarity breeds contempt' is true."

"I disagree." Ryan slid a finger down Charlie's cheek. "There's been chemistry between us since the first time we saw each other. You can try to deny it, but I felt how you responded to me when we kissed. Yes, I've found other women to be attractive and liked things about them in the past." He shifted to look into her face. "I've never had this chemistry and the bond that I feel with you. I don't intend to ignore this electricity between us."

"Electricity! You feel it too?"

"Oh yeah, I feel it." *I feel it right now.* "You're going to have to yield to it someday, to see where this attraction will lead us. If you don't, you and I will both regret it the rest of our lives." He paused a moment. "Did you mean what you said the other day about living without regrets?"

Charlie's eyes misted. "Yes."

He rose. "Come on. I'll take you back to your car." He reached down and helped her to her feet.

Charlie wiped her eyes and smiled. "What time will you pick me up?"

"Six-thirty, you know how parking is at the civic center." Ryan grinned and bumped her in a playful manner with his shoulder. She rammed him back with her hip, but harder.

"Whoa, I'm a Homicide Detective you know." Ryan teased. "I could have you arrested for assaulting an officer."

"Try it." Charlie hipped him again and grinned

At least I won this battle. He still felt the heat from her close contact with him. *I like this out of control feeling, and I hate it at the same time.*

He opened the door for Charlie. He smiled when he saw her reach over to unlock his door. After he had fastened his seatbelt, he pulled away from the curb. He took a deep breath and forced his attention north, toward his brain so that he could drive.

CHAPTER 41 - STALKING

It was Friday night. For most of the residents of Huntsville, it was a time to party after a week of hard work. The Huntress wasn't out for a good time — she was stalking.

She strolled into Wyatt's and saw it was full of cowboy wannabes and local good-ole-boys. The uniform for the night was Stetson hats, western shirts, jeans, boots, and giant belt buckles. Most of the women appeared hard-edged, yet hopeful.

She had chosen to wear black jeans, blood-red boots, and a tight western-cut shirt with pearl snaps. *I fit right in,* she thought with satisfaction.

The lead singer was belting out Tracy Byrd's song, "Watermelon Crawl," while line dancers stomped and twirled with their thumbs stuck in their belts.

The place stank of cigarettes and beer. The Huntress waved her hand in front of her face in a vain attempt to clear the air around her.

She was weaving her way among the tables, her eyes focused on the bar when a man snagged her by the arm. Off balance, she plopped on to his lap.

"What the hell!" Irate, she turned, ready to pepper him with verbal buckshot.

"Oh, Darlin', you're the hottest thing I've seen here tonight. Where've you been all my life?" he slurred, fixing his gaze on her cleavage.

The Huntress rolled her eyes. *How cliché can he get?* However … he was the correct age and the right amount of drunk. *The perfect victim.*

"Are you here alone, cowboy? What's your name?" She placed an arm around his shoulders and snuggled against him, and felt him harden against her thigh. *Good, he's not too drunk to perform.*

"Stan," he said, rubbing a hand up and down her back. "I'm here with my buddy Pete."

"Where's Pete now?" she asked, allowing him to explore.

"He went off with some little filly about twenty minutes ago. I haven't seen hide nor hair of him since. I think he took her out to my car if you know what I mean." He gave her a knowing wink. "Ya wanna work something out, Baby?" He slid his hand up to squeeze her breast.

This is a brazen one. "Sure, but I want you all to myself. Do you have a place we can go to be alone?" She didn't remove his hand.

Two men at the next table were watching; their eyes fixated on the hand squeezing her breast. The bald one licked his lips. The other adjusted his pants. Her lust meter shot from a five to an eight. She felt herself go moist with desire.

"Sure, Baby." Stan glared at the two men, making it clear the woman was his. The men shifted in their seats and averted their eyes.

She wiggled on his lap. "Where's your house?"

He puffed out his chest. "I live out in the county in a trailer, on two acres of my own land."

Still squeezing her breast like an exercise ball, he lowered his head to taste her. The Huntress placed her hand under his chin and stopped him. She waved her index finger back and forth.

"If you're going to do that in here, you'll have to share me." She nodded toward the two voyeurs, who averted their eyes once again.

"I'm not sharing anything." His voice dropped several octaves, deepening into a belligerent tone. "Let's go! Where's Pete? I've gotta find Pete. He's got my car."

She frowned. "I'm not interested in Pete. You either come with me now, or I leave with one of them." She dislodged his hand from her breast and stood.

A decisive man, Stan took her by the hand and led her toward the exit.

They reached her Mustang. "I'll drive." Stan pinned her against the driver's door and fumbled to grab her keys.

I don't think so, idiot. She crooned, "Come on, Sugar, I don't want you to get pulled over by some cop and spoil our fun by going to jail." She pulled out her shirttails and slid his hand under her shirt to her bare breast, to divert his attention from her keys.

The diversion worked. Stan moved her arms upward, and the Huntress crossed them over the top of her head, allowing him full access to her body. Weaving on unsteady legs, he slid his other hand under her shirt, cupping both her breasts.

"Let's see what we have here." Stan removed his hands and ripped open her shirt, the snaps popping like gunshots. He stepped back for a better view. After leering at her, Stan spun her toward the car. He ground his pelvis against her ass and reached around her, pinching her nipples. The Huntress rubbed against the fender, palms on the hood, lost in the sensation.

She didn't see anyone, which was a relief, yet a disappointment. She closed her eyes and remembered her freshman year in high school.

****

It was almost midnight. She giggled as Brent, the senior quarterback, pulled her into the boys' locker room at the school. She'd always wondered what it was like in there. She wrinkled her nose at the smell of sweat and gym socks.

He pulled her around the corner into a square area of wooden benches with gray lockers lined along the walls. There stood the football team of her high school. She tripped to a stop. Her face flushed hot. She felt unsure — shy under the gazes of all those guys.

"I've got a surprise for you, Baby. Remember how you told me your fantasy about dancing naked for the football team?" Brent smiled and gestured to his teammates, palm up. "Here they are, and they're willing to be your audience." He reached around her and cupped a breast, massaging it as he nibbled her neck. She felt a tingling of desire race through her body.

Someone turned on some music. The driving beat filled her body. Tentative at first, she looked back at Brent. He smiled and nodded as his hand began to rub his crotch. She stepped up on the wooden bench in the center of the square. She stood unsure for a moment and then remembered how she'd danced for her father for money.

Looking down at the eager faces, she began to gyrate. The whoops and wolf whistles of the team emboldened her.

"Take it off, Babe," yelled Brent, above the cacophony of voices and music.

"Get out your money, boys. This isn't a free show." She pulled her shirt over her head to thunderous applause. She whipped the adolescent males into a frenzy. Feeling strong and bold, she stripped one article of clothing at a time. Their faces were rabid with desire — desire for her beauty. Money fluttered to the concrete at her feet.

After she had danced naked for a while, Brent pulled her off the bench and bent her over. She knew what he wanted. She put her hands on the bench to steady herself and arched her back. Brent dropped his pants, smoothed a condom over his erect penis, and moved behind her. He matched his thrusts to the cheers of his teammates. "Brent! Brent! Brent!"

****

The Huntress smiled at the memory. As an exotic dancer, she loved enticing men while she performed. She enjoyed the power it gave her to see them make fools of themselves, while they took turns placing money in her G-string.

Opening her eyes, she glanced around. The parking lot looked empty. *Good, no witnesses.*

Stan turned her around and lowered his head.

The Huntress raised his chin. "Let's save a little for when we get to the trailer."

If I don't get this show on the road now, he'll be done before we make it out of the parking lot. She shoved him off, unlocked the door, and slid into the car.

Stan stumbled his way around the front, bracing himself on the hood for balance. A malicious grin slid across her face. *I can mow him down now, but that wouldn't be nearly as much fun.* Smirking, she unlocked the door, and Stan half fell into the car. Not waiting for him to fasten his seatbelt, the Huntress peeled out of the parking lot.

They left behind the lights of the city and entered a dark, deserted two-lane road. Stan grabbed her shirt. She yelled and swatted him, which caused her to veer into the other lane. She regained control of her Mustang and checked the rear view mirror to see if any cop cars loomed behind her.

He pawed at her again.

"Stop, you're gonna make me wreck!"

"I want it off! I wanna see those tits!" he bellowed.

With his help, she managed to remove her shirt and drove down the road topless. Stan had his head between her and the steering wheel, his mouth claiming one breast and his hand the other.

"You sure make it hard to concentrate on driving. I need you to sit up and tell me where to turn." She shoved him up, so he could see above the dashboard.

They turned right at a closed convenience store and eased down a narrow two-lane road for about a mile. They turned left down an even narrower road that ended in the front yard of a single-wide trailer.

"Nice trailer," she said, without conviction.

"I got it after my divorce. The bitch got just about everything else." He struggled out of the car, staggered, and grabbed the top of the door to regain his balance.

"Was it your first marriage?" She was curious, although she wasn't sure why. She closed the door to extinguish the light and let her eyes adjust so she could check her surroundings. *Mama always said, "Better safe than sorry."*

"My fifth. Let's go inside." He grabbed one of her breasts and squeezed. She pushed him off her again and headed toward the small deck built on the front of the trailer. Stan made it up the stairs, but he couldn't seem to get the key in the lock.

"Here, give me the key and let me do it." Aggravation flavored her tone as she reached for the key.

Stubborn, Stan pulled away and placed his shoulder between them.

"Honey, I only want to help because I just can't wait for you much longer," she crooned, as she rubbed up against him. "I'm getting cold. See how pointy my nipples are?"

It worked. Stan handed her the key.

"Nice ass," he said, as she bent to better see the keyhole that lay in shadow. He reached over and patted her.

With some effort, they made it to the bedroom. She managed to undress him while he fumbled with her jeans. After fitting himself with a condom, he shoved her on the bed and straddled her. Thrusting, he groaned, "Oh god! Oh god! Oh god," and passed out on top of her.

Unsatisfied and aggravated, she thought, *No wonder he's been divorced five times.*

She squirmed out from under him and managed to roll him over. She found her purse beside the bed and shifted items around inside until she heard the clink of the handcuffs. She held them up and beamed.

Now the real fun begins.

CHAPTER 42 - REBELLION

Charlie glanced at the clock. It was time to lead group therapy. Tonight she had Group 1 which consisted of ten people, and Marti had Group 2.

It was Monday, which made Charlie the bearer of good or bad news. Several patients would repeat a week in the program because they hadn't completed the required number of AA or NA meetings the week before. The patients always felt the staff nit-picked these issues, but part of the treatment process was to maintain clear rules and consequences. Marti had the task of breaking the news to group 2.

Charlie grabbed the blue binder to record the information for Group 1 and sat it in the chair at the front of the room. She walked across the hall to her office and collected her dry erase markers from her desk drawer. The facility policy was to remove the markers to a secure location to prevent the patients from stealing them to huff. She placed the markers on the rail of the whiteboard behind her chair. Picking up the binder, she took her seat.

The patients sat in chairs along the remaining three walls, in the shape of a horseshoe, staring at her.

Charlie opened the binder, pen in hand, and said, "Brian."

"Here, clean and sober," he replied. After a few days of being in the group, the members learned to report their status as *clean and sober,* or *I relapsed.*

Charlie spotted him in the center. "How many AA or NA meetings since Thursday night group?"

"Two."

"Tracy."

"Clean and sober with one meeting." Tracy sat to Charlie's left. "Melissa?"

"Here, clean and sober," Melissa replied.

"How many AA or NA meetings have you attended since last Thursday's group?" Charlie asked making a note.

"One," said Melissa.

Sniffing the air, Charlie caught a whiff of alcohol. "Has anyone been drinking?"

Skimming her gaze across each patient's face, Charlie looked for a clue. Everyone looked stunned, except the gangster wanna-be sitting in the corner. He slouched in his chair, sighed and examined the fake gold Rolex that dwarfed his skinny wrist.

Charlie stood and placed the book in her chair. Starting on her right, she walked past each patient. She smelled Mexican food, pizza, breath mints, coffee, and cola. She stopped. Melissa smelled like beer with a mouthwash chaser.

"Melissa, have you been drinking?"

She pulled her hair forward and twirled it around her index finger. "Nope, not me."

"This is your last chance to be honest." Charlie remembered how Melissa had stomped out of her office last week.

"I *said* not me." She jutted her chin forward. "It must be somebody else."

Charlie decided not to reply and continued her sniff check. As she approached Janice, she noticed that she looked down and wouldn't establish eye contact. She made a mental note to suggest that Janice receives a drug screen.

Satisfied that no one else smelled of alcohol, Charlie excused herself and walked to the front office. *I need the Breathalyzer.* She found it and returned to the group room.

Ten pairs of eyes locked on to the machine in her hand. One pair had gone wide with apprehension — Melissa's.

Tearing open the plastic cover, Charlie pulled out the sanitary plastic mouthpiece and inserted it into the machine. The sound was loud in the quiet room.

"Take a deep breath and blow until the light turns red." Charlie handed Melissa the Breathalyzer.

After Melissa had finished, breathless and coughing, she handed it back to Charlie.

"It's .12. You've been drinking, Melissa."

Melissa crossed her arms and looked defiant. "Your machine's broken."

Ejecting the mouthpiece with a pop, Charlie opened another and snapped it into place. Inhaling a deep breath, she blew until the light turned red. Showing the reading to Melissa, Charlie said, "It reads .00. Melissa, you're already repeating week one of the program because you didn't attend enough twelve-step meetings last week. Now you've relapsed." Charlie watched for her reaction to the news.

Melissa's eyes blazed with anger. "No one told me I had to attend those. I thought that was optional."

Charlie saw Barry, who was sitting next to Melissa, roll his eyes and shake his head. There were several titters elsewhere in the group. Melissa turned, glared at the group members, and slid down in her seat.

Charlie's tone was calm but firm. "You and I know you received that information."

Her slouch conveyed the message, "See if I listen to anything else you have to say today, Bitch." Melissa gave her a drop-dead, narrow-eyed glower that chilled her to the marrow.

Charlie felt her internal danger meter rise. *Calm down. She's upset. It's all part of the process of breaking down denial and correcting self-destructive habits.*

Melissa slid a glance in Charlie's direction. "How many saw Dr. Stone on the news?"

Charlie froze. *Where's she going with this?* She scanned the faces of the patients in the room. Some looked confused, others uncomfortable.

"Did you know she works for the police?" A vicious smile was pasted on Melissa's face.

There was a quiet rumble of voices as the patients talked to each other.

Charlie raised her hands. "Quiet, please." She shot Melissa a look. *What are you up to now?*

"For those of you who don't know, I work as a part-time consultant and psychological profiler for the Huntsville police," she announced. "As a therapist, I am required by law to keep confidential anything you say, either in the group or in private sessions, subject to the limitations listed in the paperwork you signed when you were assessed. Let me reassure you now that I take that requirement seriously."

Some of the patients looked at her with relief, others with suspicion.

"Does anyone have any questions?" Charlie scanned their faces and waited.

No response, other than people shifting in their seats.

"In that case, let's continue."

Fortunately for Charlie, the rest of roll call went well.

"Let's take a few minutes to process Melissa's relapse," said Charlie. "Does anyone have anything to say?

Mark, who'd just completed an inpatient treatment program, explained, "Clean and sober means no alcohol or drug use of any kind."

"I think that's a bunch of bullshit. I just had a few and stopped." Melissa glared at Mark. "If I was an alcoholic, I couldn't stop."

Jack, who sat to Melissa's left, piped up. "I agree with Mark. This is my second time in treatment. There were times I managed to stop at a few drinks, but there were just as many times that I couldn't. You're like me, Melissa, more of a binge drinker. I'm in control, and then boom, I've relapsed. That's what sent me back to jail. You have to leave it all alone — booze, reefer, pills — all of it."

Melissa sat slumped, arms crossed and scowling, while the other group members attempted to help her see options such as going to AA, NA, or calling a sponsor, as ways to avoid a relapse in the future.

It's time to move forward. Charlie raised a hand for quiet and let her gaze roam across each face. "Tonight's topic is anger management, an important part of maintaining your recovery."

"And keeping your ass outa jail," said Brian. Several patients chuckled.

Mark spoke up. "While I was in treatment the first time, they kept harping on releasing resentments about past harm. I thought it was a bunch of bull at the time, but I think my resentments played a part in my relapse."

Melissa rolled her eyes. "If you forgive and forget, it just means people can hurt you again." She raised her chin and shot Charlie a defiant glare.

"Forgiveness for the past doesn't mean absolution for the future," Charlie replied. "There are other ways we can protect ourselves without hanging onto our anger. Unresolved anger just causes more harm to everyone."

Melissa harrumphed and bobbed her foot.

Charlie ignored her and continued, "Anger's like a brick wall, an antiquated defense system that doesn't protect us from hurt. It does block all the good things like happiness and love from getting through." Charlie sketched a bright yellow smiley face bouncing off a brick wall. "The best defense is a high dose of self-esteem and excellent boundaries. It's important that we not hurt others or ourselves."

Melissa's dark eyes shot stilettos toward Charlie. "I don't care who I hurt."

The hairs rose on the back of Charlie's neck as her internal alarm system clanged. She fixed Melissa with a penetrating look that said, we *will* be discussing this later.

"You need to learn to chill, girl," said Janice, waving her hand in the air. "You're waaay too intense."

****

After the clients had left the building, Charlie and Marti sank into chairs in the front office.

"I hate Mondays," said Marti.

Charlie pulled a scrunchy off her wrist and pulled up her hair. "Me, too. Tonight was really bad."

"Yeah? It couldn't be worse than my group. I had two people fail their drug screens, so I had to deliver the bad news. They both pouted for two hours because they had to repeat a week in the program."

Charlie frowned. "I hate it when people cop an attitude because they did something wrong."

Marti rolled her chair from side-to-side. "What happened in your group?"

Charlie gave an exasperated sigh. "I smelled the beer, so when I did the walk around, guess who it turned out to be?"

Marti rubbed her forehead. "Our little gangster wannabe?"

"No, but he caught a random drug screen tonight." Charlie rubbed her temples. "I can't wait to see what that shows." She slung a leg over the arm of the chair. "Guess again."

Marti shifted forward in her chair. "Not Janice?"

"I didn't smell beer on her. Besides, she's a wine drinker. However, I do suspect she's relapsed on pills because she couldn't look me in the eyes tonight. She had a guilty look. You know the one."

Marti nodded, and ran her hand through her hair. "Damn, who's doing that group tomorrow night?"

"Susan, I think."

"I'll fill out a form for a drug screen so that Susan can give it to Janice tomorrow night in group. Don't keep me guessing, who was drinking?"

"Melissa."

"Again?" Marti looked surprised. "That's her second relapse. The team will probably recommend inpatient treatment for thirty days."

"All these relapses, is this a full moon cycle or something?"

Marti swept a lock of hair out of her face. "In fact, Saturday was a full moon."

Charlie stood and put the Group 1 book on the shelf in Nellie's office. "To make things worse, Melissa sorta threw a veiled threat my way."

Marti stood, a serious look on her face. "What kind of veiled threat?"

"She was angry, again. She shot me a deadly look and responded to something I said about not hurting others with, "I don't care who I hurt."

Marti crossed her arms. "Are you going to let her get away with that behavior?"

Charlie walked out of the front office with Marti on her heels.

"I gave her *the look*. I think she knows she can expect a confrontation during our next therapy session."

After she had turned out the light, she locked the office door, and they walked side by side, checking each room they encountered to verify the building was empty.

"You know how it'll go," said Marti. "She'll claim she was angry and didn't mean anything by it."

Charlie heaved another sigh. "This is a tough business. I'm considering leaving substance abuse counseling and switching back to mental health. Depressed and anxious people at least want your help."

Marti shook her head. "You act like every patient who relapses or screws up is your personal failure. You're a therapist, not a mechanic who can fix people and make them stop self-destructive habits." Marti stretched and yawned. "I swear I'm going to buy you a 'savior of the world' cape."

Charlie felt embarrassed. *She's right.*

Marti stopped and placed her hand on Charlie's arm. "Janice was sexually abused by her grandfather. I need to discuss a treatment plan with you to help her deal with her sexual addiction and the abuse. She admitted it to me this week. If she relapsed, that might be why."

Charlie frowned. "I suspected sexual abuse. I'll help in any way I can. I feel awful that her case had to be transferred that way."

"Has she been cleared as a suspect yet?" Marti's tone was hopeful. "If she has, I can transfer her case back to you. I get the feeling that she would prefer you to me. It's just little things that she says from time to time."

Charlie shook her head. "Her attorney is still refusing to let her give a DNA sample. That reminds me, Melissa also announced that I worked for the police and made it sound like I'm spying and making reports. I never thought there would be a conflict of interest when I accepted the profiling position."

Marti looked concerned. "What will you do if Max forces you to make a choice between here and the consulting position?"

"I could always open a private practice. Would you be interested in branching out with me?"

A slow smile spread across Marti's face. "Let me think about it."

They turned out lights as they headed toward the rear exit.

I was the bearer of bad tidings for several people tonight, Charlie thought. She remembered Melissa's malevolent glare and shivered. Feeling a little spooked, she scanned the parking lot to make sure it was safe.

CHAPTER 43 - ANOTHER VICTIM

On Tuesday, Charlie and Marti were waiting for their lunch to be served at their favorite Chinese restaurant.

The waitress placed a shiny metal teapot with two cups on the table just as Charlie's phone jangled the song she'd assigned to Ryan.

"Uh, oh, Detective Tingle." Marti grinned and reached for the teapot.

"Hi Charlie, bad news, there's been another murder." Ryan's voice sounded defeated.

Damn, she thought. "Do you need me to come?"

"Yes, as soon as possible." Ryan gave her the address and directions.

Charlie grabbed the pen and paper she always carried in her purse and jotted down the information. "Got it. On my way."

After Charlie had disconnected the call, Marti asked, "What's wrong?"

Feeling a little queasy, Charlie said, "There's been another murder. I need to leave now. I've lost my appetite anyway."

"You *will* catch this murderer, Charlie. Don't worry about this," Marti gestured toward the tea. "You go on and don't blame yourself. It's not your fault."

Charlie nodded. "Thanks Marti, I'll buy you lunch next time."

****

The trailer was a standard single-wide that had seen better days. Rust crusted one of the corners, and some of the skirtings were torn away. After signing in with a Madison County Sheriff's Deputy, Charlie walked up a set of concrete steps to the porch, where another deputy handed her a Tyvek suit, booties, mask and gloves.

She entered the living room and looked around. The dim space reminded her of a saloon. A black vinyl bar with swinging wooden doors led to an eat-in kitchen that had a surprising number of cabinets. The dishwasher's green light indicated a completed cycle. Charlie noticed the neatness of the place.

To the left, a long dark hall with rooms opening off to one side led to the other end of the mobile home. Moving down the hall, she looked into the first bedroom on her left. *He must have been in the National Guard. All his Army kit is piled in the corner.*

The next room was a bathroom. It contained double sinks with mirrors, a tub shower combination, and a toilet. *Hmmm, both the seat and cover are down on the toilet. Most men leave both up. Did the other bathrooms at the previous murder sites have the seats and covers up or down?* Her stomach began a gymnastic routine, performing a backward somersault. *I'm glad Ryan caught me before lunch instead of after.*

Rubbing her stomach to settle it, she passed the rear exit door on the right, washer and dryer on the left. The master bedroom occupied the full width of the end. Unlike the rest of the trailer, the bedroom was bright and cheery with white paneling, large double windows, and light blue draperies. A light blue carpet covered the floor. The brightness made the cruelty of what had happened more stark and real.

This time Charlie wasn't sure she could control her stomach. Bile stung the back of her throat. With her eyes watering, she gulped it back down. She swiped under her lower lashes with the back of her index finger.

Like the others, the victim was beaten, castrated, and defiled, only the damage to this victim was noticeably more extensive. She doubted there was a bone that wasn't broken. *The killer's rage seems to be increasing.*

Blood splattered on the white paneling, creating a horrid pattern in the well-lit room. The heat and the intense smell didn't improve the situation. She remembered what one of her FBI trainers had told her. "Murder isn't a pretty sight, and it doesn't smell like roses, either."

Ryan looked up and noticed Charlie standing in the doorway.

"Charlie, are you okay? You're white as a beach on the Gulf."
He moved across the room to place his hand on her shoulder in a comforting gesture.

Joe Sparks glanced up and frowned. "If you're gonna puke, take it outside. Don't you dare contaminate *my* crime scene."

"This is the Madison County Sheriff Department's crime scene," said a man with attractive brown eyes. His eyes twinkled with welcome. "I'm Mike Jarvis, the sheriff. I'm glad to have you on board for this investigation."

"Nice to meet you, Sheriff. I apologize. I was about to eat lunch when I received the call. A growling stomach and murder aren't a good mix."

"Better than a full one," said the Sheriff.

Charlie turned back to face Ryan. "This is the worst one yet, except there's no flies and maggots."

"We have a possible witness," said the sheriff. "Pete Jemison went out Friday night with the victim, Stan Myers." He looked over his shoulder at the body. "Jemison met up with a woman, and they were involved in Myers' car when Jemison looked up and saw Myers getting into another car with a woman he described as a 'knockout brunette.'"

Ryan touched her back. "We waited until you arrived to interview him."

The sheriff looked Charlie in the eye and tried to establish intimacy with his gaze. "Pete Jemison and Myers work — worked — for the same construction company. Because of the downpours yesterday, they didn't work. Jemison came to pick up Myers for work this morning, but he didn't answer his door. Jemison had a key, so he let himself in and found this." He waved an open palm toward the bed the way models exhibit a prize on a game show.

Ryan shook his head. "Just like the others, the victim knew what was happening. The lacerations on the wrists from the cuffs are severe." He placed a hand in his pocket and jingled his change.

Charlie's stomach was starting to cramp. She began rubbing circles over it. "It looks like he tried his best to escape."

"I noticed the place was real clean. I'm sure it's been wiped down. We'll likely have trouble finding prints."

She tried to hide her feeling of horror as she examined the victim's injuries more closely. "Was he wearing a condom?"

The sheriff nodded. "Sure was. We've already bagged it."

"I noticed that both the seat and lid were down on the toilet. Was that the case at the previous murder scenes? Do you guys remember?" Charlie looked from Ryan to Joe.

Ryan looked curious. "I'm not sure. I can look at the crime scene photos."

"Do you think that's further confirmation that the murderer is a woman?" asked the sheriff.

"Men leave both seats up. Most women leave the seat down. An OCD female would put the lid down, too. It just caught my attention today, for some reason. Where's the witness?" Charlie looked around but saw only deputies and forensic techs.

"In my car. We plan to take him back to the courthouse and question him further." The sheriff pointed in the general direction of his vehicle. "So what do y'all know so far?"

"The previous victims had sex with the same female, according to the DNA. Both samples were AB negative blood types," said Ryan.

The sheriff scrunched his nose. "This guy reeks of alcohol. Probably less able to defend himself."

Joe spoke up. "The other two victims were drinking, too. Sheriff, we'll make sure you get a copy of Doc's profile and will coordinate with your office on this case."

"It's getting crowded in here." Charlie started backing out of the bedroom. "I'll wait outside. Let me know when y'all are ready to go to the courthouse."

She drove to the nearby convenience store, her car window open so she could feel the breeze. It reminded her of a typical mom and pop grocery. There were holes in the parking lot and two beat-up gas pumps in the front.

A bell tinkled above her head as she pushed open the door. Dust danced on the sunbeams coming through the pollen-dusted front windows. The only items not covered with dust were the chips, candy, sodas, cigarettes, and cases of beer. Glass-door coolers lined the walls.

Charlie chose a cold ginger ale to settle her stomach and some other drinks for the guys. She lugged them to the old-timer behind the counter.

He honked his nose into a large red handkerchief and stuffed it in the back pocket of his overalls. His smile revealed tobacco-stained teeth framed by a gray mustache. "Howdy, that'll be ten dollars and eighty cents." He shifted the wad of tobacco lodged in his cheek from one side to the other, picked up a rusted coffee can from the floor, spit brown liquid into it, and turned to place it behind the counter.

Charlie scrunched her nose. *Yuck!*

"There's lots of excitement round here today. Are you with those folks investigatin' that murder?" His gaze traveled to the HPD lanyard hanging from her neck.

Unsure of how to respond, Charlie focused on the drinks on the counter. "Yes, I am."

"What a shame. Stan was a good-ole-boy, even if he drank a mite too much." He looked sad and shook his head.

"Stan had a drinking problem?"

"Oh yeah, I'm not aimin' to speak ill of the dead or nothin'. Stan kept me in business as far as beer was concerned. See that stack of cases over there?"

The man gestured with his head as he placed the money in the register. Charlie tracked his gaze to seven cases of beer.

"I ordered that every week for him. He went through almost a case a day, except when he was in jail."

Charlie made a mental note to ask Ryan about the victim's criminal history.

"That Stan, he liked women as much as he did beer, but he never had much luck with keepin' one around very long. He was divorced five times." He shook his head again. "I figure no woman takes it well when she plays second to alcohol." He pronounced it *al-kee-hol*.

"I'm sure the neighbors around here appreciate your store being so close," Charlie commented. "It must be ten miles to the nearest grocery store. How late do you stay open?"

"On weekdays I stay open to 10:00, midnight on weekends. So this happened after midnight."

"Why do you say that?"

"It gets lonely here at night, so I sit here where I can watch the comin' and goin' of traffic. No car turned down this here road after Stan left to go to town."

"Thanks, Mr...."

"Jones, Elias Jones."

"Mr. Jones, I enjoyed our talk."

On the drive back to the murder site, it all began to make sense. *By waiting until midnight or one o'clock in the morning, our killer can be sure that the intended victim is intoxicated and that most neighbors will be asleep.*

With care, Charlie lifted the paper bag. The drinks inside shifted, making little clinking noises. Grabbing her large purse, she headed back toward the trailer. Now that she'd had a break, she felt better.

Joe and Ryan slammed out the door. Both looked pasty.

Ryan pulled off the mask and scrubbed his hand across his face as if he could wash off what he'd just seen. "What I wouldn't give for a cold drink right now."

"I thought y'all might feel that way." Smiling, Charlie handed each man a cold drink from the sack.

Joe looked surprised. "I may have underestimated you, Doc."

Ryan gave her a warm smile. "Thanks, Charlie, it couldn't have been better timed."

Mike Jarvis came tromping down the wood stairs. "Did an angel of mercy bring us some cold drinks?"

Charlie smiled as she held up the bag. "I'll make sure everybody gets one, Sheriff."

He blocked her path and took the brown sack from her. "Call me Mike." He winked and grinned. "I'll take these. They can't be taken inside. I'll just yell to let the guys know they're on the porch."

Charlie backed away, frowning as an uneasy feeling clawed its way down her spine. She turned in time to see Ryan shoot lightning bolts toward the sheriff's back with his gaze.

Unaware of the animosity, Joe chugged down his soda. He wiped his mouth with the back of his hand and belched. "That hit the spot." He belched again and whacked Ryan on the back. "What's wrong with you, buddy?"

"Nothing," Ryan muttered.

Charlie wasn't sure how she felt about Ryan's reaction to the sheriff's flirting.

Mike Jarvis trotted back down the steps to join the group.

When he was close enough to hear, Charlie said, "The store owner, Elias Jones, was brimming with information. He wanted to gossip, so I let him talk." Charlie let her gaze roam across the three men.

"What did he say?" said Ryan, as he pulled off his protective gear.

"Stan had a case-a-night addiction to beer and was a known womanizer. He was married five times. Mr. Jones saw no one go down this road before midnight."

"Good work, Dr. Stone." The sheriff sidled close to her. "I'll send one of my men down to talk with Mr. Jones to make an official report."

She stepped to the side to create distance. "Glad to help, but I just listened. People tend to talk to me for some reason."

"Let's leave the forensics crew to finish their work, and go question Mr. Jemison. I'll meet y'all at the courthouse," said Jarvis. "You're welcome to ride in with me, Dr. Stone."

"Thanks, but I brought my car."

Charlie drove away, relieved to leave the crime scene. *I wonder if Stan Myers has any family or friends to mourn his death?*

CHAPTER 44 - PETE'S INTERROGATION

Charlie entered the Sheriff's Department interrogation room, curious to see how it differed from the one at the Huntsville Police Department. This one contained a large wooden rectangular table, heavily scarred by years of abuse. Six wooden chairs surrounded the table. Bright fluorescent lights reflected off the institutional green painted walls.

The men filed into the room. Sheriff Jarvis had Mr. Jemison sit at the head of the table. The Sheriff and Joe sat to Jemison's left, Ryan and Charlie to his right. Charlie sat close enough to smell Ryan's Polo cologne, hoping the scent would clear the smell of death that was still teasing her nostrils.

Sheriff Jarvis turned on the tape recorder and announced the date, time and attendees. "Pete Jemison, a witness with information regarding the wrongful death of Stan Myers, is present, and the interview is being recorded. Mr. Jemison, do you agree to have this interview taped?" Jarvis waited for confirmation.

"Yeah, I do," said Jemison. If the wide-eyed look combined with his slouch was any indication, he was hung over, in shock, and scared half to death. He had the lean, muscled look, work-roughened hands, and deep tan associated with the construction industry. He was wearing jeans, a blue flannel shirt over a white tee shirt, and a cap that read "Smile if you aren't wearing panties."

Charlie made an obvious show of reading his cap, and then gave him the look she reserved for her patients when they carried on side conversations in group therapy. It was effective in the group and worked just as well here.

"Wh…. Oh! Sorry, ma'am." He removed the cap and shoved it into his lap, blushing through his tan.

At a nod from the sheriff, Pete began. "Well, it was Friday night —"

"The seventh of May?" clarified the sheriff.

"Yeah. Stan and I had plans to go clubbing in Huntsville. I have a pickup, and it has all my tools in it, so we went in Stan's car, and he drove. We went to Wyatt's, and I met this hot little number. Stan gave me the keys. When I went out to the parking lot, he was still sitting alone and drinking. I was doing just fine in the car if you know what I mean." He smirked and gave a conspiratorial wink to the sheriff. "We made sure to park back in the shadows, out from under those damn orange lights."

He paused and took a drink of water. Some dribbled down the front of his shirt, and he wiped it with his hand. The sheriff nodded for him to continue.

"This woman had on the bra from hell, so I had to sit up in the back seat to get a better angle on it. That's when I saw Stan with that brunette. She was parked right underneath one of those orange lights. They tussled a bit, and Stan had her backed against the car."

Joe was writing notes on a yellow legal pad. "Where was he in relation to the woman?"

"He was in front of her, at first. Later he was behind her, reaching around to the front." Jemison demonstrated as if he was reaching around a woman and made squeezing motions with his hands. His gaze moved around the table. When he met Charlie's eyes, he dropped his hands and cleared his throat.

"Are you sure it was your friend, Stan Myers?" asked Joe.

"Damn sure. You see, when I saw what was going on, I sat up straighter to watch the show. I guess Stan saw me moving in his car, 'cause I saw him grin and nod. He ripped her shirt open. If it had buttons, he must have popped them all off. He angled her to face me. She wasn't wearing a bra. They fooled around for a while. She had her hands on the hood. Stan had her bent over the fender and was grinding on her from behind. Then they got in the car and left. You know, I think she liked him doing her like that, right out in the open for anybody to see."

"What makes you say that, Pete?" Charlie tilted her head and picked up her pen.

"Because she let him do that to her for several minutes, right there in the parking lot. I thought she was going to hump the paint off that fender. When she got free, her shirt was still open, showing her tits, and she didn't even bother to pull it together, she just got in the car."

Charlie considered what she'd heard. It added a new dimension to the profile. The perp could be working as an exotic dancer or a stripper, someone comfortable having lots of skin exposed.

Ryan cleared his throat. "Did the lady with you see anything?"

"Naw, she was flat on the backseat with me straddling her."

"Pete, this sounds like a woman who would catch your attention. Did you notice her in the club while you were in there?" Charlie twirled her pen between her fingers.

"Man-oh-man, she was a looker!" He nodded his head up and down with emphasis. "If I'd seen her first, I might be the one dead today, instead of Stan." Realization must have hit home by the haunted look in his eyes.

"Describe her to us, Pete. How tall was she, how big?" Sheriff Jarvis gestured with his hands, encouraging him to be more descriptive.

"She came up to Stan's nose, and he was 6'4. She was wearing tight dark jeans and a light-colored western shirt. She had fluffy long brown hair." He made gestures around his head indicating a full hairstyle.

Charlie leaned closer. "How long was her hair?"

"I'd say, as long as yours," he said.

"Was she small-boned, large-boned, fat?" Charlie probed his memory.

"Actually," he squinted his eyes, "she looks a mite like you, but with brown hair. Slender, pretty, with big um...you know."

Ryan cleared his throat again, diverting Pete's attention toward him. "Did you notice the car? What make, model, color, or tag number?"

"It was a dark-colored car, maybe green. It's hard to tell the color of anything under those orange lights. It was a mid-sized car. I didn't get a tag number. It was too far away for that."

Ryan tapped his pen on the table. "Can you recall anything else about the lady or the car? Were there any dents, bumper stickers or anything else unusual?"

Jemison stuck his tongue out the corner of his mouth and looked at the ceiling tiles, as though the answer was written across them. "Nope, I can't recall anything else unusual that I haven't already told y'all."

Jarvis asked, "Pete, do you remember what time you saw your friend get in the car?"

Charlie suspected Sheriff Jarvis hoped to pin down the possible time of the murder.

"Yeah, sorta. When I got Stan's car keys, I looked at my watch to see how much time I had before the club closed at two. It was almost one o'clock. I remember thinking I didn't have much time to…convince the lady. We were out in Stan's car maybe fifteen minutes when he came out."

The interrogation ended, and the sheriff took Pete Jemison to a different area of the department to work with a sketch artist.

"If y'all don't need me, I have some errands to run." Charlie pushed back her chair and stood.

"Sure, I'll get in touch with you later," said Ryan.

CHAPTER 45 - JOE'S ACCUSATIONS

"So what's your theory, Joe? Do you think Charlie started murdering men so that she could start her consulting career?" Ryan's throat felt strained from trying to control his mounting anger. "Do you honestly think Charlie is wearing a brunette wig and killing alcoholic men?"

"There have been cases of firemen starting fires so they could put them out," said Joe. He was standing across the table from

203

Ryan. "She does work with alcoholics." He leaned forward and rested his hands on the table.

Ryan raised his voice. "What have you got against Charlie?"

"I don't have anything against her, but you saw the way Jemison looked at her. Have you looked at the sketch in progress? It looks more like Doc every minute."

Frustrated, Ryan ran his hand through his hair. "Have you considered that he just left an interview where Charlie was the last woman he saw? Besides, that sketch looks like Janice, too." Ryan knew he sounded peeved. *I need to tone it down before someone comes to find out what the ruckus is about.*

Joe growled, "There are too many coincidences."

Ryan shifted his weight and crossed his arms. "Like what?"

Joe counted his points off on his sausage fingers. "She wears the same size shoe as the perp. Size five isn't a typical size, you know. Jemison thinks she looks like the woman he saw in the parking lot. You're the one who told me she has AB negative blood like the killer. Oh, I almost forgot. She drives a dark green mid-sized car."

Ryan shook his head. "How many dark green mid-sized cars are there in Huntsville? You're grasping at straws, Joe."

Joe held his arms out, palms up. "Ryan, what do we know about this woman anyway?"

"She's a highly qualified professional and a good person. You're way off base here, Joe. Everything you mentioned is circumstantial."

"Be careful, buddy, you're thinking with your dick, not your head," Joe grumbled. "I hope I'm wrong, but I don't think I am."

Ryan's face felt hot from suppressed rage as he backed away. Unwilling to hear any more accusations against the woman he'd come to realize he loved, he said, "You're wrong Joe. I'm out of here." He turned and stormed out the door and down the hallway.

"Ryan!" Joe called after him.

He never slowed or looked back.

As he walked to the parking garage, he thought about Charlie and all the things Joe had said to him. Despite his protests, a faint, niggling doubt settled in Ryan's gut. He wondered if Charlie owned a long brunette wig.

CHAPTER 46 - FIRST DATE

Feeling like Cinderella, Charlie stood in front of the full-length mirror. She shifted left, then right. Turning around, Charlie looked over her shoulder, giving every detail a critical inspection. Pleased with the reflection before her, she sighed. Resting a hand on her hip, she bounced it a few times and smiled, feeling vampish. "Ryan Roberts, I hope you're ready for this dress."

She wore intense make-up for this special evening. She had emphasized her eyes with smoky shadow to make them the focal point of her face. Her lipstick was a darker shade than usual and highlighted the fullness of her lips

Her dress, a long sheath of black beaded silk accented with gold and silver beading across the front and shoulders, molded to her curves. The cut-out in the front exposed a hint of cleavage. The back was scandalous, exposing her entire back almost to her bottom.

She had pulled her hair up in a tumble of cascading curls. Dangling rhinestone earrings completed the picture of elegance.

The doorbell rang. Charlie jumped.

She put a hand to her chest, as though to settle her pounding heart. "Calm down," she told herself. She glanced around to make sure everything was in order.

Spanky raced from the room as the doorbell chimed again.

When Charlie entered the living room, she could hear Ryan sweet-talking to Spanky through the door. Spanky pranced and whined.

If her tail wags any harder, it'll knock her off her feet. Charlie grinned at the thought.

She swung the door wide and in her best sultry voice said, "Hello!" She formed a seductive smile and stepped back to give Ryan the full effect.

"Wow!" Ryan gawked, mouth unhinged. "You look great. Hell, you look better than great."

Spanky was doing her happy dance around Ryan. He bent to pet her. The pup squirmed as if in ecstasy.

"Thanks. You look…very handsome indeed." In his navy dress uniform, with a short cutaway jacket and trousers with stripes down the side, Ryan looked the epitome of masculine.

Charlie cocked a hip, placed a French-manicured hand on it, and winked. "I'll just get my wrap."

Ryan's grin widened. "I love a punctual woman."

Charlie heard him gasp as she turned her back to him to retrieve the wrap and evening purse she'd left draped over the arm of the sofa. She could see him in her peripheral vision. He looked ready to drool.

She felt him tremble as he placed her wrap over her shoulders. *Geez, I hope he has enough blood flow left to his brain to drive.*

Spanky gave her a soulful look. Charlie reached down and fondled her velvety ears. "We'll be back home later, Spanky. Be a good girl." Charlie heard her pup's pitiful whine as she closed and locked the door.

CHAPTER 47 - CHARLIE MEETS SARAH

Arm in arm, Charlie and Ryan entered the North Hall of the Civic Center. At one end of the room, a raised platform boasted the traditional head table. Round tables for eight, graced with white linens and black napkins, dotted the room at regular intervals. Candles glowed inside hurricane glass cylinders set on square mirror tiles and surrounded by burgundy silk magnolias.

At the other end of the room, a platform for the band nudged against the wall, behind a portable dance floor that looked large enough to accommodate about half the attendees.

Somehow Charlie hadn't expected so many people. *Ohmygod, why did I wear this dress?* Feeling exposed and shy, she felt reluctant to surrender her wrap. It was one thing to stand in her home in a sexy dress, and quite another to parade it in front of a room full of strangers.

Taking a deep breath to calm her zinging nerves, she allowed Ryan to check her wrap with an attendant for safekeeping. Ryan offered her his arm, which boosted her courage.

He walked tall and proud, clearly happy to have her by his side. Charlie firmed her chin and stepped forward with a confident air that belied her tap-dancing heart.

"Let's say hi to the Captain," Ryan suggested. "Then I want you to meet Joe's wife, Sarah."

"That's fine with me." She smiled up at his handsome face.

The captain stood near the head table with his arm around a woman who was a foot shorter, even in heels. His formal uniform served to make him appear even taller. This was the first time she had seen him since the interview with Sherry Harper.

Ryan nodded. "Captain and Mrs. Strouper, how are you tonight? Mrs. Strouper, that's a pretty dress."

"Thank you, and who is this lovely lady?"

Captain Strouper answered, "Honey, this is our new consultant, Dr. Stone. This is my wife, Vanessa."

Vanessa wore a black gown with a daring neckline. Her hair was upswept in an elaborate pattern of copper curls. Charlie felt better about the bold back of her dress.

"I like your dress, Vanessa. It's very becoming on you." Charlie exchanged a handshake and found Vanessa's grip to be firm and confident.

"Thank you. I understand your input has been valuable in this serial killer case." Her gaze flitted between Charlie and Ryan.

"I'm delighted to hear that. I'll feel much better when we catch the killer." Charlie gave the captain and his wife a smile.

"Won't we all," said the captain.

"Excuse us, Captain." Ryan pulled her away. "There are Joe and Sarah." He gestured toward the other end of the room. "I can't wait until he sees you in that dress!"

Charlie stiffened, feeling unexpected dread. *Do I have to? Joe's been so cantankerous toward me lately.*

Sarah was wearing a beaded pink gown that reminded Charlie of a mother-of-the-bride dress. Her only accessories were a single strand of ivory pearls and matching pearl drop earrings. Joe was standing several feet from Sarah, engrossed by the band as they set up their equipment.

Good grief, by the size of those speakers we'll all be deaf by midnight, thought Charlie.

"Hi Sarah, I want you to meet our new consultant, Dr. Charlene Stone." Ryan placed his arm around Charlie's shoulder and smiled.

Sarah offered her hand. "Hello, Dr. Stone, I'm happy to have the opportunity to meet you." She gave Charlie a conspiratorial wink. "Any lady that can put a bee up my Joe's butt has to be interesting."

"Please, call me Charlie." She felt a prickle of embarrassment as she wondered what Joe might have told Sarah. "That shade of rose pink is wonderful on you."

"Thank you. Our youngest daughter is getting married in less than a year, so I thought it would make a great dress for her wedding."

Charlie winked. "I bet Joe liked the idea of you wearing that dress twice."

"I see you have him pegged. That did ease his pain." Sarah laughed.

Joe swallowed some of his drink and turned. When he saw Charlie, he choked and coughed, his eyes bulging.

Ryan pounded on his partner's back while Sarah rolled her eyes to the ceiling.

"Joe!" Sarah reached across and hit him on the arm with her small beaded evening purse, causing him to slosh some of his drink over his hand.

Joe backed out of range. "Calm down and stop beating me to death." He looked like a red-faced fire hydrant stuffed into a dress uniform.

Ryan was grinning at his partner's plight.

For her part, Charlie felt no mercy after Joe's gruff behavior toward her in the past. She was relieved that Joe offered no comment on her dress. *Perhaps he's afraid Sarah will beat him to death with her handbag.*

"Let's find a table." Joe pulled on his collar in an attempt to stretch it. "My feet hurt in these shoes."

"Oh, don't you start whining," scolded Sarah. "You're dancing with me tonight. I didn't wait all year for this, just to sit at a table and watch everyone else have a good time."

Joe stepped aside to let Charlie pass. She shot him a sideways glare as she moved past him. *Don't get cranky with me tonight. I plan to have a good time.*

They found a table and took their seats. Sarah and Charlie sat next to each other, chatting as they watched the other couples mingle before dinner.

Sarah smiled and leaned closer to Charlie. "Ryan seems quite taken with you. He's brought different ladies to this function over the years, but he's never had that twinkle in his eye."

"Really? I like him, too. Joe, however, doesn't seem to like me *at all*. He's always so cranky. Do you know why, Sarah?"

"Joe respects your skills, he's just traditional and doesn't think women should work. He had a hissy fit because I started a little part-time office position at our church. He's snubbed our minister for the past three Sundays."

Charlie's brows rose in surprise. "You're kidding!"

"He doesn't know what to do with women. Even our daughter Regan baffles him. Truth be told, Joe is all about the job." Sarah sighed. "I knew this when I married him. He cut a dashing figure back in those days." She patted her cushioning. "I looked pretty good too, back then."

The waiter arrived with four dinners, bringing conversations to a temporary halt. He placed a plate in front of Charlie, Sarah, Ryan, and one of the other guests, leaving Joe without food.

"What the hell," Joe complained. He downed part of his drink and crossed his arms.

"It's probably part of your Karma, for the way you behaved earlier." Sarah gave him a sweet smile and took a bite of her chicken. "Yum, this is *so good*, too bad you haven't gotten yours yet." She winked.

Joe was the last person at their table to receive his dinner. The aggrieved expression left his face the moment his food landed in front of him.

The after dinner speeches were coma-inducing. Charlie stifled a yawn and glanced over at Ryan, who looked bored.

Joe nodded off to sleep in his chair. This wasn't too obvious until he started to snore — in loud snorts. Sarah had to jab him with her elbow to wake him.

"What? What?" Joe sat up bleary-eyed and knocked over his water, which cascaded over the edge of the table into Sarah's lap.

Sarah gasped and jumped up, water dripping to the floor. "Joe!" She swatted him with her purse. Charlie passed napkins to Sarah to soak up the water. Ryan held his stomach laughing.

"For goodness sakes Sarah, it's just water," Joe hissed.

The awards were more interesting, although Charlie knew none of the recipients.

The Mayor announced, "Our next award is for the most solved homicide cases for the year. The winners are…Lieutenant Joe Sparks and his partner, Detective Ryan Roberts."

The hall resounded with applause. Both men strutted to the front to receive their awards, shoulders squared, heads held high. Charlie and Sarah smiled at each other and clapped with enthusiasm.

"Did you know they were getting this award?" Charlie inquired.

Sarah shook her head. "Did you?"

"No, but it's pretty cool."

Sarah hooted as Joe received his plaque. Charlie applauded and whistled for Ryan. He met her eyes over the heads of the audience and grinned, holding his plaque high. Both men received slaps on the back after they left the stage. They shook the hands of their fellow officers while walking back to their table. Their proud posture and glowing faces said it all.

"This is great! Why didn't you tell us you were getting an award?" Charlie reached over and gave Ryan a congratulatory hug.

"I didn't know. I knew we were in the running, but I didn't know we'd won." Ryan's eyes glowed.

"Oh Joe, I'm so proud of you, Sugar Bear." Sarah threw herself into Joe's arms and gave him a big hug and kiss.

Joe beamed, pink staining his cheeks. "Okay Sarah, that's enough." He untangled her arms and looked around.

The awards ended, and the band at the other end of the auditorium began playing. All conversation was reduced to bellowing across the table. After a few songs, the band slowed the tempo.

Ryan leaned across the table. "Dance with me, Charlie."

He took her hand and led her to the dance floor. Following Ryan's example, Joe invited Sarah to dance.

Charlie's heart was racing like a runaway train as she stepped into Ryan's arms to dance. His embrace felt so warm and safe that she began to relax. She could feel his hand burning on her bare back. She began to shiver with excitement as the tingle began.

"Are you cold?"

She smiled up at him. "You're warming me up. I may self-combust, so watch out."

Ryan uttered a soft groan and pulled her closer. She inhaled his cologne and sighed, closing her eyes.

"You fit so perfectly in my arms." He hugged her closer.

For that moment, it was just Ryan, the music, and the dancing. Everything else ceased to matter.

As the dance ended, Charlie opened her eyes and saw Joe talking to the captain. He pointed at her, a scowl on his face.

Good Lord, she thought, *what have I done wrong now?*

Ryan pulled her close as a new song began, and Joe disappeared from her mind.

Charlie and Ryan were still dancing when Joe and Sarah found them to say good-bye.

Joe looked droopy. "Sarah just wore me out with all this dancing."

"Party pooper, you didn't even dance that much." Despite Sarah's complaints, it was obvious from her shuffle that her feet were hurting.

CHAPTER 48 - THE DISCUSSION

It was close to midnight, and the ball was winding down. Charlie and Ryan were among the last to leave.

He rubbed his stomach. "I'm starving."

"Me too. It was all that dancing." Her blue-grey eyes twinkled as she smiled up at him. "I've had so much fun."

Such beautiful eyes.

They drove to Denny's on University Drive and split a large breakfast combination, teasing each other the whole time.

They had finished the meal and were lingering over coffee when Charlie shot Ryan a serious look. "I need to talk to you about something."

"Uh oh, those are fatal words in a relationship." Ryan sat back. "What did I do?"

Charlie shook her head. "Ryan, it's not you, it's Joe. I can't seem to do anything right according to that man. I think he may try to get me fired."

Ryan's face grew hot as he remembered his argument with Joe. He paused and looked down at his coffee cup. "I'll talk to him." *Again!*

Charlie ran her index finger around the lip of her mug. "Will it do any good?"

Ryan shifted in his seat. "Don't worry about it."

Charlie looked dubious. "I'll try, but this job is important to me."

CHAPTER 49 - RYAN WINS

Ryan and Charlie sat in companionable silence on the drive home. He took her hand in his and held it all the way to her house. It felt so comfortable — so right in his.

They stood outside her front door as she fumbled for her keys in the tiny purse. Feeling nervous, he shifted from foot to foot and ran his hand through his hair as she unlocked her door.

"May I come in for coffee?" He moved closer, his heart pounding like a bass drum against his ribs.

"We just finished coffee. Aren't you tired?" She was smiling just a little, her face glowing beautiful and mysterious in the moonlight.

"I've got my second wind. Besides, I'm off tomorrow … well, today." Ryan slid his hand up and down her back, tracing her vertebrae.

"Okay," she sighed, shivering. "I'm getting cold."

"I'm sure I can chase away that chill." He focused his gaze on her with spoon-bending intensity.

Charlie opened the door, and Spanky leaped and whined, delighted to see them. When Charlie bent to pet her, she flopped on her back. Laughing, Charlie stroked her stomach.

"Hello, Spanky girl," Ryan cooed, as he bent to scratch Spanky's ears. *She's such a good dog.*

Charlie stood and smiled. " I'll go start the coffee. Be right back." Before he could say anything, she was gone.

What can I do to set the mood? Remembering that she was cold, he turned on the gas logs in the fireplace to create a warm and cozy glow. Satisfied with the effect, he collapsed on the sofa. Spanky leaped up beside him and snuggled close.

"I see you won over my dog." Charlie placed a loaded coffee tray on the table.

"If I can only win over her mistress."

Charlie sat erect and poured the coffee. She added cream and sugar to her cup and stirred. Placing the spoon in her mouth, she licked it clean.

He watched, admiring the grace of her movements and feeling his voracious need for her. She held out his cup of coffee with trembling hands and smiled.

Ryan took the cup from her and placed it back on the tray. *Damn it. I don't want coffee, Charlie. I want you.*

He slid his hand along her cheek and settled it on the back of her neck. Her eyes grew huge, but she didn't pull away when he leaned toward her.

He kissed her with tenderness at first, then with more passion. Kissing this woman was the most sensual experience of his life.

"Charlie, you're so exquisite. I've wanted to kiss you since the first day I saw you," he murmured in her ear, as he kissed her neck.

Charlie ran her fingers through his hair. He groaned his approval. She slid her hands under his uniform coat and moved it over his shoulders. He freed himself from its bondage, and let his eyes roam from her face to the hint of cleavage revealed by her dress.

Taking both of her small hands in his, he turned them over and kissed her palms, continuing to each finger. He felt her shiver.

He'd thought about this moment so many times and knew the possible consequences for both of them. Staring into her eyes, he said, "Charlie, I'm not going to force you into a situation you may regret tomorrow. I don't want to stop what we've started here, but if you want me to leave, I will."

Gripping her hands, he thought, *ask me to stay.*

Charlie's eyes misted. A small smile played on her lips.

Please, ask me to stay. He felt ready to burst inside. *What will I do if she says, go?*

Reaching up, Charlie loosened his tie and pulled it out from his collar. He held back, enjoying the ecstasy of the moment. She unbuttoned his starched shirt with slow, deliberate care and eased her hands inside.

He moaned, thrilled to feel her touch on his skin. The sensation of her cool fingers entangled in his chest hair almost drove him to action. Instead, he held his breath, making the sensation of her touch and the beating of his heart more intense. She helped him remove his shirt. The cool air made her hands feel hot as she slid up his chest, over his shoulders and down his back.

Reaching around her, he unzipped her dress and eased it forward over her shoulders. She stood, letting the dress drop to a pool of fabric at her feet.

He let his eyes roam over her smooth skin and admired her full breasts. He felt himself grow hard. Her waist seemed so tiny compared to the flair of her hips. His eyes feasted on her beauty as they slid down past the black lace thong she wore. He could feel his heart throbbing in his cock as his gaze journeyed over her shapely legs. *Perfection.*

He stood and enveloped her in his arms and kissed her as if he could absorb her inside his core. Taking him by the hand, she led him to her bedroom.

CHAPTER 50 - TEARS OF RELEASE

Charlie snuggled against Ryan's left side as he lay on his back. Her head rested on his shoulder, and she'd thrown her leg over both of his. *I feel so safe for the first time in* .... She couldn't remember how long. She could feel the steady beat of his heart and the warmth of his skin. She smiled to herself. *The man is like a personal heater.*

She wasn't sure what words described how she felt because to be truthful, she had mixed impressions. She knew she didn't regret her decision to make love to him. It seemed almost inevitable. She did worry about the possible fallout.

She craned her neck to look at his face. His eyes were closed, and he seemed so relaxed, his features almost child-like in the glow of the candles. His fingers traced patterns on her skin like the flitting of butterfly wings.

A swell of emotion was building inside her that she recognized. A hodgepodge of hurt, anger, betrayal, humiliation, grief and fear coiled together like a venomous snake. She'd been denying its presence and shoving it down for over a year, but now she could no longer control the emotional monster. Sobs wracked her frame as it exploded through her body.

Oh terrific, we've just had great sex, and I'm crying. But she couldn't stop.

Ryan bolted upright, his eyes wide with alarm. "Charlie, what's wrong?"

She tried to speak, but she was sobbing too hard. The emotion was pouring over her in waves and waves: Grief over the deaths of her mother and father, and her anger at them for dying. The humiliation she'd felt when she'd caught Nathan with Eric, and the pain of realizing that her marriage had been a lie. The anguish of all her losses — of family, of trust — roared through her, and she was helpless to stop it

Ryan gathered her in his arms like a child. "Whatever it is, you can tell me." He held her close and rocked her, and at last her tears brought healing.

CHAPTER 51 - WAKING ALONE

The phone jangled Ryan's signature tune.

Charlie shot awake. She looked for him, but then remembered that he'd already kissed her goodbye this morning after being called into an emergency meeting. *So much for our day together.*

The phone jangled again.

"Where is it?" Charlie sprang from the bed and rushed toward the dresser, where the phone lay plugged into the charger. En route, she slammed her toe into the chest at the foot of her bed.

"Damn!" Tears sprang to her eyes, and she held her toe, hopping on one foot. Limping the rest of the way, she grabbed the phone.

A warm tingle coursed through her body as she answered. "Hi, Ryan."

"Charlie, you need to come down to the precinct," said Ryan. His tone was serious.

"What's happened? Has there been another murder?" Her heart slammed down to the pit of her stomach.

"Not a murder. It's complicated. Come as soon as you can." Ryan's tone sounded so stiff.

"Okay, I'll see you in a bit." Frowning, she set the phone back on her dresser.

One glance in the mirror confirmed that she wasn't leaving the house without a shower. She slipped under the stream of warm water and felt her muscles soften. She smiled, remembering the night before. *If nothing else happens between us, last night will be worth it. No regrets.*

Her thoughts shifted to this morning's phone call. *I wonder if it was about the case?* She lathered her hair and turned her back to the steaming spray to rinse it. The warm water felt so good.

An idea hit her. She lowered her hands and stood in the foggy shower, letting the hot water cascade over her body while she thought. She pondered the case and the similarities between the three victims. *Of course! Why didn't I see it sooner?* It was so simple.

"All the clubs are country music establishments that cater to people in their thirties and older. The killer hasn't repeated a pickup in the same location." Hearing her words echo off the tiles made it seem clearer somehow.

Turning off the water, Charlie toweled dry and wrapped the damp towel around her. She limped to her office, turned on her laptop, accessed the search engine, and keyed in her request. When the list came up, Charlie copied and pasted the list into a Word document and printed it.

Holding the paper, she returned to the bedroom and placed it on the dresser. Once she was back in the steamy bathroom, she wiped the fogged mirror and looked at herself. *I look the same, but I feel different, lighter. It was a very cathartic evening.* She blow-dried her hair and applied makeup. After slipping into jeans and a coral shirt, she put on her running shoes, wincing as she tied them. Her toe still throbbed.

Charlie returned to her office with the sheet of paper and researched her list on her laptop. There were only three clubs left that catered to the thirty and older patron. They were the Honkey Tonk, Lonely Hearts, and Busters. In all likelihood, one of these clubs would be the next hunting ground for the killer.

Excited about her new theory, Charlie grabbed her phone and purse and hobbled toward the door.

CHAPTER 52 - AMBUSHED

Charlie made it to the precinct and headed straight to Ryan's desk. Her toe was feeling somewhat better. She limped up behind Ryan and touched his shoulder.

He jerked and whirled around. Charlie's smile faltered when he didn't smile back. "What's going on?"

Ryan shook his head. "Let's talk in private." He led her to the conference room and closed the door.

Charlie asked again, "Ryan, what's going on?" She clutched her paper in both hands.

Ryan ran his hand through his disheveled hair. "Joe thinks you're the killer. He's convinced the captain to take you off the case until you provide a DNA sample and a list of your alibis."

Charlie gaped, speechless with dismay.

After she had processed what he told her, she said, "I know Joe doesn't like me, but this?" She waved her arm as if the problem resided within that room. "I can't believe it!"

The door opened, and Joe walked into the room. Scowling at Charlie, he crossed his arms and settled back on his heels.

With balled fists cocked on her hips, Charlie faced off with him. "I can't believe you think I'm the killer. I'm on your side, remember?" Angry tears sprang to her eyes. *Damn you and your warped suspicious mind.*

Joe looked immovable. "Too many coincidences here, Doc. We're going to need some DNA."

Charlie looked to Ryan, waiting for him to come to her defense.

Ryan shot Joe a dirty look and turned toward her. "Charlie, we finally found some prints at the last murder scene. They don't match *anyone* in our system." He turned his angry gaze back on Joe.

Charlie crossed her arms. "Aren't my fingerprints in your system?"

Joe stood like a rock, frowning at her. "The prints are only partials. Hard to tell much based on what we recovered. Are you giving us a DNA sample or not?"

Charlie lifted her chin. "I have nothing to hide, take your sample." She sliced Joe with a look that was sharp enough to disembowel him.

Joe opened the conference room door and waved Mike inside.

The tech looked from Joe, to Ryan, to Charlie. She hadn't seen him since he'd removed a condom crawling with maggots from

David Street's battered penis. She had the impression he was as uncomfortable now as he'd been then.

Joe crossed his arms. "Don't just stand there. Get on with it."

Mike gave her an apologetic nod. "Sorry, Doc."

"Not your fault, Mike." Charlie gave him a brief smile to assure him there were no hard feelings and opened her mouth. He swabbed the inside of each cheek.

After Mike had left, Charlie turned to Ryan. "I think I may know where the killer —"

Joe interrupted, holding up a hand. "Doc. You're off the case until you're cleared. Leave. Now."

Ignoring Joe, she took a step toward Ryan and held out the page in her hand. "I think I may know —"

Joe interrupted again, wedging himself between her and Ryan. "You. Are. Off. This. Case. Do you understand? Do *not* make contact with *anyone* in this department until you're cleared. That includes Detective Roberts." Joe cocked his head in Ryan's direction.

Charlie looked at Ryan, but he wouldn't meet her eyes. The muscle in his jaw flexed as he audibly ground his teeth.

Joe continued, "I suggest you document your alibis for the times of the murders and contact an attorney. Oh, and don't leave the area. We may be bringing you in for questioning, *soon*."

Ryan stood glowering at his boss and partner. His hands balled into fists.

"I can't believe this shit! I've almost figured it out, and you won't listen to me?" Charlie raked Joe with a glare that should have skinned the hide off his body. She didn't look at Ryan again. Stiff with rage, she squared her shoulders and left the conference room.

She hobbled to the captain's office, but he wasn't there. *Coward,* she thought. *You let Joe do your dirty work for you.*

Feeling like a volcano about to rain molten ash on anyone close by, she limped down the center aisle of the bullpen. All the detectives avoided her gaze.

Her face burned with humiliation as she stood in the empty elevator. Hot tears trickled down her cheeks as she limped grumbling to the parking lot. She would have stomped, but her toe ached too much.

"I guess it's up to me to track down this killer. So be it." Harboring enough anger and determination to power the city lights of Huntsville, Charlie straightened her spine and limped to her car.

CHAPTER 53 - THE HONKEY TONK

The Huntress knew she was in good-ole-boy territory when she pulled into the parking lot of the Honkey Tonk. The lot was a sea of pickup trucks. Dressed for the occasion, she wore her tightest jeans, a fitted red western shirt, boots, and a cowboy hat. She checked her hair in the rearview mirror and unsnapped a few pearl buttons on her shirt.

As she approached the entrance, several men wearing Stetsons parted like the Red Sea to make a path for her to enter the door.

"Oowee, darlin', come home with me tonight," said one guy, grinning like a half-lit fool.

She eyed him up and down. His offer interested her, but he was blond and not what she was looking for, at least not tonight.

Enveloped in the haze of smoke and lights, the band was cranking out a classic country tune. Couples on the crowded dance floor snuggled close, swaying back and forth.

The Huntress ignored most of the men who noticed her, choosing to stay focused on finding her prey.

The band finished a slow song and started a new one with a faster beat. The floor filled with line dancers moving in sync, their thumbs anchored in their belts She decided to join the dancers and eased into the front row. The Huntress turned and slid to the right. She saw a man staring at her. She met his gaze.

The man's face went a dark red. He dropped his gaze to his beer.

He looked to be about forty-five. She guessed he'd be about six-feet tall, maybe two hundred pounds. The flannel shirt over a crew neck t-shirt and jeans labeled him as a good-ole-boy rather than a cowboy wannabe. Other than needing a shave, he was the right age, the right coloring, the right everything.

The music ended. The band put down their instruments and took a break. The Huntress threaded her way to his table. Pasting a dazzling smile on her face, she rested a hand on her cocked hip.

"Do you mind if I sit? I hate to perch at the bar." She pointed at the chair next to him.

Looking rattled, he gestured toward the empty chair and knocked over his beer.

"Oh, hell!" He flushed even redder.

"Here, let me help you." She leaned across the table and helped him soak up the beer with napkins.

His eyes riveted on the swell of her breasts where her blouse gaped open.

A shy one. I'll have to coax him in without scaring him off.

A waitress bustled over, wiped up the remainder of the spill and raked the wet napkins onto her tray. Satisfied that the table was dry enough, the waitress plopped another beer on the table and hurried away with the dripping towel. The Huntress watched with surprise as the man chugged down his entire replacement beer.

He put down the empty mug and wiped his mouth on his sleeve. "Would you like a drink?"

"I'd love a Corona with lime."

He rolled up both sleeves, revealing his well-muscled forearms. "It's getting warm in here."

She smiled as she trailed her fingertips over a prominent vein pulsating under his tanned skin.

While she nursed her beer, he gulped down two more. The more he drank, the bolder he became, alcohol overriding his shy nature.

She sat pretending to be fascinated with the bar scene, as he slid glances her way.

"My bad, I forgot to introduce myself." He tilted his head. "My name's Zack Bailey."

"Zack. I like that. It's a friendly name." The Huntress smiled and flipped her hair over her shoulder.

"I sure would like to be your friend." He winked and took another swig of his beer.

A slow song started. "I just love to slow dance. Would you dance with me?"

He frowned, a crease forming between his brows. "I'm not much of a dancer."

She took his hand. He shook his head. She pulled him to his feet anyway. He was weaving a bit as she guided him to the dance floor.

As they swayed to the music, the Huntress snuggled close and looked into his eyes. "Do you have a house or someplace we can be together?"

He grinned down at her. "I sure do, honey."

"Do you live alone?"

"Yep."

"Suppose we go there, now." The Huntress placed a seductive smile on her lips and rubbed the back of his neck with her hand.

"Okay, but let's get a beer to go." He took her hand and plowed a path toward the bar, dragging her in his wake.

CHAPTER 54 - SURPRISE

The Honkey Tonk was the last club on Charlie's list. By the time she swung into its packed parking lot, it was thirty minutes past midnight. Backing into a shadowed space far from the club, she turned off her lights and sat there a moment, gathering her courage.

She uttered a quick prayer and opened her car door. Phone in hand, she was navigating her way among the parked cars when her sore toe clipped a concrete parking barrier.

"Shit!" Charlie managed to break her fall by grabbing at a pickup's side view mirror. She watched in horror as her phone arced gracefully through the air and crash-landed somewhere in the shadows between two nearby vehicles. On hands and knees, Charlie searched with frantic intensity between the vehicles for her phone. She found it and with shaking hands powered it on.

Thanks to its protective case, it wasn't broken. Sighing her relief, she thought, *What am I doing here? I should go home.*

She heard a man's voice and a woman's lilting laughter. Popping up for a peek, she saw that the woman had long dark hair. *This could be the perp! But I can't see her face.*

Charlie eased forward until she could see the car. *It's dark green!*

Car doors closed and the engine cranked to start. Charlie rose from the pavement with plans to follow that car.

Another vehicle gunned into the parking lot, and she ducked. She saw the beams of its headlights illuminate the aisle close to where she sat huddled between two large pickups. A dark green SUV rolled past her. Charlie thought she recognized the driver. Peeping around the bumper of the parked truck, she saw the Colorado license plate.

Melissa? What are you doing here?

CHAPTER 55 - SEX AND HANDCUFFS

The Huntress followed Zack's directions, maneuvering through the streets until they reached University Drive. He directed her to turn north on Jordan Lane, which eventually turned into Highway 53. She noticed that the stars shone like diamonds against the black velvet sky out here, away from the city.

Zack pointed. "Turn right here, at that gas station with its lights off."

She drove down a narrow two-lane road lined by trees and brush.

Zack pointed toward a small house, covered in white vinyl siding. "This is it, on the left."

It had a tiny covered front porch with three black wrought-iron posts. A white plastic chair squatted near the door with what looked like a coffee can next to it. A yellow lawn tractor sat in the middle of the uncut yard, Johnson grass sprouting through its wheels.

"Drive around back," Zack told her. "I always park in the back and go in the kitchen door."

Her tires crunched on the gravel of the driveway as she followed his instructions. The sound of the crackling stone seemed unnaturally loud in the honeysuckle-scented night.

The lights of her car skipped across an old Pontiac Sunbird propped on concrete blocks and a Ford 150 pickup parked at the back of the property. The nearest neighbor appeared to be miles away. Frogs, crickets, and cicadas created a deafening cacophony in the woods that surrounded the house on three sides.

Just what I need, she thought with a wicked smile.

Zack opened the passenger door, fell out of the car, and lay sprawled on the grass. She leaned over to see what had happened and laughed.

"It's not funny." He dragged himself up by the doorframe. "I stood up too fast. My medication makes me feel dizzy."

She opened her door and grabbed her purse.

Zack gained equilibrium by placing one hand on her car's roof, and the other on the top of the door. "My keys are in here somewhere." Fumbling in his pockets, he pulled out a ring of clanking keys and held them high.

She walked around the hood and reached for the keys, but he yanked them out of her reach. Throwing a heavy arm across her shoulders, he said, "Come here, pretty lady."

The full moon spotlighted their progress as they weaved up the steps. After several failed attempts, Zack unlocked and opened the door.

She walked into the kitchen and shook her head with disgust. *Shit, it looks like a fraternity house after a party.*

Zack staggered to the bedroom and fell on the unmade bed.

She followed him into the room. *When did Zack last change these sheets?* She felt repulsed.

She got on the bed and straddled him with her knees. He reached up, grabbed the front of her shirt, and ripped it open. "I like it rough," he grunted.

She wondered where the shy guy she'd first met was hiding. *Apply booze and create a monster.*

"I like that you don't wear a bra, it makes things easier." With work-roughened hands, he explored her body and then pulled her down to suckle her breasts. When he came up for air, she sat erect and ripped his shirt open. Buttons flew in all directions, pinging off the walls and tinkling on the hardwood floor.

Crawling off, she gyrated her hips in a bump and grind as she performed a striptease. Zach's gaze remained glued to her every movement. She leaned over, breasts swaying, and unbuckled his belt. He scrambled out of his jeans and boxers. Her eyes widened at the sight of his length and girth.

Before she could put a condom on him, Zack stood, wavering, and picked her up. She wrapped her legs around his waist. Holding her ass, he staggered a few feet to the dresser and set her on top. Leering at the reflection in the mirror, he pulled her to the edge and thrust deep inside her.

Already slick with desire, the Huntress cried out with pleasure and clawed his back. Blood seeped from the scratches and trickled down. Ramming her hard, he wrapped one arm around her and squeezed her breast with the other in time with his thrusts.

They reached a crescendo at the same moment. She collapsed against him, her chest heaving. Sated, he slid out of her, dripping semen on the floor, and pushed away from her.

He collapsed on his back among the crumpled sheets, smiling, in a partial stupor.

She slid off the dresser and reached in her purse for her father's handcuffs. Crawling back onto the bed, she examined the headboard. It was solid wood, except for a thick decorative pole in the center. Sitting astride him, she maneuvered his hands toward the pole. Her breasts dangled near his mouth as she stretched to handcuff him to it. The click of the cuffs triggered a flashback.

****

"No, please don't hurt her. I'll make you happy," Chastity pleaded, trying to drag her father away from her sister.

"Get off me, Baby Girl. Melissa has to learn her place." He shook her off his arm, placed his palm in the center of her chest, and pushed her to the floor.

Melissa fought like a cat, with flailing arms and legs, teeth and nails. Their father was too strong. He threw Melissa face-down on the bed and pinned her with his weight. After cuffing her to the iron bedstead, he shoved pillows under her to raise her hips. Bile rose in Chastity's throat as she listened to her sister's futile attempts to avoid her fate.

"I wouldn't have to do it this way, Melissa, if you took your birth control pills and cooperated like your sister." He crawled off the bed and started undressing. "Baby Girl, get those clothes off, sit over there, and play with yourself where I can see you. You know what I like."

Tears running down her face, Chastity stripped and climbed on the bed. She placed her back to the headboard and spread her legs, facing her father. She had no choice. If she didn't, he would get mad and hurt Melissa worse.

"Keep those eyes open, Baby Girl. I want you to watch. I like it when you watch."

Smearing cooking oil on his penis with his hand, he spread Melissa's cheeks apart and rammed himself inside her. Melissa screamed, her face red and contorted.

With each stroke, he grunted and she whimpered. The assault completed, he withdrew. Melissa collapsed, sobbing.

"It's your fault. I can't take a chance on you getting pregnant. Stick your butt back up in the air."

Melissa sobbed and cringed, shaking her head.

"Get it up, or I'll stick it up your ass instead, your choice. I don't know why you make me do this to you."

Shaking, tears and snot dripping to the sheets, she crawled to her knees.

"You'll thank me for this someday, when you find a husband. You'll be all broke in and ready to go."

Grabbing his nightstick, he raped her with it.

****

Zack's eyes snapped open. "You like it rough too, hon'? Well, you'll have to give me a little time to recover." Raising his head, he attached his mouth to her aching breast. Her vagina tingled. Rubbing against him, she climaxed again.

She pulled free and smiled with sadistic glee. "You don't know rough, yet."

CHAPTER 56 - THE CHASE

Charlie hurried back to her car, keeping low so as not to be seen. *I don't understand what Melissa is doing here?* She reached her Honda and peered over the fender of the black pickup parked next to her. Melissa's car was still idling.

The man and woman in the dark green Mustang convertible turned left out of the parking lot. Melissa's Cherokee pulled forward and turned in the same direction.

Charlie scrambled to her feet and fumbled her car key into the door lock with a shaking hand. She tumbled into her car, sped through the parking lot, and turned left.

There they are! Charlie spotted the Mustang and Melissa's SUV several blocks ahead. She followed them at a distance down University Drive. Her quarry turned onto Jordan Lane with Melissa five car lengths behind. *I think she's following the same Mustang I am.*

Staying back, Charlie pursued both vehicles, feeling both frightened and foolish. Her mind raced. *What am I going to do when I catch this mystery woman? What will I say if she calls the police? Even worse, what if Melissa is involved in these murders?*

They left Huntsville behind, and the road turned into Highway 53. The Mustang turned right on a street marked by a closed gas station on the corner. Slowing to a crawl, Melissa turned into the gas station and stopped.

Charlie drove past, hurried down the road to a break in the median, and executed an illegal U-turn. By the time she headed back in the right direction, Melissa was already turning down the street to follow the Mustang.

Charlie turned off her lights and followed. Aided by the moon's light, she crept down the pavement, taking care not to trigger her brake lights.

Taillights flashed red some way ahead of her. When she reached the area where she thought she'd seen them, she saw the Cherokee parked in the front yard of a small white house. Melissa was nowhere in sight.

Charlie drove on to the end of the street, where an abandoned wreck of a house leaned close to collapse, its caved-in roof yawning in the moonlight like a hungry mouth. She used its driveway to turn around. Then, with all the stealth she could muster, she eased the Honda to the edge of the woods surrounding the white house and yanked hard on the parking brake to stop its forward momentum. She shoved the gearshift into park, powered down her window to listen for danger, and turned off the ignition.

She turned off the dome light and slipped out of the car. She closed the door as quietly as she could and stood for a moment to listen again for anything that might forewarn of danger.

The sounds of the insects and frogs in the area deafened her, drowning out the thunder of her galloping heart. Her tongue felt glued to the roof of her dry mouth. She shoved her keys and phone into the pockets of her jeans and tried to decide what to do next.

CHAPTER 57 - HELP ARRIVES

Chastity reached in her bag, tore off a piece of hot pink duct tape, and placed it over Zack's mouth, enjoying the dawning panic in his eyes. Gliding from the room, she opened the back door and let in her twin sister.

"What took you so long?" asked Melissa. She was holding their dead father's black nightstick.

"I was enjoying myself," said Chastity. "This one's a live-wire, and he's hung like a horse."

"I fail to see what you find so fascinating about dicks." Melissa leaned over and kissed her sister's mouth. Her eyes darkened when she saw the red marks on Chastity's breasts. "He hurt you. That asshole hurt you. He'll pay for that."

Chastity smiled with malicious delight. "I agree. He must be punished."

Melissa strode into the bedroom behind Chastity, slapping the nightstick in her hand. Zack shifted his gaze from one identical twin to the other, his eyes going wide. Chastity could smell his terror. *Good. He deserves to feel fear, just the way we did.*

CHAPTER 58 - SNEAKING A PEEK

Charlie tiptoed toward the house, avoiding the gravel driveway and keeping close to the cover of the woods. Fireflies twinkled around her as she moved through the tall damp grass, the faint noise of her steps lost in the sounds of nature that seemed to move in waves through the woods. She swatted at a mosquito that buzzed past her face, uncomfortably aware of the way the saturated bottoms of her jeans clung cold against her lower legs.

Bam!

Charlie flinched, her hand flying to her mouth to hold in a scream. *That came from inside the house.*

Crouching low, she scuttled crab-like toward the house. When she reached it, she stood and flattened herself against the side of the dew-dampened siding. Aware she was hyperventilating, Charlie stopped and placed a hand on her chest. *Calm down.* When she regained control, she strained to hear inside. The rising and falling cadence of the insects drowned out any conversation from within the house.

Hunkering low, she eased over to a window and peeped inside. She saw a kitchen with dirty dishes piled high in the sink and an empty pizza delivery box lying open on a table. Ducking out of sight, she let her eyes adjust to the dark. Bending even lower, she crawled under the window to the other side.

She was standing to go to the next window when her right knee popped. She froze. *Did they hear that?* She stood and listened, rubbing her knee. After a few minutes, she shuffled toward the next lit window.

Once again, she dropped to one knee. Grasping the windowsill for balance, she stole a glance inside.

CHAPTER 59 - ZACK MEETS THE CUTTER

Melissa had her hair pulled up into a ponytail, which swished like a pendulum with her every move. Chastity watched as she stripped off her clothes, folded them into a neat pile, gathered Chastity's clothes, and placed both sets of clothes outside the room. Bloodstains were difficult to remove from clothing. They'd discovered that after the first murder.

Zack was staring at the policeman's baton in Melissa's hand as if hypnotized.

Melissa slapped the stick on her other palm. "Isn't this every man's dream — identical twins?"

Chastity grinned to see Zack flinch. She gestured toward her twin. "Zack, my name's Chastity, and this is my sister, Melissa." She reached over and dragged her long nails down his chest, leaving bloody claw marks.

"I hear you like rough sex, Zack. Is that true?" Melissa slammed the nightstick against the headboard near his head, denting the wood. It sounded like an explosion in the small room.

His eyes looked ready to pop from their sockets. His chest heaved as he thrashed, trying to escape.

"Let me tell you what we're going to do to you tonight," Melissa crooned. "First, I'm going to ram this baton up your ass, so you'll know how it feels to have a big dick rammed inside you." She created a circle between her index finger and thumb, sliding the black stick in and out.

Zack shook his head, eyes pleading. The pink tape reduced his begging to a muffled garble.

"I'm not going to be nice to you, the way my daddy was nice to me. Noooo. I'm not going to grease it down first." She gave him a malicious grin and repeated the in-out pantomime.

Zack's eyes were glued to the two-foot-long nightstick. He was sweating heavily.

"Then I'm going to make you feel pain like you've never felt before." Melissa slapped the baton into her hand again. "You've been a bad boy, so you deserve to be punished."

Zack twisted and bucked. Blood slid down his forearms where the cuffs sliced his flesh.

Eyes gleaming, Melissa lowered her voice into a menacing tone. "Then I'm going to cut off your bad boys and stuff them down your throat."

She reached into Chastity's bag and drew out a long, gleaming butcher knife. The light glinted off the ten-inch steel blade as she waved it around, grinning like a maniac. She laid it on the dresser. Turning back toward him, she pulled her lips back in a hideous caricature of a smile. "You see, Zack, Chastity's the Huntress, but I'm the Cutter. We're like female lions, we hunt and kill as a team."

Zack kicked out at Melissa, missing her by inches. Chastity inhaled, her hand covering her mouth, as her sister's eyes narrowed. Melissa had a vicious temper when she was drunk.

Snarling, Melissa cracked the baton on his knee. His eyes bulged, and he screamed behind the duct tape.

Chastity gave Zack a wicked grin. "That's right Zack. You're going to die." She turned and sat down on the bedrooms lone chair. "Don't worry. It won't be fast."

He mumbled from behind the tape. As he struggled, the handcuffs sliced him more.

Chastity laughed with excitement, increasingly aroused by Zack's pain and terror. She glanced over at her sister and saw a demented look creeping into Melissa's eyes. "No need to hurry, Melissa," she soothed. "We have plenty of time."

A rattling sound caught Chastity's attention. She leaped to her feet when she saw Zack grasp the pole he was cuffed to with both his hands.

He heaved with his full weight. The center pole broke free with a *crack*.

Chastity screamed. With a muffled roar, Zack gripped the pole in his shackled hands and swung at a surprised Melissa like a power batter in the major leagues. The pole slammed into Melissa's jaw, knocking her sideways. She hit the floor in a heap, out cold.

Chastity couldn't stop screaming. Zack gathered himself and turned to face her. The rage in his face froze her, as though her feet were nailed to the hardwood floor. Zack rose and swung, grazing the side of her head with the damaged pole.

Chastity swayed, seeing double. She was dimly aware of her blood spraying across Zack's face as pieces of broken pole went flying. Pain flashed to life and burned a path across her head, nauseating her. She dropped to the floor, cradling her bleeding head in her hands.

Unable to move, she watched as he fell back on the bed, his face contorted in pain. He struggled to a sitting position and peeled up one corner of the duct tape on his face. Grasping it between his large fingers, he took a deep breath and yanked.

"Ahhh!" Hair and skin ripped from his face, leaving a red rash.

With a grunt, Zack managed to get off the bed. He started to run, but his knee gave way. He crashed to the floor with a yelp of pain. "Damn!" He cradled his knee in his palms and rocked from one side to the other.

Chastity sobbed, head in her hands, as she watched Zack drag himself, clawing with his hands, to the living room. His retreating form was blurring in and out of focus.

She knew she'd ripped the phone from the wall. *We have time.*

"Son of a bitch!" she heard him yell from the living room. *I have to get up and stop him….*

CHAPTER 60 - STUNNED

Charlie stood stunned, unable to process what she was seeing. Melissa, her patient, was naked and slapping a round black stick in the palm of her hand. *If she's the killer, then the guy I saw leave in the green car is probably handcuffed to a bed in that room.*

She saw Melissa raise the black stick and move out of sight. She heard the crack of breaking bone and a man's muffled shriek.

Lightheaded, Charlie dug her nails into the vinyl on the windowsill to steady herself. Her mouth tasted bitter. She heard Melissa's voice in her mind, *"I don't care who I hurt."*

Dear God, help me. What should I do? She prayed silently. *Ryan!*

Tugging her phone from her jeans, she sprinted away from the house to call him. When she got him on the line, she recounted what she'd seen in an urgent whisper.

"What the hell are you doing there?" Ryan bellowed.

"She's going to kill him if you don't do something," Charlie warned him. She gave him the address and hung up to call 911 as he'd directed. Then she hastened back to the window and chanced another look.

She heard a scream and a muffled roar. Melissa staggered into view, holding her face, and fell to the floor with a thud. Someone was screaming.

Charlie wondered, *Who is killing whom?* Without a weapon, she felt helpless. *Why did I leave my pepper spray in the car?*

She hunched over and scrambled toward the front of the house, trying to avoid the gravel drive that might give away her location. Her foot slid in the wet grass, and she slammed facedown onto the ground, the air knocked from her lungs. She clawed at the vinyl siding to pull herself up. Swaying on noodle knees, she coughed and sucked in air, then staggered onward, still fighting for each breath.

She had just made it to the front yard when the front door banged open. She froze, hoping her stillness would hide her. A massive naked man stood silhouetted in the doorway. Moonlight glinted off handcuffs as he hobbled out, using a large stick as a crutch. He half-slid down the front stairs, swearing and howling with pain.

When he saw her, his eyes grew round with alarm. Fueled by high-octane adrenaline, Charlie raced to the man. "We have to get out of here before she kills us both. Let me help you. My car's over there."

She half-dragged him to her car. Leaning him against the back door, she unlocked her car, opened the door, and stuffed him inside. He yelped with pain and cursed like a demon.

She eased the door closed and jumped in the driver's seat. The car stuttered when she turned the key.

"Not now, dammit!" she cried in frustration, tears wetting her cheeks. She swiped at them, shot an apprehensive glance toward the house, and tried again. It coughed once and died.

Banging on the steering wheel, she begged, "Come on baby, start. Please God, let it start."

The engine roared to life. Charlie rammed her foot on the gas pedal, fishtailing down the street. She could smell the burning rubber from the friction of her tires.

"I'm Dr. Charlie Stone," she gasped, still short of breath. "I'm a consultant for the Huntsville Police Department. Is there a neighbor nearby who can help us?"

"Turn right at the next road," said the naked man. He was cradling his bloody knee.

The tires squealed as she turned the corner. She raced down the street.

"Turn right into this driveway," he bellowed.

Whipping the wheel to the right, she skidded to a stop, leaving a plume of dust from the gravel drive behind her.

"The Taylors live here."

Charlie nodded and fumbled with the door handle.

"Thanks for saving me back there."

"Thank me later…"

"I'm Zack."

"Right. For now, we need to get you some help, Zack."

CHAPTER 61 -SLEDGEHAMMER OF PAIN

Chastity opened her eyes. The light caused jolts of pain to zing through her head. She closed them to reduce the agony, while she tried to remember what had happened.

Fuck! She sat up to look around. A sledgehammer of pain hit her, and she rolled to her side to vomit. After a moment, she lifted shaking fingers to probe the spot that pounded near her temple. She flinched in pain when she touched it. Pulling her hand away, she stared at her bloody fingers. *My blood.* She watched, fascinated, as more blood dripped to the floor.

A groan near the foot of the bed caught her attention.

Melissa struggled to a sitting position, holding her jaw with one hand. She, too, leaned over and heaved. Wiping her mouth with the back of her hand, she slurred, "I'm gonna kill that sonofabitch, but he's gonna suffer first." She explored the swollen contusion on the right side of her face.

In a quavering voice, Chastity said, "Melissa."

Melissa looked up. "Chastity?"

Chastity shifted to wedge herself in the corner for support and put both hands to her head. "I'm hurt." She started crying, her tears mingling with the blood was still spattering on the wood floor.

Through vision blurred by her head injury and her tears, she watched as Melissa crawled to the bed, clawed her way up, and stood. She swayed like a flower blown by the wind and wobbled to the bathroom. When she reached the doorway, she stopped and retched again.

After a moment, Melissa eased herself down on the side of the tub. She pulled a towel from the rack nearby and wet it using the tub faucet. Clutching the towel, Melissa got to her feet and stood still for several seconds, her free hand holding the wall for support.

Chastity waited as Melissa worked her way to her, once again using the bed for support. At last, Melissa was beside her, wiping the blood from her face with the cool, damp towel.

"Let me see. How bad is it, Chastity? Are you okay?"

"Ow! It hurts — real bad." Chastity sobbed, her chin trembling.

"Don't worry. He'll pay for this. Hold this to your head to stop the bleeding. I busted his kneecap. He won't get far."

Melissa vomited again. "I have to sit on the bed and let my vision clear. Then I'm going to find that guy, and we'll finish what we started."

CHAPTER 62 - THE TAYLOR'S

Frantic with fear, Charlie pounded on the door. Zack struggled up the stairs and collapsed — naked, bloody, and handcuffed — on his neighbor's doorstep.

The light came on. Mrs. Taylor opened the door, looked down, and screamed. "Oh my gosh! John! Come quick! It's Zack!"

John rushed to the door. Pushing his wife aside, he stopped and stared.

"Hell, man, what happened to you?"

Charlie spoke up. "I'm Dr. Charlie Stone, a consultant with the Huntsville Police Department. There's been an attempted murder. Can you get Zack in the house?"

Reaching down, John helped Zack hobble inside.

"Close and lock the door. They tried to kill me!" Zack's voice was hoarse, his expression wild with fear.

John glanced outside to see if anyone was approaching. Then he slammed the door shut and locked it. As he helped Zack hobble to the sofa, he told his wife, "Martha, call 911."

Just then, Zack bumped his injured knee on the coffee table. He clutched his knee, his scream a high keening sound. Charlie watched in helpless dismay as he passed out and slid under the coffee table, bumping his chin on its edge before he reached the floor.

CHAPTER 63 - THE SEARCH

Chastity helped Melissa search the house. Zack was nowhere to be found.

Chastity moaned, "He could be anywhere!" as she struggled into her clothes.

Melissa's face contorted with rage. "How could you let him go!" she shrieked, throwing anything within her reach across the living room.

"It wasn't my fault!" Chastity screamed back. The yelling made her head hurt. She reached up, pressing her hands over her eyes until the nausea passed. Her throat felt raw.

Melissa handed Chastity her purse. "We've got to catch him. Come on."

They stumbled down the front stairs, clinging to the railing for support.

"I'll check the back." Chastity ran her hand along the side of the house for support as she waded through the damp grass to her car, still parked where she'd left it near the rear porch. She opened the back door and bent to retrieve her flashlight from the floorboard of the back seat. Excruciating pain blurred her vision, and a wave of nausea slammed into her stomach. Bile gushed from her mouth onto the beige upholstery of her back seat. *My Mustang! What next?*

Still retching from the smell, Chastity straightened and closed the door. Flashlight in hand, she stumbled toward the abandoned vehicles on blocks. After fifteen minutes or so, she gave up and returned to the front of the house, where she found her sister sitting in a lawn chair near the front porch.

"We lost him," said Chastity, her spirit sinking with defeat. "We lost him." She could feel panic creeping up on her.

"Shut up!" Melissa snapped. "Let's get our stuff out of the house, and get the hell out of here."

All Chastity could think was, *I can't go to jail. What're we going to do?*

They returned to the house, and in a frenzy, gathered their things.

CHAPTER 64 - HELP IS ON THE WAY

Charlie sank down on the sofa before her legs could give way under her, her nerves still singing with adrenaline. Her wet jeans were smeared with mud and blood.

Martha rushed past her to place a blanket over Zack, who was still lying unconscious under the coffee table. John shifted the table out of the way, so that she could cover him.

"At least he's not feeling any pain," Martha said, as she ran to the house phone. She punched in 911.

Charlie leaned over and pressed her fingers against his neck to check his pulse. Then she lifted each eyelid to check his pupils. "His pulse is steady, and his pupils are equal and reactive."

John nodded, grabbed the phone from Martha's trembling hand, and told the operator the nature of the emergency and his address. "We need an ambulance. His knee is injured, and he has blood all over him." John's tone became gruff. "Hell, lady, I don't know where the blood came from."

Charlie shifted a throw pillow, dug her phone from her pocket, and speed-dialed Ryan.

Ryan answered. "Charlie, where are you and what's happening?"

"I have Zack, that's the victim, at a neighbor's house. We called 911, and they're sending an ambulance. Melissa busted his knee. It looks like he'll need surgery." Charlie told Ryan the Taylors' address. "It's one street north of the crime scene."

"Are you all right?"

"Other than high on terror, I'm fine. When will you be here?"

"I'm only two miles away, and a Limestone Sherriff's deputy is en route. I'll call you when I know something more."

Martha stepped in front of Charlie, leaned over and handed her a glass of water.

"Thanks." Charlie realized she had blood on her hands. She took a sip and set the glass down on a coaster. "Martha, may I use your restroom?" She held her hands out for inspection.

"Certainly, dear. Follow me."

Helping Charlie to her feet, she led her to the bathroom, gave her a washcloth and towel, and left. Charlie washed the blood from her face and hands. Toweling dry, she felt better.

She heard the sirens and dashed out of the bathroom.

CHAPTER 65 - IT'S THE COPS

Chastity and Melissa were leaving the house when they heard the sirens. They froze for an instant and stared at each other.

Chastity wailed, "Oh God, what're we going to do?"

Melissa gave her a grim look. "We run now and set up in another state. Get in my Jeep!"

Charged by panic, Chastity yanked open the door of Melissa's Jeep and threw her things into the back seat. As Melissa fastened her seatbelt, she scrambled into the front passenger seat.

Gravel sprayed in all directions as they accelerated out of the driveway. The rear end of Melissa's SUV fishtailed, then the vehicle found traction and barreled down the road.

Wrenching the steering wheel, Melissa made the turn onto Highway 53. The Jeep rounded the corner on two wheels, throwing Chastity against the passenger door.

Chastity was the first to spot the police car. It was coming from the other direction, slowing to turn from the main road to the road they'd just left. "Ohmygod, it's a cop!"

"Shit!" said Melissa. She slammed her foot on the gas and accelerated to a dangerous speed as the patrol car screeched to a halt.

"What're we going to do? What're we going to do?" Chastity screamed. She squirmed around and clutched the headrest, squinting to see out the rear window. She sagged back into her seat. "He's following us."

"We're going to keep going," said Melissa. "We have no choice. Do you want to go to jail?"

"No," Chastity whispered, clutching the dash.

CHAPTER 66 - THE PURSUIT

Charlie heard the siren reverse directions.

"Sounds like the sheriff's deputy is in pursuit," said John.

Zack had regained consciousness and was sitting on the floor, his back propped against the sofa. He rubbed his chin with a confused look.

"Can you take care of Zack?" Charlie asked the Taylors.

"Well, sure." Martha nodded and pulled the belt tighter on her robe.

Charlie knelt beside Zack. "The police are going to need your statement. While it's fresh in your mind, try to write down everything you can remember about tonight." She stood. "Better yet, do a voice recording on the Taylors' smartphone, if you can."

Zack nodded. Charlie grabbed her purse and phone.

She was yelling Ryan's name at Siri when John asked, "Where're you going?"

"To help catch a killer." She raced out the door and down the steps.

Ryan answered.

"What's happening?" she demanded.

"Joe's on his way. The suspects just turned onto Highway 53, heading toward Ardmore. A sheriff's deputy is pursuing them. I'm almost there."

"I see you!" She waved at him.

He skidded to a halt in the Taylors' drive. She hopped in and fastened her seatbelt, as he backed up and screeched down the road like his gas tank was on fire. As Ryan turned onto Highway 53 toward Ardmore, Charlie spotted an ambulance racing toward the intersection.

CHAPTER 67 - STOP!

Utility poles flashed by at blinding speed. Chastity began to hyperventilate as she eyed the speedometer. Melissa was barreling down Highway 53, a narrow two-lane road that led to Ardmore, at ninety miles an hour.

Melissa adjusted her seatbelt. "If we can get into Ardmore, we can cross over into Tennessee. They won't be able to stop us once we hit I-65. We can jump off the interstate, find some back country roads and be home free." She glanced at Chastity and focused back on the road.

Stiff with fear, Chastity nodded yes. That was a mistake. The motion caused her vision to swim and her head to ache even more.

"I think I have a concussion." Chastity forced the words past the golf-ball-sized lump in her throat.

"I think that asshole broke my jaw. It hurts like hell. Why the fuck didn't you handcuff him better?" Melissa was gripping the wheel so tightly her knuckles were white.

"It's not my fault the headboard fell apart." Chastity rubbed her forehead.

Melissa entered Ardmore and slowed to seventy miles an hour. The speed limit sign flashed past — 45 mph.

Chastity turned again, kneeling in her seat to check the progress of the sheriff's car behind them. An idea struck her. She reached between the seats, stretching to snag the strap of her purse on the back seat. Dropping back into her seat, she dug through her purse for her smartphone. She turned it on and brought up a map program to search for possible escape routes.

Melissa took her foot off the accelerator. Chastity glanced up and stiffened in her seat. "Cops!"

The flashing blue lights bounced off the windshield of their SUV. The cruiser was blocking the right lane of Railroad Street, the road closest to the concrete train trestle.

Melissa growled, "Shit, they're blocking us from getting to the interstate."

Chastity dropped her phone and dug her nails into the dashboard. "Slow down!"

"I'll ram that police car if necessary." Melissa tightened her grip on the wheel, jammed her foot on the accelerator, and swerved to the left.

Spike strips glinted in the streetlight.

"Stop!" Chastity arched her body, pushing on the floorboard with both feet. The speeding Jeep missed the front fender of the cruiser but hit the spike strips. Chastity shrieked as her hands flew to cover her face.

Air hissing from its tires, the Jeep careened out of control and skidded into the concrete wall supporting the trestle. Metal struck concrete with a sickening crunch.

CHAPTER 68 - THE CAPTURE

Ryan and Charlie pursued the two suspects for miles. Feeling agitated and helpless, Charlie rolled down her window to cool her flushed face. They were approaching the small town of Ardmore when the deputy's car in front of them swerved off the road. Charlie flinched. Digging her nails into the door handle, she pumped the nonexistent brake on the passenger floorboard. The deputy regained control and swerved back onto the road ahead of them.

They entered Ardmore and slowed. Flashing blue lights bounced off the store windows as they passed.

The railroad trestle came into view. Charlie cringed when she saw Melissa's SUV. Its hood was crumpled against the buttercup yellow concrete.

"Good, it looks like Ardmore got the roadblock up in time," said Ryan. He brought the car to a halt beside the deputy's car, close to the scene.

The Ardmore officer moved from behind his vehicle and approached the suspect's car in a crouch, with his weapon grasped in both hands.

"Put your hands on the wheel, now!" The officer bellowed.

Both Ryan and the deputy exited their cars and crouched behind the driver's side doors, their weapons were drawn. Charlie scrambled from the car and ducked behind the rear fender.

The Ardmore officer reached the wrecked Jeep and looked in the window. He raised his hand as a signal and yelled, "All clear," as he holstered his automatic.

Charlie saw Ryan holster his weapon and sprinted to the Jeep. Melissa's battered body lay sprawled across the hood amid glittering particles of safety glass. Her head was twisted at an unnatural angle. Charlie checked for a pulse anyway. Nothing. *She's gone. She must have died on impact.*

"Three to Ardmore, I need to get some responders and an ambulance en route," the officer said into his walkie-talkie.

Its speaker crackled. "Roger that."

The officer nodded a greeting to Charlie. Leaning in, he checked the driver's pulse. "This one's still alive."

Ryan came up to the Jeep and looked in. "I'm surprised she didn't wreck before now. She was driving like a demon escaping from hell." He shook his head.

The deputy radioed the situation to his Lawrence County dispatcher. Blue lights and sirens pierced the predawn darkness.

CHAPTER 69 - TWINS

Charlie moved to the driver's window and looked in. She sucked in a breath as she saw the two-inch burn scar on the forearm of the woman behind the wheel. She looked back at the body on the hood. *That's not Melissa. Melissa's alive!*

She reached in and took Melissa's hand. She could tell by her labored breathing that it took Melissa's complete focus to take her next breath.

"Chastity…where's…Chastity?" Melissa coughed up blood.

"I'm sorry, Melissa, she's gone." Charlie squeezed her hand. Easing her hand up her wrist, she felt Melissa's thready pulse.

"Dr. Stone?" Melissa gasped for breath and coughed again.

"Yes, I'm here. Save your breath. Help is on the way."

Blood dribbled down her chin. "Do… you… still believe I can… be saved?"

Tears welled in Charlie's eyes. "Yes, I do."

"God… I'm sorry," she gasped. "Please…. forgive me… my sins."

"I'll pray that God forgives you, too, Melissa," Charlie soothed. "Quiet now. I hear the sirens."

Tears were streaming down Melissa's cheeks. The Ardmore officer, clad in his dark blue uniform, stepped past Charlie and looked at Melissa through the shattered windshield.

Melissa saw him. Fear and despair on her face, she whimpered between gasps, "Don't… hurt me…Daddy. Don't…hurt me… again."

She took one last rattling breath, and her hand went limp in Charlie's grasp.

CHAPTER 70 - CHARLIE FACES JOE

Charlie bowed her head. When she raised it, tears tracked down both cheeks. She released Melissa's arm and looked one more time at Melissa and the twisted body on the hood. *Twins. Melissa never told me her sister was an identical twin.*

Melissa, in a tee shirt and jeans with her hair pulled back in a ponytail, was dressed as she had for so many therapy sessions. *Only this time, she's covered in blood.*

The Ardmore officer stepped closer to Charlie. "She's just died, ma'am, they're both dead. Did you know them?"

"I knew the driver." The tears dripped unheeded off Charlie's chin. She felt shattered, like the broken glass scattered across the crumpled hood of the Jeep, as she stepped back to let the emergency personnel do their job.

Ryan stepped past her and leaned in closer to compare the two bodies. "I'll be damned. They're identical." He scrubbed his face with his hand and shook his head.

Releasing her breath in a sigh, Charlie palmed the tears off her face. Her shoulders slumped. She felt deflated and raw. It was a blow to realize that one of the killers had been in a therapy session with her just a few days before, and she had never realized it. *Melissa wasn't the type to dress up and seduce men. Janice seemed the most likely candidate to be a seductress.* An expression Charlie's father had often used came to mind. *"If it had been a snake, it would have bitten me."*

The EMT's were pulling Melissa's body from the Jeep when Joe arrived on the scene with his sirens blazing and slid to a stop. He climbed out and lumbered toward the wreck. When he reached Ryan and Charlie, he stopped and swept his gaze over the bloody wall, down to the limp body on the hood, to then rest on the body being laid on a stretcher.

His jaw dropped. *"There are two of them?"* Upon further inspection, he exclaimed, "They're identical twins!"

Ryan nodded, rubbing the back of his neck.

"Did they kill the guy?" asked Joe.

Charlie straightened her shoulders and shoved her hair out of her face. "No, but they sure as hell tried. Zack is on his way to the hospital with a shattered kneecap. I asked him to start writing out his statement, while his memory is fresh."

Squinting at Charlie, Joe asked, "What are *you* doing here? What do you know about this? I thought I made it clear that you're off the case."

Charlie stood tall and lifted her chin. "Why Joe, I was solving *your* murder case, saving a man's life, and clearing my name. I did a killer job of it, too." She spun on her heel and stalked away.

"Well, I'll be damned," Joe said behind her. "I'll bet we have our killers. This wreck will save the taxpayers the cost of a jury trial. I only wish I knew why they did this."

Charlie stopped and turned in time to see Joe shake his head as if the whole situation baffled him. *I have a pretty damn good idea why* she thought. *Due to the laws requiring confidentiality, I may be one of the few who will ever understand.* Aloud, she said only, "Violence begets violence, Joe."

"Ain't that the truth?" Joe nodded and hitched up his pants.

Ryan walked to Charlie and took her hand, "Are you okay? You're crying." He studied her face for a moment. "You knew her, didn't you?" he whispered.

"Don't ask me questions you know I can't answer." She walked into his arms and sobbed, not caring who saw her in his embrace.

CHAPTER 71 - ENDINGS AND BEGINNINGS

It was a breezy, sunny day. Charlie and Ryan held hands as they zigzagged their way among the graves to the twins' funeral tent. One of those modern memory gardens, it was blanketed with flat granite grave markers and devoid of trees. The deceased would bake for all of eternity beneath the blazing southern sun.

Ryan shielded his eyes to look up at the contrail left by a passing jet. "It's funny how things turned out."

"Funny, 'ha, ha' or funny 'peculiar'?" Charlie chose her path with care, trying to avoid sinking her black dress heels into the red clay.

Ryan squeezed her hand. "Funny, like strange."

"I agree. One minute, Captain Strouper was chewing me up one side and down the other for doing surveillance without backup while I was off the case. The next minute, he nominated me for a medal of commendation and asked me to join his Sexual Assault Task Force."

"Yes, that *was* strange. Then there's Joe." Ryan shook his head.

"I couldn't believe he apologized." She stopped and looked up at Ryan, smiling. "You think Sarah beat him with her purse until he agreed to apologize?"

Ryan smiled back. "I believe you impressed him. He was shocked after you gave him your statement. When he received Zack's written statement, even Joe admitted that you used your head and kept your cool under pressure."

Charlie shook her head. "I wasn't cool," she told him. "I was terrified."

When they reached the tent, there were five mourners, and two flower arrangements, one of which Charlie was sure was hers. The twins would lie next to their mother and father, a broken family once again united.

The priest gave a short, generic eulogy, the kind given when the minister had never met the deceased. He shut his Bible and offered condolences to an older lady seated in a chair at the front. Turning to clap the funeral director on the back, he ambled away, soon followed by everyone but the lady, whose hair was the color of raw cotton.

She rose with difficulty from the metal chair and shuffled to the coffins, across the bright green fake grass covering the gravesite. Bowing her head, she placed a hand on each before making the sign of the cross. When she turned, Charlie saw that she was weeping. She looked exhausted, with dark smudges under her eyes.

Charlie stepped with care over the uneven ground and offered her hand to the woman, intending to give her condolences.

Ryan trailed behind her.

The woman took her hand. "I'm Lucy Smither, are you Dr. Stone?"

Charlie paused, surprised that this woman knew her name. "Yes, and this is Detective Ryan Roberts." Charlie gestured toward Ryan, who had moved to her side.

Ms. Smither shook Ryan's extended hand and turned back to Charlie. "I'm Melissa and Chastity's, aunt. Thank you for the lovely flowers."

"I only wish I could've done more."

"I raised them after their father's death," Ms. Smither went on. "Melissa told me about you. I received the impression she gave you a hard time at the beginning."

Charlie remembered the session where Melissa had almost made her lose her professional calm by playing with that gum wrapper. Her glance slid over to the caskets. "I'll admit there were times …" She shook her head. "Melissa appreciated what you did for them."

Ms. Smither smiled, but it didn't lift the anguish from her eyes. "She would be glad to know you cared enough to attend her funeral. Did you know Chastity, too?"

The image of Chastity's broken body lying on the hood of the Jeep flashed through Charlie's mind. "No, I never met her." *Not alive, anyway.*

Ms. Smither nodded. "Melissa and I talked a few weeks ago. She said she told you some things about her childhood, and that her nightmares stopped." A tear rolled down her wrinkled cheek. "She carried so much pain."

"I'm glad I was of some help," Charlie replied. "I only wish I had known her before all this started. Maybe we could have worked through what was wrong so that no one would have died."

Reaching into her large leather handbag, Ms. Smither pulled out a fat brown envelope and handed it to Charlie. "These are Melissa's diaries. I planned to bury them with her, but I think she would want you to have them because you're someone who would understand."

Charlie took the envelope, surprised by its weight. "Are you sure you don't want to keep them?"

"No. I read several pages and couldn't bring myself to read the rest." Ms. Smither paused and glanced back at the coffins. "I prefer to remember them as teenagers. Please read them. My girls weren't all bad." She clutched her purse in a tight grip. "You know, I never had any children of my own. The girls were all I had."

Charlie slid the envelope into her purse and slung it back onto her shoulder. "If there's information here that could help the FBI's Behavioral Science Unit, may I share it?"

Ms. Smither nodded. "Those diaries belong to you now. If you think it could save lives, share them."

Charlie took her hand and held it for a few minutes. They looked into each other's eyes, two women who had tried to rescue a pair of damaged girls but failed.

"Thank you for trying to save Melissa." Holding a tissue to her mouth, Ms. Smither turned and walked to a white car.

Charlie sat in the metal chair Ms. Smither had vacated. *It's still warm.*

Ryan sat beside her and reached for her hand. She sat for some time thinking about life and death.

At last, Ryan squeezed her hand. "Charlie, are you okay?"

Charlie returned the squeeze. "You've been asking that a lot, lately."

The grave workers lowered the caskets into the ground. Each thumped as it reached the concrete vault.

"You seem fragile. I'm sure it was a shock to discover that one of the killers was also your patient."

The funeral director and the grave workers loitered in the shade at the rear of the tent, waiting for them to leave so that they could complete their task.

Charlie stepped forward and knelt between the two graves. She grabbed handfuls of red clay in both hands and slowly crumbled it into both graves while she prayed for the twins. In her mind she said, *Melissa and Chastity, I wish I had known you as children. I wish I could have helped you both.*

At last, she dusted off her hands, rose to her feet, and brushed off the knees of her pants. She turned and nodded to the caretakers of the deceased. Then she walked over to where Ryan stood and took his hand.

As they strolled back to the car, she said, "You never did explain how you discovered that Melissa was my patient. That was confidential information."

"When I ran the Twins' priors, Melissa's conviction for DUI came up, along with the name of her probation officer," Ryan told her. "I placed a courtesy call to Constance to let her know she could close her file. She told me that she thought Melissa was doing better since she'd started the outpatient program with you as her therapist."

Charlie stopped and looked up at Ryan. "When you work in substance abuse treatment, there are always patients in your program who will die. Addiction is a hungry monster. I've had patients die from health problems, suicides, accidents, and drug deals that went bad. I've never had a patient who was a murderer."

Ryan nudged her. "At least that you know about."

Charlie nodded. "True. Have you ever heard any of the light bulb jokes?"

"Yeah."

"There's one about psychologists, and I finally understand the answer."

Ryan tilted his head. "What's the answer?"

"It only takes one psychologist to change a light bulb, but the bulb has to want to change." A strange chill ran up her spine and enveloped her, causing her to shiver. She turned to see if someone was behind her. No one was there.

Ryan stopped and turned to follow her gaze. "And if the light bulb doesn't want to change?"

"It extinguishes itself." Tears glistened in her eyes, threatening to cascade down her cheeks at any moment. She paused a moment to gain control of herself.

"This one hit me hard, Ryan. I'm burned-out, and I'm ready for a change."

Ryan held her by the shoulders. "You aren't going to stop consulting, are you?"

"No, I don't think so…I'm not sure. I need to get away to think. Captain Strouper wants to talk to me tomorrow about expanding my role with the department. I know that I want to stop working with substance abusers. I'm tired of seeing people commit slow suicide."

Charlie swiped at the tears that had begun streaming down her cheeks. Ryan handed her his clean handkerchief. This brought a brief watery smile to her face, but then she lost control and sobbed, shoulders heaving. Ryan folded her into his arms and rocked her.

Resting his chin on the top of her head, he said, "There's some good news. Zack was released from the hospital today. He's one lucky guy that you showed up when you did."

"I don't know what I would've done if he hadn't gotten loose. The only weapon I had was pepper spray, and it was in my car. Captain Strouper was right, what I did was stupid. Thank God it worked out." Charlie wiped mascara from under her eyes.

"Zack signed a statement identifying the twins as the ones who attacked him. All three cases are now closed."

They reached the car. Smiling, Ryan led Charlie to the passenger door and opened it. "I think you need a jolt of Java."

Charlie slid into the seat and smiled up at him. "Leave it to you, Ryan Roberts, to see coffee as a cure to all that ails the world."

Ryan cocked a brow. "You mean it's not?"

"My friend Marti is convinced it's salsa."

Ryan laughed.

As Ryan drove to Mullins, Charlie turned her mind from the dead and considered the future. She knew she had a long journey ahead of her. Some hard decisions loomed about her life and career. *At least I won't be alone,* she thought. *There are my friends here and in Birmingham, and Spanky.* She glanced to her left and smiled. *And now — there's Ryan.*

THE END

253

Preview of Deadly Lessons

Please enjoy a preview of the next Charlie Stone Crime Thriller.

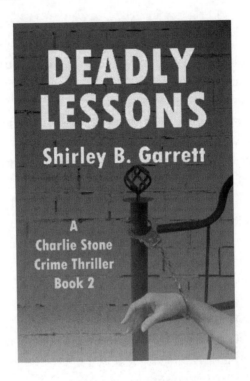

DEADLY LESSONS

CHAPTER 1 — STALKING

"A good person consistently does the right thing at the right time, in the right way, and for the right reason." Aristotle

A red Miata convertible veered into the dimly lit parking lot. The Trainer leaned to the right to get a better view through his van's dirty windshield. One of his legs had fallen asleep, so he rubbed it to ease the burning sensation. He'd been sitting for over an hour waiting for a suitable woman to become his next student.

An elegant blonde clad in a business suit slid out, exposing an expanse of thigh. She beeped the remote lock and walked toward the store with her phone pasted to her ear.

The Trainer shook his head. *There she is, a "Miss Independent Woman." Driving her fancy sports car and wearing a business suit. She's walking in those high heels like she owns the world, and her pussy don't stink.* His hands tightened on the steering wheel. *I'm the one to teach that bitch her place.* As the woman approached, he listened to her conversation through the open window.

"Janie, I need those documents completed by Monday morning. I have to be in court by eight." The woman cocked her head and listened. "I know it's almost ten on Friday night. I didn't say you have to do them tonight, but I need them no later than Sunday." She disconnected the call and dropped the phone into her purse.

Her designer heels tapped a brisk rhythm on the asphalt. She tracked toward the Healthy Foods store like a grocery-seeking missile and disappeared inside.

The Trainer started his white van and pulled it around to back in next to her Miata. His hulking vehicle blocked the view of the tiny car from the store.

He leaned forward and rested his forearms on the steering wheel. *When did all these swanky grocery stores invade Huntsville? When I left Alabama, Winn-Dixie was as fancy as it got.*

Ten minutes later, he spotted the woman through the plate glass window as she approached the self-checkout. Her long, blond hair cascaded past her face as she bent to scan her items.

The Trainer did a visual check of the lot to make sure the area was still clear. Satisfied, he grabbed a plastic bag that contained a cloth pretreated with Sevoflurane, and slipped it into his pocket. He'd stolen a bottle of the anesthetic from a vet's office and had researched how to use it. He'd only used a few drops, but nonetheless was glad the van's windows were open.

His future student strode through the automatic doors into the parking lot.

There's the uppity bitch now. He slipped out of the sliding door and left it open. He'd disabled the interior lights weeks ago. Hiding at the rear of the van, he watched her progress.

The woman shifted both bags to her left hand as she looked down, fumbling with her purse. Focused on fishing out the key fob, she didn't seem to notice the vehicle backed in next to her. She beeped open her Miata.

The Trainer pulled the rag from the plastic bag. A sweet smell permeated the air. He whipped his arms around the startled woman. She managed one gasp before he slapped the cloth over her face and dragged her between the vehicles.

Ducking and squirming, she jammed her foot on top of his. The spiked heel of her shoe slid off his heavy, steel-toed boot.

He widened his stance.

She jabbed him with an elbow.

The Trainer grunted as it scraped his ribs. He shifted the rag over her nose and mouth as she drew a breath to scream. Tightening his hold, he lifted her off the ground.

She kicked both feet into the air.

Off balance, he backed against the side of the van.

A shoe flew off her foot. It thudded off her car and slid to the asphalt. She flailed her arms. A bag clocked the Trainer on the side of the head.

He shook his head to clear his vision. "You stupid cunt!"

He held fast, feeling her struggle lessen as the drug invaded her system. She dropped limp into his arms.

The groceries fell to the ground along with her keys.

Breathing hard, the Trainer eased her down to the pavement. He stood holding his ribs and glanced around. With a grunt, he hefted her into the van and tossed in her purse. He slipped the rag back in the bag and sealed it. After a final glance to check for witnesses, he jumped in and slid the door shut.

The woman moaned, teetering on the edge of consciousness. The Trainer rolled her over and jabbed his knee in her back, to hold her down while he bound her extremities.

The Trainer licked his lips and grinned. "Yessiree, you're gonna figure out who's in charge now, 'Miss Independent Woman.' It's time you learned your place in the world, and I'm the one to teach you."

CHAPTER 2 — CHARLIE'S VISITATION

Darkness spread like India ink as the thick clouds rolled to obscure the moon. Several flat, polished grave markers reflected the fingers of moonlight that poked through the clouds. A dark figure sat cross-legged on one of the graves, backlit by a ray of faint light.

"Who are you?" Charlie Stone dug her nails into the flesh of her crossed arms. *If this is a dream, I need to wake up.*

The figure answered, "I can't move on until I save you."

Charlie darted glances around the cemetery and stepped back. "Save me ... from what?"

The shadowed figure continued, "I must also help you save them. He took the first one."

Charlie shook her head. "Who is 'he' and who did he take?" Damp cold seeped through her clothing and chilled her. She rubbed her arms, trying to dispel it.

The dark figure levitated an inch off the stone. "You'll know soon."

Charlie's eyes went wide and she backed up several steps. "Who are you? Is this a dream?"

The figure held its arms out. "You're more open to me in your dreams. I know now that you tried to help me, that it wasn't psychobabble bullshit. I was too far gone. You know that by now, since you read my diaries while you were at the beach."

Charlie stiffened. *This is not possible.*

"Despite all the bad things that I did, all the people I murdered, you prayed for me." The face remained in shadow and unrecognizable. "I heard what you said about my father on the phone to that cop, Ryan. You're right — a father shouldn't beat and rape his daughter."

Charlie's hands covered her mouth.

"I asked for forgiveness, so I have this chance. I must pay my debt. I'm here to warn you. You tried to save me. Now I'll try to keep you and them from harm — if you'll let me."

"I don't understand…"

The image disintegrated, and the earth reclaimed it with an audible sucking sound. A moonbeam spotlighted the rectangular stone where the shrouded figure had levitated seconds before.

Charlie trod over the uneven ground to read the inscription. The name on the polished stone shook her to the core.

* * *

Charlie shot awake and clutched the covers to her chin. *It's her.* Heart pounding, she fumbled the switch on the lamp and glanced around the room. *I'm home.* A week at the rented condo in Gulf Shores had disoriented her.

After jamming her feet into the moccasins by the bed, Charlie grabbed the robe from the chair, belted it over her sleep shirt, and snatched her phone off the bedside table.

Spanky, her eight-month-old beagle puppy woke and shook herself, tags clanking. She followed Charlie as she checked the rest of the house for intruders.

Satisfied that she was alone, Charlie walked into the living room and collapsed into the recliner. Spanky jumped into her lap and licked her nose before circling to settle with a sigh.

Charlie ran both hands through her long, blond hair. *So much has happened in the past two months. Heck, the last year.*

It all began when Dr. Charlene Stone completed her training with the FBI to become a community psychological profiler, and was hired by the Huntsville, Alabama, Police Department as a part-time consultant. Her first case involved the murder of a local DJ and soon turned into a hunt for a vicious serial killer.

Burned out from her work as a substance abuse therapist, Charlie turned in her resignation at the Hope Returns Treatment Center at the end of July. Her friend and colleague, Marti Hathoway, agreed to open a private practice with her. After they found an office they could afford in a decent location, Marti turned in her resignation from the treatment center. They planned to move in this week.

Nightmares about the serial murder case had haunted Charlie until she took a weeklong vacation at the beach. The sun and waves were a soothing balm. She'd slept late, read the killer's diary written when she was a teen, jotted her feelings in her journal, received several therapeutic massages, and had eaten key lime pie. The nightmares had stopped. She had closure.

At least I thought the nightmares were over and I had closure. After checking the time on her phone, she dialed Marti. *It's only eleven-thirty. She's probably still awake.*

Made in the USA
Columbia, SC
02 April 2024

33503670R00146